About Roland Cheek's Western Sagas

Stan Lynde, much loved Western writer and creator of the cartoon strip Rick O'Shay says of Roland's *Echoes of Vengeance*: *"Cheek paints his young protagonist's odyssey with a deft hand, portraying the values of courage, principle, and friendship on a canvas as broad as America itself."*

Fine Western author Richard Wheeler has this to say of Roland's Western writing: *"Like Louis L'Amour, Roland Cheek knows how to start a story at a gallop and hold the reader to the last page. He writes richly and authentically about the Old West, drawing from an encyclopedic knowledge of his subject."*

The Billing's Gazette says of *Bloody Merchant's War*: *"… Cheek takes the struggle beyond the usual disputes over land, animals and political power, beyond the race and divisions that leave [Jethro] Spring caught between the Native American blood of his mother and the so-called civilized world of his white father. While all these elements drive action in the novel, what sets the book apart is the struggle for men's souls."*

The Tulsa World has this to say of *Lincoln County Crucible*, the conclusion of Roland's two Lincoln County sagas: *"Roland Cheek has used the history of the Lincoln County War and gives it a fresh twist. The dialogue is extremely well-done and the action scenes are alive with excitement."*

Roundup Magazine, publication of the Western Writers Association, says of *Gunnar's Mine*: *"… another page turner from Cheek with characters that possess all three dimensions and are tough to kill. Any reader who likes action, adventure, and a plot with more twists than a sidewinder will love Gunnar's Mine."*

Now comes *Crisis On the Stinkingwater*, fifth book in Roland Cheek's sweeping *Valediction for Revenge* Western series featuring the adventures of wanted murderer, Jethro Spring, outcast progeny of a Blackfeet mother and mountain man father. Crisis On the Stinkingwater takes place in northwestern Wyoming's lonely Stinkingwater Valley. It's a tale pitting a lonely homesteader against land claimed by a lawless cattleman.

Non-fiction Books by Roland Cheek

Learning to Talk Bear

Phantom Ghost of Harriet Lou

Dance on the Wild Side

My Best Work is Done at the Office

Chocolate Legs

Montana's Bob Marshall Wilderness

CRISIS

ON THE

STINKINGWATER

CRISIS
ON THE
STINKINGWATER

ROLAND CHEEK

a Skyline Publishing Book

Copyright 2004 by Roland Cheek

Cover design by Laura Donavan
Text designed and formatted by Michael Dougherty
Edited by Narelle Burton

Publisher's Cataloging in Publication

Cheek, Roland.
   Crisis on the Stinkingwater / Roland Cheek: author ; Narelle Burton:
editor.— 1st ed.
      p. cm.— (Valediction for revenge ; 5)
      ISBN: 0-918981-12-3

      1. Frontier and pioneer life—West (U.S.)—Fiction.
      2. Cattle ranching—West (U.S.) 3. Homesteading—West (U.S.)
      4. Northwestern Wyoming—Fiction. 5. Western stories.
      I. Title.

      2003

ISBN: 0-918981-12-3
Library of Congress Control Number 2004091681

Published by   Skyline Publishing
                  P.O. Box 1118
                  Columbia Falls, Montana 59912

Printed in Canada

Dedication

To Bill D. and Mary and Heidi and Mark and Dan, all long-suffering spouses of the very special friends who help Jane and me bring our books into being.

THERE IS SO MUCH GOOD IN THE WORST OF US AND SO MUCH BAD IN THE BEST OF US, IT HARDLY BEHOOVES ANY OF US TO TALK ABOUT THE REST OF US.

—proverb posted on the wall of an all-night diner where the author occasionally stops for coffee.

⇒ Chapter One ⇐

I rid up ol' Clark's Fork o' the Yellowstone that spring of '83, an' looked around. T'warn't the first time I was thar and I hoped it wouldn't be the last. But a coon my age has to think it likely he'll face the Reaper some day, what with injins and varmints 'round most every corner.

The reason I come, so I told m'self, was t'look over the fairest place on God's green earth for at least one more time. Sunlight Basin hadn't changed much since the last time I was there a-workin' for Morgan back in '80. But Sunlight Basin warn't whar I was goin'. The Southfork of the Stinkin'water was.

Morgan hisself was a okay cowboy if you liked the breed. He'd drove cows into Three Forks buffler country some years afore, and I hitched up one winter I was hungry. Seems like he'd had some injin trouble, Morgan had, and was lookin' for somebody could help. Since I was long on time and short on backstrap, I allowed as I might be the Angel Gabriel a-sent to deliver old Morgan from the devil's hand.

Bein' beset by devils he called Bannocks, old Morgan jumped at m'offer and we hit a right smart agreement—if I could keep injins from his cows and his topknot, Morgan would supply all my worldly wants.

Now many a run-down ol' mountain stomper ain't a-lookin' for nothin' more, so I signed on with a holler and a handshake and grubstaked out o' Morgan's camp for three winters afore he tooked my advice and moved to the forks of the Stinkin'water whar I knowed the grass was stir-rup-deep and the water fit for drinkin' if you boiled it first.

Life couldn't a-been better for this ol' rascal. Then Morgan turned out to be a pot-likker and sold his outfit to a pansy-bottomed eastern pilgrim what I'd heered existed, but never knowed the kind. Bein' as me'n Pansy Bottom didn't hit it off real loud, I got to thinkin' about other places I been. So I just up and rode away.

I ate buffler hump in the Bearpaws, elk rib in the Crazies, dog meat in Paiute tipis, and dog salmon on the Lochsa. I looked most of it over purty good; up by the big blue lake o' the Kalispels and down into Salt Lake country, what used to be a fine place to winter 'til it got filled up with God-rotted Mormons. I was over to whar the Yellowstone dumps into the big river and I was down to Henry's Fork o' the Snake. It was up in the Bitterroot country in Montana when I got to thinkin' about the purtiest place God ever made, and I figgered three years without eyeballin' the Stinkin'water was longer than long enough.

I first hit the Stinkin'water back in the winter o' '40. I was a green-eared young'un of twenty-one, fresh from a North Caroliny dog patch, and Richard was a plumb keen mountain wizard with the know-how of a timber lobo a-hind him. For all my green-as-grass and for all his wild-place smarts, Richard was one o' the swellest gents I never did meet. He had the patience of a wild critter and spoke so soft a man had to lean close to listen in on gab th'owed his way. He moved like a cat and was plumb keen with any kind o' weapon come to hand. Most of all, howsomever, Richard just never made mistakes and he was some punkin' for a young'un to learn from.

Other fellers called him Dick, but I never did. Way that come to pass was plumb fancy. Him and me, we'd been out for a couple o' days when I asked him his name. He says "Dick."

"Dick," I says. "I never afore heered o' no mountain man name o' Dick."

"Fine," says he. "Just call me Richard."

So Richard it was. That quiet, slender feller teached me more in the years him and me watched each other's backsides than I picked up all the rest o' my life—leastways up to now. I learned about beaver and injins and mountains and rivers and prairies and deserts. I seen buffler by the thousands and tiny pink flowers what looked like a fancy woman's slipper. Richard teached me how to read moccasin tracks to tell the grade o' injins and whar t'look for water in dry country if a man's throat turned parched and his ears fixed to shrivel. He teached me how t'read mountains and how t'have eyes in the back o' my head, same as t'front. And he showed me all the places he figgered was plumb best on God's green earth.

Jackson Hole was purty; no arguin' that. So was the Big Hole east o' the Bitterroot Divide, as was his favorite, the Medicine River country west o' Fort Benton. But of all the places he showed me, I liked the Big Horn Basin best, and the Southfork o' the Stinkin'water best o' that.

———•—•———

Pansy Bottom was still there, I could see, layin' as I was up on the timbered hill east o' the forks o' the Stinkin'water. Spirit Mountain the injins called it, but the white man, in his infernal wisdom, hung Cedar Mountain on it. Ain't no wonder a smart coon learns to like injins better.

Well, if Pansy Bottom was still there—and I could see him out in a little round corral with his fancy stud horse—then Snake Eyes was there too, else Pansy Bottom woulda been run plumb outen the Stinkin'water by now.

Howsomever, I didn't come t'see Pansy Bottom, nor his snake-eyed honcho. All I wanted was t'take a look at the Southfork, maybe clear up t'the Thorofare country. Afore I did, though, I needed a fret o' t'baccy and coffee, and maybe a bean or two from ol' What-his-name's store at Marquardt Town down below.

So I snapped my eyepiece shut and picked m'self off the ground. Then I runned a hand down m'buckskins t'knock off a little dust and twigs; no use t'look plumb tacky when you hit your first jerktown in two months.

On the way down through the juniper brush to m'hoss, a whirrin' clatter come from off to m'right. He was gray-diamond and cross-hatched, all coiled and a-shakin' his tail in the center like a Mexican gourd dancer. He was maybe three feet long and 'bout that far off, near as I could tell. "Yep," I says to him. "Ol' Snake Eyes down below has the same kinda look you got, and I'll bet he's twice the danger."

———•+•———

The sign over the door read: A. JUDSON - GENERAL MERC. Then I recollected the squinch-eyed little runt what runned the place. I reckoned him and me is about the same growth. But I'm screwed down 'cause o' injins and growly bears and goin' without buffler hump and fat ribs for too long to a stretch, while 'A. JUDSON' is small in build 'cause he's small in ever' other way, too.

A. JUDSON was a-talkin' to a feller I didn't know when I shoved open the front door and swaggled in. Old

A. JUDSON looked at me and curled his lips into a sneer—just like he allus did.

Well, I knowed right whar t'baccy and coffee and beans was, and I figgered I could take a tad o' sneerin' for a short dab, then be shut o' the place, and shut o' the smell o' 'A. JUDSON - GENERAL MERC'.

But the first thing I heered after the door slammed shut ahind me made me calc'late to check out the price o' shirts and pants and all kinds o' foofaraw whilst I listened on....

"You mean he stepped right in against a drawed gun of Levi Bunting's?"

Snake Eyes! I thought.

"I know. It's hard to believe." A. JUDSON beginned.

"And you mean he took away Bunting's gun and broke his arm to boot?" the feller I didn't know asked in disbelief.

Snake Eyes? I asked m'self and I wandered closer t'look on the washtubs, rub boards, brooms, and mops.

"I couldn't hardly believe my own eyes either!" said A. JUDSON.

"What kind of by-Jesus whopper is this nester, anyway?" asked the feller I didn't know.

Are they talkin' 'bout the same Snake Eyes I know? I wondered.

"What was it he said again?" asked the feller I didn't know.

"Well," beginned A. JUDSON, "he just walked up to Burroughs' table ..."

Pansy Bottom! I thought.

"... where Bunting ..."

Yep, that's sure as hell the Snake Eyes I know.

"... Morton and me were sitting. And he done it as big and bold as if he had a squad of Sheridan's cavalry behind him. Then he flat told Burroughs he was homesteading Blood Canyon."

Takes guts, I thought.

"And everybody just sat there?" asked the feller I didn't know.

"Everybody was stunned for a minute," said A. JUDSON. "Then Bunting jerked up and started for the stranger. It was Burroughs that stopped him that time, probably because his lady friend is in the country and he don't want no trouble right now. Then that crazy home-steader bastard just wheels and walks out of the saloon."

I was sortin' stovepipes along the west wall 'cause I needed a little time t'waller over ever'thing I heered into proper order.

"But, then, he came right back in?" asked the feller I didn't know.

Whoopee! I thought.

"Came in with a gun on his belt and a smile on his lips," said A. JUDSON. "Didn't use either of 'em, though, 'cause the smile stayed on when he took Levi's gun away and broke his arm."

"Whoopee!" I let slip out loud.

"And the sonofabitch was still smiling," said A. JUDSON, "when he turned back to Burroughs and told him his mind hadn't changed a bit—that he'd already taken up a homestead at Blood Canyon and figured to live there until he was ready—on his own—to leave."

The feller I didn't know just hung his head and shook it in wonderment. D'rectly he raised up and asked, "What is it that Burroughs and Bunting will do now?"

I snorted at that whilst pokin' around amongst the picks and shovels and stuff. *Hell's bells, there ain't but one thing Pansy Bottom and Snake Eyes can do, and that's t'get after that gutsy feller and th'ow him off.* "And he'll be plumb lucky if that's all they do!" I ended up out loud.

Both feller I didn't know and A. JUDSON turned to look at me. Then A. JUDSON says to the feller I didn't know, "Burroughs was well soaked last night when he left

Morton's place, and Bunting has a broken arm. I don't know what they'll do, but I don't expect it'll be today that it happens. However long it takes, though, I can't imagine them letting anybody stay up the Southfork very long."

"Especially with what he did to Bunting," feller I didn't know said as he pulled off his hat and runned finger thru hair sparse as mine.

"I doubt the man is still in the country," A. JUDSON said as he turned to look at me. "Dammit, old man! You've pawed over everything in the store. Do you want something or don't you?"

"Cain't seem t'find t'baccy, coffee, nor beans," I mumbled. "Don'tcha carry none o' that stuff?"

CHAPTER TWO

Washburn saw them when they were a speck topping the rise on the road to Marquardt. He shaded his eyes against the mid-morning sun, then picked up the slop bucket, hobbled down the steps, and limped to the rear of the cookhouse where he pitched the bucket's contents into the bug-infested ditch. On his way back up the steps, he set the bucket down on the porch and, wiping hands on his grimy, once-white apron, again stared up the road. They were close enough now that Washburn could tell the easy-cantering horse was a fine-lined buckskin, and that its rider seemed as if he had a taproot through the saddle and into the buckskin's guts.

Bunting spotted the oncoming rider, too. He paused while crossing from the blacksmith's shop to the tack shed, also shading his eyes against the sun, watching.

The buckskin broke from a canter into a steady trot as he neared the ranch. When horse and rider passed beneath the ranchyard arch, it settled into a swift walk, each step kicking up little spurts of dust.

The foreman's hands were on his hips, legs spread, chin tucked against chest. Washburn knew that stance; wondered why the sonofabitch was mad already so soon in the day. *Something happened in the smithy,* he decided.

The quick-stepping buckskin, head swinging in rhythm with each stride, passed the bunkhouse and soon was abreast the cookhouse, apparently heading for the main house. With a little imagination, Washburn figured that horse and rider could've been a single animal; one of those half-horse, half-human critters from an old fable. The man's buckskin shirt and trousers and moccasin-style boots nearly matched the color of the buckskin horse, even without the coat of road dust covering both. Then Levi Bunting let out a roar!

The stranger gave his reins a flick and the buckskin stopped in its tracks. The man tipped back his hat with a thumb and ran a forefinger around the inside of his red-checkered neckerchief. Washburn could tell his hair was dark and needed trimming. In due course, the rider clucked at the buckskin and the pony started forward.

Again Levi Bunting roared. Again the stranger checked the horse. The voice was soft, but it carried. "It's the owner I'd like to talk to."

Levi stomped forward, thumb hooked into his gunbelt. Washburn wondered if the stranger had any idea how near he was to plucking a harp. Schulte came around the corner of the blacksmith's shop—trust the ugly, beer barreled bastard to belly up to trouble.

"We're not hiring saddle tramps," Bunting snarled.

The stranger smiled, white teeth actually flashing in a bronze face covered with stubble. "Not looking for work," he said. "I merely want ..."

The foreman's voice softened and the cook could catch only bits and pieces. "You're uncommonly dumb, mister. We're not furnishing beans to grubline riders either."

That was a surprise to Washburn. The Lazy T Bar always observed common ranching courtesy. Then the shambling blacksmith loomed grinning at Bunting's side, clenching and unclenching ham-sized fists.

"Not riding grubline either, Mr. Bunting. All I want to do is talk to Mr. Burroughs for a minute."

Washburn scratched his own unshaven stubble while mulling over the fact that this stranger knew both Bunting and Burroughs by name.

The foreman could've told the stranger that Ellis Burroughs was gone from his ranch; had in fact been gone for some weeks. As a ranch owner with one of the few healthy cattle herds after the terrible winter of '82-'83, savoring Chicago's delights as a guest of one of the premier meat-packing firms was a benefit difficult to decline. Instead of sharing that information, however, Bunting growled, "You got thirty seconds to get off this ranch before I have Schulte here drag you from that hammer-headed buckskin and throw both of you off separate."

Schulte's grin widened and he stepped forward.

The stranger's eyebrows arched as he reached into his shirt pocket, took out a cigar, bit off its end and fumbled for a match which he struck on his saddlehorn. While he was so engaged, the buckskin stretched its nose to the ground and blew noisily through its nostrils.

"He's yours," Bunting said to Schulte.

Schulte started forward. Then Jethro Spring clucked to his horse, spinning him like a top and trotting him away.

Bunting glanced at Washburn. "You got two choices, Cookie," he snarled. "You can get the hell to work, or you can get the hell off this ranch. Be all right with me if you did the last one."

Washburn snatched up his empty bucket and disappeared into the cookhouse, screen door slamming behind.

"You want I should saddle a horse and go after him?" Schulte asked.

Bunting kicked at the dirt and growled, "Schulte, there ain't a horse in the corral big enough to carry you, let alone take you to any blue ribbons in a damned horse race." *Lord knows, Schulte isn't the brightest star in the Lazy T Bar's firmament,* the cook thought, watching the sunlit yard from behind the screen door, *but he's sure as hell the biggest.* At six feet three inches and two hundred and sixty pounds, Isaac Schulte was, in fact, the largest individual for one hundred miles in any direction. In addition, the man brawled for sheer sport, had a noted short fuse and a sufficiently slow wit to take him into serious trouble without the necessary brains to get him out. Washburn figured the blacksmith was a perfect tool for the ranch owner and his foreman to manipulate at will. The cook stoked his stove and stirred a pot of beans simmering on one corner. While doing so, he recalled how the dull-witted blacksmith had stunned Ellis Burroughs' favorite saddlehorse with a single blow from his ham-like fist. True, the stallion was a tad flighty anytime someone fiddled with his feet. But to stun a horse using just a fist! Washburn shuddered.

Burroughs had been furious. The stallion was an American Standardbred of impeccable bloodlines. Fortunately the stallion got his feet under him and appeared only wild-eyed and terrified. It was Levi Bunting that interceded for the blacksmith. Washburn overheard them talking at the cookhouse table while he prepared supper.

"C'mon, Ellis, Schulte's got no more brains than that horse—not as many, actually. Besides, the horse ain't hurt and Schulte knows he's up to his ears in a pigsty. Give him another chance and you've got the biggest, toughest bastard in all Wyoming on your leash."

"I suppose," Burroughs mused, "there is something to be said for taming such a brute."

"Want me tell him to stop packing his bedroll?"

Bunting asked.

Burroughs slapped the table. "Go ahead. But I warn you, he's in your parole; one more time out of line and Caesar's conquest of Gaul will seem more recent history."

Still, the penitent blacksmith oozed tribulation. Though Bunting controlled Schulte on the ranch, it took but one of his roaring, destructive drunks to demonstrate the man could not be trusted in town except under close surveillance. Overall, though, it was obvious Ellis Burroughs took a great deal of pride in breaking Isaac Schulte to heel; obvious that having the big blacksmith at his beck and call gave the young ranch owner a sense of power. *I wonder if he thinks of Levi Bunting the same way?* Washburn asked himself. *Or me? Or how about all the other folks in this godforsaken country?*

→ Chapter Three ←

Ellis Burroughs met
Levi Bunting in a
smoke-filled cattleman's club in Cheyenne. Burroughs,
scion of one of Saratoga's wealthiest summer families, was
lured west by tales of fortune and adventure lurking among
western horizons, as well as the allure of lusty men and
women dwelling therein. With the blessing of his father—
and his substantial financial backing—the younger
Burroughs first explored the Texas Panhandle. But Charles
Goodnight proved to be an obstinate, durable and most of
all, capable old man, and it quickly became apparent to the
younger Burroughs that Goodnight would permit no
ambitious, well-financed competitor near Palo Duro
Canyon.

Goodnight and Burroughs parted as friends, however,
and it was the Texas cattleman himself who suggested
Cheyenne as the proper place for an enterprising young
man to begin looking over northern ranges.

So it was that Burroughs spotted the swarthy stranger

as he approached through the haze of a smoke-filled, dimly lit room. The newcomer was tall and broad-shouldered, and he weaved through the crowd with a lazy grace. He pulled out a chair, reversed it, and straddled it without a by-your-leave, coming immediately to the point.

Ellis Burroughs never learned how Bunting knew he was interested in acquiring a cattle ranch, but it was soon apparent they were of similar bent. And before the evening ended with copious quantities of Irish whiskey swilled amidst a swarm of charming maidens from Annie Laurie's, Levi Bunting was segundo of the extensive, yet-to-be-acquired, Burroughs ranch holdings.

Bunting led his employer to the upper Stinkingwater country in far northwestern Wyoming. The way his segundo explained it, the headwater country of the Stinkingwater River was fertile land for cattle, bounded on the west by that monument of recent legislative idiocy, Yellowstone National Park, on the northwest by the near-impassable Beartooth Mountains, and on the south by the newly created Wind River Indian Reservation.

Bunting explained how the country up both forks of the Stinkingwater River was taken by a few small ranchers struggling for survival, with varying degrees of success against the rugged land and inhospitable elements. He also pointed out that many of those ranchers had little more than squatter's rights to the land they claimed and he thought an aggressive, well-financed operation could purchase one or two of the smaller holdings and expand from there. How the expansion would be accomplished was never revealed, as well as being of little consequence to either man.

Burroughs and Bunting settled into temporary quarters in the little hamlet of Marquardt, letting it be known that they were interested in acquiring ranch property. Two weeks went by without a single nibble.

"What is wrong with these people?" Ellis Burroughs

asked in exasperation. "Every one of them is living on the squalid edge of survival. Why would intelligent beings living so close to perpetual poverty maintain such a facade of independence?"

Then Bunting heard that Morgan might be interested in selling if the price was right. "But," Levi warned, "ain't none of 'em comin' in with their hats in their hands, so you'd better figure on visiting him, not the other way around."

Morgan proved to be crusty, and when Burroughs finally consented to visit the rancher, the young easterner thought him a thief as well. "Your asking price is absurd!" the younger man protested, tromping out when the old cattleman refused to budge, trailed by his foreman. But ten days later, with no other offer in sight, the two men returned to come to terms with Morgan.

With the transfer, Ellis Burroughs became the owner of twenty-seven hundred acres of fine bottomland situated at the juncture of both forks of the Stinkingwater River. And with the Lazy T Bar brand came the customary grazing rights in the hills between the Northfork of the Stinkingwater and Sunlight Basin, even farther north. Also included in the purchase were five relatively useless hands who'd accompanied Morgan when he ventured into the Stinkingwater Country soon after Indian rampages were checked and the Bozeman Trail reopened.

Recognizing their grazing lands to the north for the valuable asset they were, Bunting and Burroughs still cast covetous eyes on the rich ranges along both sides of the Southfork—ranges that, added to their existing holdings, could play a major role in the rise of the Lazy T Bar to a place in Wyoming's sun.

Bunting left immediately after the Morgan purchase for Chugwater, Cheyenne, and Laramie to obtain the kind of cowhands he felt appropriate for the Lazy T Bar. Meanwhile, Ellis Burroughs prodded the uncommunicative

Dankin, Morgan's holdover foreman, to throw a few steers south of their former range.

On Bunting's return with six hard-looking hands from the Medicine Bows, Burroughs justified Dankin's absence. "Until I let him go, Dankin never said fifty words to me. All I ever got was a curt nod, or a shake of his head when he disagreed with me. And he was altogether too stubborn about moving steers south."

"We're better off shut of him, Mr. Burroughs," Bunting replied. "Word's out now, and pretty quick we'll have our choice of hands."

"At least Dankin could throw a rope. But that wrinkled old idiot who rode in moccasins and Indian leggings could hardly so much as haze a steer back from a quicksand wallow. His saddle was even a Civil War McClellan with no horn— he couldn't rope if he knew how. And that museum piece of a rifle! God, how could the man be useful with that equipment and his poor attitude?"

"My, you are wound up, ain't you Mr. Burroughs?" Bunting murmured.

"Dankin tried to tell me old Buttercut—that was his name—was valuable watching Lazy T Bar cattle in the mountains. Washburn even reckoned the old man was a bonafide mountain man who could read tracks and oncoming weather; he also claimed the old man had lots of Indian friends. But frankly, I doubt the old fool's credentials for I've known some real mountain men, like Buffalo Bill Cody for instance, and the old man had no dash or flare like those real men who spent their lives doing the extraordinary."

Bunting chuckled. "I'll get rid of him for you."

"He's gone. He was gone when I let all the holdovers but the cook go. Pulled out two days before, without so much as a by-your-leave. The rest of them were gone thirty minutes after I gave them notice; almost as if they were packed and ready. Washburn said I'd miss them at roundup, especially the old supposed-to-be mountain man."

"Why not make it a clean sweep and get rid of the cook, too?" the foreman asked.

"Levi, Levi. If we let them all go, the neighbors might talk. Besides, I like his crabapple strudel."

Bunting laughed. "Won't be no neighbors to talk, Mr. Burroughs, when we get our way."

In the short term, however, with the approach of winter and time being short, the men of Lazy T Bar contented themselves with a general roundup. It soon became apparent that it wasn't an easy chore for new men riding strange country, and when the tallies came in, Ellis Burroughs smoldered.

"This is far short of what I'd been led to believe existed," the ranch owner cried, waving the tally sheet. "I thought you and Morgan did a survey before purchase."

His foreman nodded, shrugging from his heavy, sheepskin-lined canvas coat and hanging it on a hook. "We did, and they were there." The man nodded again, before adding, "They're still there, too. We just didn't get 'em all."

"What, then, are you going to do about it?"

"Already sent four of the boys out in pairs to look some more. But they came back when this storm hit. When it's over, we'll try some more." The foreman pulled off his flat-crowned hat and shook snow from it. "It may be fate and it may be hate. But our day's yet to come."

Burroughs threw the tally sheets to the floor. "This better not be all, Mr. Bunting, or there could be more changes made on this ranch!"

Bunting's black eyes narrowed. He wiped the remaining snow from his hat with a forefinger, then carefully reshaped the brim. "Don't pee until your water comes, Mr. Burroughs. We're doing everything we can do and trying some things we can't. If we don't come up with the cows to match your numbers, the fault might not be all ours. It could mean you should've let the old hands go after roundup, 'stead of before."

———•◦•———

Ellis Burroughs and Levi Bunting began Lazy T Bar's march to prominence in the spring following purchase of the ranch from Emmett Morgan. To begin, the Lazy T Bar drove only enough cattle north of the river to maintain claim to that country, while the rest of the herd was moved south and west of the ranch, into the Stinkingwater's rich Southfork grazing lands.

As expected, their move was not undisputed. Thomas Bledsoe, for instance, was not amused. The Englishman laid claim to the area around the creek named for him and swore he'd defend his grazing rights. Legal briefs were filed in Rock Springs, but before a trial date was set, Bledsoe was killed by his horse—dragged to death while riding alone. "A Higher Authority," Ellis Burroughs was heard to say, "transferred uncontested title to the Bledsoe Creek range to the Lazy T Bar."

Old Marquardt and his three touchy sons were another problem. Marquardt declared no T Bar cow would graze the Kittleson Mountain foothill range claimed by his Plus Four brand. Then Levi Bunting and several Lazy T Bar hands happened upon the younger two Marquardt boys changing T Bar brands to Plus Fours. With the evidence produced—thirteen cattle with Lazy T Bar brands clumsily made to look like a Plus alongside a Four, a running iron, and culprits caught red-handed—it looked like an open and shut case.

Fortunately for the two Marquardt rustlers, Ellis Burroughs withdrew charges against them when old Marquardt conveniently agreed to drop claim to the contested range. In hindsight, given their subsequent protestations of innocence and the high regard in which old

Marquardt is held among the local populace, Burroughs thought he also should've demanded that the Marquardt clan leave the Stinkingwater. But the all-important thing was T Bar stock grazed the entire Kittleson Mountain foothills.

Other problems arose that second summer, but the growing crew of the Lazy T Bar seemed to handle every situation. As Ellis Burroughs later told a Denver Post writer who profiled his meteoric rise:

"Levi Bunting turned out to be an excellent judge of men, and the best seemed to gravitate our way. Naturally I always paid top wages and no doubt most good men prefer being associated with a successful venture."

The Lazy T Bar's success wasn't only limited to expansion, however. Ellis Burroughs also took considerable pride in instituting the first cutting and stockpiling of wild hay in all northwestern Wyoming. "I attracted a great deal of ridicule from more experienced ranchers that first season," Ellis told the journalist, "but they have little left to laugh about after this devastating winter of '82-'83."

Burroughs culled only the oldest cows for sale with the steers, and introduced pedigreed shorthorn bulls into his herd. The third summer men of the T Bar were ready to throw stock even further south and Burroughs' crew numbered eighteen.

Swenson resisted their first drive into Ishawooa Canyon by turning the drifting T Bar cattle and hazing them back. Then Swenson came to town for the annual Fourth of July celebration and he was drinking. Harsh words were exchanged between the Swede and Levi Bunting. Guns were drawn in anger and the Ishawooa rancher drowned in his own whiskey-drenched blood.

The informal inquest demanded by Bunting and held that same day, exonerated the T Bar man because of a preponderance of testimony and evidence that he'd drawn only in self defense. There were, however, dark whisperings that Bunting was a killer and that Swenson stood little chance in a gunfight, even if sober.

Circumstances were different when Swenson's two tough Texas cowboys stormed into town to avenge his death. The tall, skinny one was noted as a handy man with a gun and some said the stocky one was just as fast. The two men, blood lust in their eyes, crashed through the batwing doors of Morton's saloon late the day after Swenson died. Ellis Burroughs, sitting at a table to one side, had time only to wonder how Swenson's men arrived so quickly. Guns blazed.

Levi Bunting was at the bar with young Cletus Wills. They jumped apart, instantly galvanized into action. Though he was caught by surprise, it was Bunting's revolver that was first to speak. Even while moving, his first bullet caught the tall gunman full in the hip, spinning him into the other gunman, spoiling that one's aim. Then Wills's and Bunting's guns blew life from the second Swenson cowhand.

After Swenson's death and the resulting shootout with his two cowboys, the Lazy T Bar experienced little active opposition to expansion up the Southfork. And when they turned eyes east, Corbin and Ashland thought it the better part of valor to dissolve their holdings on Trail Creek for a pittance of their worth.

Thus, only Andrew Kittleson's spread stood between the T Bar and unlimited expansion east, down the Stinkingwater. Andrew Kittleson, however, presented a different sort of a problem for the men of the Lazy T Bar. Despite having a Stinkingwater mountain range named for him, the man was a sitting District Judge who was judicially responsible for most of western Wyoming and held court in far-off Rock Springs.

"This is out of my league," Levi Bunting said. "Be nice to fold the Double O Connected into the Lazy T Bar, but it's too big a risk to take on an outfit owned by a judge."

Ellis Burroughs drummed fingertips to desktop. "Make him an offer."

"I did. Twice. He don't even bother to answer."

Burroughs frowned. "Then I shall visit 'His Honor' in his lair."

A week later, Ellis sat across a dining room table from white-haired, bulldog-faced Judge Andrew Kittleson. The judge finished reading the contents of a packet the younger man had presented him a few minutes before.

"You're trying to blackmail me, aren't you, you bastard," the judge growled, "about something that happened thirty years ago. I could have you arrested, stick you in a jail cell, throw the goddamn key away."

Burroughs nodded. "I am, and you could. However, Judge, the information contained in that packet would surface, as sure as God made little angels. Do you want that? Besides, I'm as well-connected in the East as you are; perhaps better. And as powerful as you are in Wyoming, you couldn't keep me under lock and key for long, and you know it."

The younger man pushed his chair back and stood. "Think about it, sir. I intend to be in Rock Springs for three more days. The offer for your Stinkingwater ranch is a reasonable one. And it includes my silence in the bargain. It's a quite fair trade, don't you think?"

With acquisition of the Double O Connected, the Lazy T Bar had virtually uncontested access to the hills and mountains between the main two forks of the Stinkingwater, and points south and east. In addition, chiefly because of Burroughs' insistence on extensive winter feeding, haying crews stacked back-up feed for T Bar cattle on the old Marquardt, Kittleson, Bledsoe, and Swenson ranch bottomlands, as well as the home ranch.

With Lazy T Bar ledgers forecasting black ink for the coming year, Ellis Burroughs accepted the packing house offer to visit Chicago.

In his diary, Burroughs wrote:

> Rising cattle prices, the result of last winter's disastrous die-offs on overcrowded ranges to the north and east, as well as a progressive operation presided over by purposeful men, have proven the practical nature of my dream.

———•••———

After his pleasant Chicago sojourn, Ellis Burroughs continued on further east, to New York and Saratoga, consulting with his father, and visiting the girl he'd left behind.

Lillian Mathers was everything he'd remembered, and more; the radiant daughter of one of his father's most trusted retainers.

August Mathers was rescued by Douglas Burroughs after the Panic of '73 left Mathers' railroad vehicle manufacturing company in receivership. It wasn't philanthropy that caused Douglas Burroughs to offer Mathers a position. Instead, it was because the man's integrity was beyond question, chiefly because of Mathers' decision to honor his company's creditors at the expense of his personal fortune.

Lillian was fourteen at the time her father was appointed to his position in the Burroughs company. She remembered how relieved she felt to be somebody once again; to be assured her family could once more spend the summer in Saratoga; to know she could continue her education at Vassar. She did not, however, understand the harsh words exchanged at the time between her proud mother and her determined father.

Since that time, Lillian had watched her father's health

decline, coming to understand why her mother was so opposed to August Mathers' taking a position with a company she claimed "destroyed him in the Panic." Eventually Lillian came to realize her father stayed so long with the Burroughs Empire because of his love for his family. Poor health eventually required August Mathers to retire, but even then he received a stipend from the Burroughs headquarters. Though her father eventually regained a measure of his health, he didn't seem eager to return to Burroughs' employment. Nor did his employer appear to care—perhaps Douglas Burroughs thought Mathers' usefulness had run its course.

The Mathers family was actually quite close to Ellis Burroughs, recalling his loyalty as a boy when the family's financial situation became apparent and their so-called friends deserted them.

Lillian had been so proud of Ellis when he wished to strike out West and not become his father's creature, as had his brother John. She, of course, thought of the virile, athletic youth with the fair complexion and blonde wavy hair as very handsome. She accompanied him to the rail station the day he went away, and just before he boarded, whispered that she loved him.

When Ellis returned to the East, he hinted of his interest in Lillian's hand and extended an invitation for the Mathers family to visit Wyoming. He was even more robust, more handsome!

"It's true! It's true! Everything we've been hearing about Ellis and his success is true."

Her father wasn't quite so sanguine, asking questions all along the way: of a rancher when they left the rail line at Billings, of the coach driver between Pryor Gap and a place called Pole Cat. August Mathers had a troubled look on his face after talking to a tall, Texas-drawling, crippled stage hand at the Ralston station. And he advised his daughter against any hasty action after talking with a gentleman named Corbin while they waited for Ellis at Corbin's ferry crossing.

Lillian Mathers loved her father very much; so much, she told him she'd rather take poison than disappoint him. But when Ellis Burroughs and three of his cowboys galloped up to Corbin's Crossing in a cloud of dust, she found it difficult to recall her father's admonitions. And that was before Ellis pushed his wide-brimmed hat rakishly back and a shock of straw-colored hair fell across his forehead.

The young rancher shook hands with Lillian's father and bowed low to both ladies. Then he introduced Levi Bunting, his first assistant, and two cowboys named Lyle and Grattner. The young man had an aura of command that, despite his common and dusty attire, was uncontestable. He apologized for not meeting the Mathers party as the stage arrived, though he offered no reason for being tardy, and said the buggy would be along soon. Then he asked the others if they would excuse while he took Lillian by the arm, guiding her down the dusty road to what he said was a newly constructed bridge that would "soon put that villain Corbin out of his stage post crossing business."

She stared up in puzzlement, murmuring, "Villain? The man was quite pleasant to us."

He laughed and led her onto the bridge. "I'm pleased, Lillian, that you and your parents decided to visit." When she smiled, he added, "I've missed you so."

She replied that she'd not changed her mind since he'd first gone west, and that she was very anxious to see his ranch. He held both her hands and said he hoped it would someday be "our ranch."

"I hope so, too," she murmured.

"What do you think of Wyoming?"

"It's beautiful—but so wild and forbidding."

Ellis smiled and asked if the stage journey was tiring.

She shook her head. "Strangely, the fresh air and wholesome exercise seems to benefit Father's health. Really, we didn't notice the demands of the stagecoach ride. Father was busy identifying wildflowers and noting rock formations, talking to anyone who would pass the time of day about the land and people. Time passed swiftly ... though I will admit," she blushed, "that I grew anxious to reach Corbin's Crossing."

Then their carriage, accompanied by yet another rider, rolled in, whereupon Ellis and Lillian returned to the others.

<hr />

No one had bothered to tell Ellis Burroughs of a nondescript, buckskin-clad stranger who'd called at the ranch a week prior to his return from the East. Therefore, the Lazy T Bar owner was as much in the dark as any other of the surrey's passengers when the lone rider created such a flurry among the T Bar's outriders.

The man leaned forward with forearms resting across his saddlehorn, his buckskin horse standing quietly at the roadside. Levi Bunting was first to spot him as he topped Listening Woman Hill. The foreman shouted to the other outriders and the two horsemen in the rear galloped around the surrey, racing over the rise to join the front outriders in surrounding the lone rider.

As the carriage rolled to a stop alongside the milling horses and riders, Bunting shouted curse words at the stranger who merely smiled, tipped his hat at the ladies and said, "Mr. Burroughs ..."

Bunting's big, steeldust gray horse crashed into the trim buckskin, staggering him and cutting off his rider's words. "You sonofabitch!" Bunting cursed. "I told you we wanted nothing to do with you!"

Ellis saw Mrs. Mathers bring a gloved hand to her mouth and felt Lillian place a hand on his arm. "Levi!" he called. "There are ladies present!"

"All I want is a word with Mr. Burroughs," the stranger began. "Just a moment is ..."

Again the gray crashed into the buckskin. This time the smaller horse shuffled his feet and maintained a balance. But when the gray backed off, Levi Bunting held a revolver pointed at the stranger's chest.

"Levi!" Ellis shouted. "For heaven's sake!"

The stranger nodded as Levi dropped the revolver's muzzle to point at the ground. Again the stranger touched his hat brim. "Thank you, Mr. Burroughs. What I have to say won't take but a minute."

Ellis weighed his response. The rancher had never before set eyes on the stranger, but his foreman apparently had. And Levi's anger seemed unbridled. Burroughs didn't care a fig about a man he'd never seen, but he had to consider his passengers and the effect an unpleasant encounter might have on them. However, there was something chiseled in stone about supporting one's employees.

Again the gray crashed into the buckskin. This time, turning his gaze on Bunting, Jethro Spring murmured, "You're getting annoying." The revolver came up.

Burroughs made his decision. "Levi! You and Wills take the lead. Grattner and Lyle, fall in behind." Then he glanced at the stranger and said, "And no, my good man. I'm otherwise engaged today, and shall be unable to converse with you." Then he slapped reins to his two carriage horses and the little cavalcade resumed its journey to Lazy T Bar's headquarters, at the forks of the Stinkingwater.

Lillian squeezed Ellis's arm, but August Mathers observed, "It sounds as though you don't have any more of an idea than we do about that affair."

The young rancher smiled over his shoulder at the elder Mathers. "As a matter of fact, I've never seen that man."

It was some time before anyone in the surrey spoke

again, then Lillian tentatively began, "Ellis...."

"Mmmm."

"That man—he wasn't armed, was he?"

He looked at her in surprise. "Why, my dear, I'm sure I don't know. I never looked."

"He wasn't," August Mathers said quietly from the rear. "At least he carried no weapon in sight, as does every other man we've seen since we crossed the Missouri for the last time."

Ellis chuckled. He split the reins and jerked his coat open. "There, see? Now you've seen another."

Lillian giggled, but the Mathers elders glanced at each other. Neither smiled.

CHAPTER FOUR

The visit by the Mathers family proved exciting for Ellis Burroughs, so much so that he radiated enormous charm towards Lillian's mother and took much pleasure in discussions with her father. To the primary subject of his interest he demonstrated a perfect blend of probity and courtliness. And the young rancher was tireless in showing off his ranch, outlining its boundaries on unrolled maps, and explaining in detail his future plans and projects.

One day Ellis Burroughs, and Lillian and August Mathers rode into the northern hills. The rancher was full of enthusiasm about the grazing potential of both the Trout Creek and Rattlesnake Creek drainages. He told them his cattle grazed as much as fifteen miles north to a mountaintop pasture called Dead Indian Meadows. "I don't know why it's called that," he said.

Then he shook his head and told them of a huge, beautiful valley beyond the hills to the north. "It's called Sunlight Basin, and I do know why it's so named." He told them the basin is claimed by an irascible cattleman named Chapman who headquarters on the appropriately named Skull Creek, a tributary to the Clark's Fork of the Yellowstone River. Again the young man shook his head.

"We had to abandon plans to place T Bar cattle in Sunlight Basin after the Chapman fellow met me at a cattleman's meeting in Billings and told me he'd shoot every T Bar cow he found north of Dead Indian Meadows. Actually, I thought it was very rude of him." Ellis trailed off, then added, "Unfortunately the man is capable of backing up words with action."

August Mathers' eyes shifted to his daughter. He raised an eyebrow.

Four days after Ellis Burroughs and the Mathers, father and daughter, made their ride into Rattlesnake Hills, Ellis and Lillian took an unescorted ride to the top of Cedar Mountain. From its crest they could see the country around the forks of the Stinkingwater. In one beautiful tableau, Ellis pointed out the Lazy T Bar's ranch complex, as well as the scramble of structures known as Marquardt. As the sun dipped to the west, Ellis held her in his arms and asked her to set a wedding date.

She shuddered, nearly succumbing. Then her father's warning and her promise to him pushed aside the moment and she told Ellis he made her very happy. "But," she said, "I must first consult with my parents about wedding plans—where the wedding should take place, its size, the number of guests. Don't you see, Ellis dear, we must draw on Mother's wisdom and Father's approval?"

The man took a deep breath and nodded. He said he understood her father's straightened financial situation and if she would allow, he'd make arrangements to cover all wedding expenses.

She gazed at the far-off Beartooth Mountains to the north and west, then squeezed his arm and murmured, "Perhaps we should return."

"Yes, I suppose it would be for the best." Then he held her horse and gave her a hand up to her sidesaddle, a gentleman all the way—one with whom any woman would be proud to share her life.

———•+•———

One day Ellis Burroughs, his foreman, and a hand named Patrick O'Brien rode into Marquardt. Before leaving, the rancher, bowing over Lillian's hand, told her they'd not be gone long. "Business, unfortunately, requires occasional attention."

She laughed and flicked the back of her hand at him. "Oh do go on, Ellis. Even if you were attending to pleasure rather than business, it would be no more than you deserve."

As the three riders cantered up Listening Woman Hill, Ellis caught his foreman watching him and smiled. "God knows, I had to get away for a few hours, Levi. Being gracious is a noble habit, but it's a poor calling."

"She's some punkin', Mr. Burroughs." Bunting spat to the side and added, "So's her momma and daddy. But you take 'em on steady and they might put some cramp to our style."

"Knock back a couple of whiskeys and play a hand or two of poker," Ellis replied, "and things will appear in better light."

They crested the hilltop and reined their horses to a steady trot. The distant hamlet of Marquardt stood out on the treeless plain. Bunting spat again and said, "The only light that'd be better for you, Mr. Burroughs, would be candlelight, and that gal layin' naked in it."

Burroughs' eyes flashed. "Watch your mouth, sir. She's a lady."

Bunting nodded, spat again and said, "She surely is."

Morton's was, as usual, boisterous. Soon after arriving,

Burroughs and his foreman began a few hands of draw poker with the mercantile owner Judson, stable owner Kluster, and saloon keeper Morton. O'Brien, situated to intercept trouble, sat at a table with two hands who worked for the T Bar during roundup. It was while Kluster dealt that Bunting growled, shoved his chair back and leaped to his feet.

Burroughs glanced up to see the same stranger who'd tried talking to him on the road, weaving through the room. The man wore faded denim trousers and a worn doeskin jacket over a pale blue workshirt. His hat was a shapeless, narrow-brimmed thing, so hard-used that holes were worn at its creases. The face under the hat might have been chiseled from granite—except for a pair of most unsettling gray eyes that darted from Bunting to Burroughs and back again. Ellis glanced down to the man's waist; no weapon was visible.

Thinking of the auburn-haired beauty waiting at his ranch, how nothing must be allowed to come between them, Burroughs murmured, "Levi! Let's hear what the gentleman has to say."

"Thank you, Mr. Burroughs," the stranger said as Bunting settled back into his spread-legs stance. "I just want to tell you I plan on being your neighbor. I've filed on a hundred and sixty acres up Blood Canyon, at the Granite Creek junction with the Southfork."

There was a gasp from the stable owner, while Morton and Judson slipped to their feet and edged away. Ellis Burroughs threw his cards face down on the table. *There isn't a shred of hope for this fool,* he thought. *Levi will kill him! And well he should!*

"As I understand it, Mr. Burroughs, to do so is my legal right. I trust there'll be no trouble between your people and me. I certainly intend to be a decent neighbor."

Bunting's black eyes were little more than hooded slits. "Have you heard enough, Burroughs, or d'you want to offer the sonofabitch the home place instead?"

Burroughs' mouth worked but nothing came forth. Eventually the stranger said, "Thank you, Mr. Burroughs. I wanted to tell you this way so's it wouldn't come as a surprise." Then he wheeled and started for the door.

"I've heard enough!" Levi Bunting roared, smashing a fist to the table. Cards and unattended drinks flew everywhere. "You'll homestead no land of the T Bar, Mister, and you'll homestead no land anywhere on the Stinkingwater 'cause your time has run out. I'm going to end our problems with you, you sonofabitch!"

Then Ellis caught his foreman's sleeve. "Levi! No! He's not armed."

Levi Bunting glared down at his boss to growl, "With or without a gun, next time I see him, he dies."

As the stranger passed O'Brien's table, the Irishman thrust out his boot. The stranger stumbled and someone in the crowd tittered. Others laughed and someone else mooed like a cow, another cackled like a chicken, and yet another let out a couple of oinks like a pig. Then the man pushed through the batwing doors and was gone.

Morton sidled back to his chair and Ellis Burroughs told the saloon keeper to cash him in. Then he said, "Forget him Levi. We'll not see that rude fellow again."

Bunting's face was flushed, but when the rancher added, "Let's have a drink on that premise—that we'll not see him again," Bunting strode to the bar and ordered a bottle and two glasses. On his way back to the table, the store owner Judson slapped him on the back and the foreman grinned, pausing to respond.

Ellis's gaze swept the room. O'Brien had tilted his chair against a nearby post and was cackling at someone's joke. Morton bent over, counting chips, Kluster down on one knee picking up glasses and cards. Hijinks and hilarity ruled all along the bar. Ellis swung eyes back to the door. He must have been the first person in the entire building to see the stranger re-enter.

The man pushed open the batwings and held them for an instant as his eyes adjusted. Then he glided inside and let them swing, heading directly for Burroughs' table.

Ellis tore his eyes from the stranger to see Levi break away from Judson, laughing at something the shopkeeper said. Burroughs tried to shout, couldn't, then returned wide-eyed to the oncoming stranger. He also might have been the first person in the building to see the revolver swinging from the man's right thigh.

A hush descended with the man's advance. Levi returned to the table, pausing to say something to Morton, who laughed and bantied with the T Bar segundo in return. Bunting thumped the bottle and glasses to the tabletop, pulled out his chair and started to take a seat when Morton gasped. The foreman wheeled, cursed, and clawed for his gun. But the stranger was too close. As the weapon cleared the holster, the man was on him, seizing Bunting's wrist, stepping backward, pulling the lunging foreman toward him and around. There was a twist, a grunt, a snap, and a scream as Bunting's revolver thumped the floor.

Holding Bunting by the collar and suspended above the floor, Jethro Spring said, "Mr. Burroughs, I hope you'll take my intentions seriously. I intend to exercise my legal right. Now you know I'm capable of doing just that." Then he jerked Bunting half-upright, spun him around, placed a foot on his rump and gave a mighty shove, propelling the T Bar man headfirst into the bar.

As Bunting crashed into the bar, the stranger spun on his heel. On his way to the door he hooked the chair of an open-mouthed O'Brien with his toe and jerked. The Irishman crashed to the floor. Then the stranger was gone.

Only the 'swish, swish' of the batwings cut the utter silence. The only things moving in all the building were myriad sets of eyes, focused first on Bunting's crumpled heap, then on the Lazy T Bar owner. It took all of Ellis's willpower to pour a finger of whiskey into a glass and lift it to his lips. O'Brien scrambled to his feet, then stood confused.

"Will you stand there all day?" Burroughs demanded of O'Brien. "See to Levi." The rancher tossed off yet another drink, proud that his hands were steady. O'Brien came to say Bunting's arm was broken and that he'd sent for old Marquardt, the hamlet's unofficial doctor. Burroughs thanked his man and tossed down another drink. A disheveled Levi Bunting staggered to the table and collapsed into a chair, grasping the bottle with his left hand and drinking directly from it.

The man sent for Marquardt returned to say the quack doctor would not come to Morton's for a broken arm. If Levi wanted it splinted, Marquardt said he would do it at his home. Bunting cursed and declared he'd ride to Powell to have the arm set by a real doctor before he'd go to the hovel of a local quack.

Kluster readied a hack while Burroughs engaged a driver.

The rancher started to order another bottle, then thought of Lillian and told O'Brien to fetch their horses. It was after dark before they rode into the T Bar ranchyard.

Though both elder Mathers had retired, Lillian waited for Ellis with coffee and cookies. "Is something wrong?" she asked after turning up the lamp.

"No, no. Nothing is wrong."

She smelled whiskey on his breath, and he seemed agitated. When she asked further, he broke in, "Dammit, Lillian, we'll talk about it in the morning."

She heard him pacing his room until at last she fell into a troubled sleep.

CHAPTER FIVE

"**S**keeters are some pesky back here in the brush," I whispers to m'self as I laid up in a patch o' small firs and studied the edge o' the cliff, fifty feet away.

Though I never seen his layout, I knowed by the sign he was still in the country. Oh he'd tried some to cover his tracks, and had done a passable job. But the plain and simple wearin' away o' balsamroot and bunchgrass and injin flower showed more'n just wild critters a-wearin' it. Nope, there was somethin' in Blood Canyon aside from elk and deer and grizzly bears. So I didn't ride in like a Mormon bishop surveyin' his rabble.

Instead, I pulled on my recollectin' cap and remembered a cliff what stuck over whar Blood Canyon opened near the mouth o' the first creek. It tooked some doin' to get m'pony 'round there, what with clamberin' over a ridge way back ahind, and thru a break in a string o' other cliffs. And it took a little time for me t'wipe m'tracks so's a mean-eyed Blackfoot couldn't foller. Now I was a-layin' still as a sunnin' snake, and m'horse was tied t'some trees far back up the crick and over a couple o' low ridges.

Bein' a careful beaver what already lived to a ripe age, I laid up amongst the trees and studied the ground 'twixt me and the cliff. T'was gettin' along late into the day and leastways three piss ants was under m'buckskins. I couldn't see nothin' t'keep me from crawlin' out on the cliff edge and takin' a peek at that feller's layout.

"Now if it was me," I said to m'self, "I'da fixed somethin' here to make it right unhealthy for them as would want t'look down over that cliff." I tooked a last look around and shoved outen my patch o' firs, stood up slow and easy and pinched off two o' the piss ants, leavin' the other to roam free since he was headed for m'ankle nohow. I moved slow and easy and m'moccasins left no mark for wild or tame critters t'see. Each step was read out aforehand and I knowed I was no more'n a whisper shufflin' up to whar I could see over the edge.

M'head was the first thing stickin' over, and it was under cover of a three-foot limber pine. I knowed that little pine'd not stop no bullet, but nobody can shoot what they can't see. And the pine was more'n big enough to cover m'head whilst I peered out o' the branches.

It was a right smart cabin, I could see, even bein' so far away as to be out o' shootin' range o' most rifles—'ceptin' m'Hawken.

Now that I was at the edge o' the cliff I could hear water fallin' out o' the rocks and splashin' into a pool below. But I couldn't see it 'cause that limber pine I hid ahind was too short to cover me iff'n I stood. Nor if I poked m'head over, the pine wouldn't cover it then, either. Likewise, I could see the tops o' some scattered cottonwoods under the cliff, but no way could I get the lay o' the land 'less I moved.

I tooked another long look around and had beginned t'crawl when somethin' caught m'eye. I studied on what I was lookin' on for awhilst, then grinned and muttered, "Dogged if'n this coon I'm a'huntin' ain't set a leetle trap and I'm near crawled into it."

The trap was a rope loop a-covered with pine needles and dead limbs, all scattered t'look like God put 'em there, even to a old time mountain beaver like m'self. The trigger was a bigger limb layin' in the middle and fine-tuned to another rope a-leadin' over the edge o' the cliff. I didn't need t'be school-raised to figger out a big log or rock was a-tied to the end o' both ropes and rigged t'balance real gentle-like. Move trigger. Drop rock. Drop rock, drop Sam over that cliff. Made me shudder t'think on it.

That's when I beginned t'think I ought to pay more attention. And it was when I reckoned t'get the hell back the way I comed before I went another way I didn't want.

It was also when I decided I'd better get a good look at the coon smart enough t'make a set that near ketched Sam Buttercut, not t'mention breakin' Snake Eyes' bones before bedtime. Piss ants nor no, I was gonna lay back in the brush 'til the smart coon comed t'check his traps.

It was dark and a quarter moon afore I got up and traipsed back to m'pony for jerky and branch water and t'lay down m'head.

Mr. Smart Coon comed the next mornin', just after daylight. The first piss ants had stirred a minute afore and I was a-layin' still as a snake at sunrise. This time, though, I was blinkin' a lazy eye a-hind m'Hawken sights. Of a sudden he was there, movin' like a shadow and only half as noisy. He carried a Winchester like he'd fetched up with it, and a Colt slung low from his right hip.

A shadow he mighta been, but it was his ground and he comed fast. He tooked a passing look at his snare and was steppin' along to a second one to m'right when he stopped in mid-stride, then went for the limber pine whar I'd spied on his cabin. Long about then was when the first sweat beginned to bead on the small o' m'back. And when he eared the Winchester hammer back was when them beads commenced t'run down m'crack.

Now I didn't figger t'make no shootin' match out o' just a friendly visit, but that eared-back Winchester and his eyes a-follerin' whar I'd crawled made it appear t'me like he warn't thinkin' a social call was in progress. With nothin' else t'do, I eared back ol' Hawken and said, "Howdy do!"

I ain't sweared to God much in m'life, but I'm a-swearin' it now—I only blinked once and he warn't there no more. One second he was there and the next second he was gone, diving over that cliff like his only choices was bein' gutted by a Hawken ball or divin' into a pile o' rocks from the top o' his cliff.

"Aw, now why did you hafta go and do that?" I said out loud as I pushed to m'feet. "Ain't no call t'kill yourself 'cause you got beat by Sam Buttercut. Shucks, there ain't never been nobody could come on top o' old Sam, 'ceptin' maybe Richard."

I walked up to the cliff edge and peered over, figgerin' on seein' the jumpy stranger's body on a pile o' rocks. What I did see, though, caused me t'leap straight back and head for m'hoss at a high lope. Y'see, there warn't no stranger a-layin' spread-eagled at the bottom—only a scalin' rope a-swingin' gentle, back and forth.

He was follerin' all right, just as I allowed he might. I saw he was there two days after the cliff meeting. I laid up high on Ishawooa Mesa and watched him ridin' a big buckskin gelding and trailin' across a rock patch whar few injins I never seed coulda follered. I studied on it some, comin' to the last to know I didn't want t'have t'put that feller's candle out. But by damn! Ol' Sam Buttercut wasn't exactly used t'havin' to run hard just to keep some young poison from grinnin' down on his carcass, neither.

Me'n Hoss had lit out up-crick only a couple of ticks and a tock after I seed the empty scalin' rope swingin' in the breeze. By then I knowed the feller I wanted to chum up to had in his head that we ain't friendlies, and might even figger us enemies. Way I thought it, me'n Hoss would spend a few days cuttin' some circles through the high country, then we'd come in on that cabin from another angle. Meanwhile, just in case the feller I wanted t'chum up with figgered we'd likely never get along and made as if t'do something about it, I allowed t'watch my backtrail.

I never seed him for awhilst after me'n Hoss run for it, but I knowed he was there. Any good mountain coon soon learns to tell when somethin' is after him, even when he can't see it. T'was about dusk that first day, whilst me and Hoss was a-runnin' from Blood Canyon that I reckoned I was a damn sight better fighter than runner. So I picked m'spot careful-like, and rode ol' Hoss on by. It was a big rock what looked over a bend o' the crick, and whar I could get a clear shot at whatever it was a-trailin' us.

I tied ol' Hoss up in a patch o' prickly spruce and checked the cap on m'Hawken. Then I started hikin' back to the rock. If his cayuse hadn't stomped a fly when it did, I'da walked right into that sticky varmint what was huntin' me, 'cause he was already at the rock!

Well, I settled back into a juniper bush, knowin' he had no way a-knowin' I was near onto him, and calc'lated m'next move. I'd reckon it fair to say m'head was a little scrambled, for ol' Sam Buttercut spent the better part o' his whole life bein' the hunter, 'stead o' the hunted. Way I saw it, I had two choices: I could cut and run, or I could circle and fight. Bein' so close on to real dark, I knowed he couldn't catch up to me and Hoss, allowin' us to build up a right smart lead. But it rankled. Ol' Sam Buttercut'd never been chased this far by white men afore—and worse, him bein' only one.

Hell with him, I thought, *I'll stay and fight!*

Deep dark comed some later and that's when I moved from the juniper. Hawken stayed, propped in the bush 'cause I crawled out with a knife in each hand. It took me a hand-span o' moon time to come up on the rock, then I waited. I'd made naught a whisper a-comin', so I figgered I had the jump on the varmint. I still didn't aim to hurt him bad, but since I hadn't yet seen him since he jumped the cliff, I never knowed if he had a pistol or not. One thing certain, a rifle warn't no good up close in the dark. And if he warn't some punkin' with a knife, it'd be all my show, 'cause knives in the dark is whar I shine.

I hadn't heard naught o' his cayuse after that first time, so I figgered maybe we both got close to the rock 'bout the same time, and he pulled his pony back t'be safe. But he knowed I was around. Of that, I was certain.

D'rectly I eased on up t'the rock and found whar he'd been a-layin'. Still warm it was, and the prickly hair on the back o' m'neck raised up wonderin' whar he be. It didn't take me long t'study out that maybe me'n ol' Hoss should a-cut and run, 'stead o' stayin' t'fight. That's when I figgered I still had half a night left t'lay some long tracks.

Took me a little spell to get back to the juniper whar I'd left ol' Hawken. Problem was, Hawken warn't there! I first thought I comed out on the wrong bush, but I knowed I ain't. And I knowed that sticky, low-down varmint what hunted me had stoled it. That was when I commenced t'worryin' about ol' Hoss. But he was standin' whar I left him—and that itself was plumb suspicious!

So I was real easy crawlin' up to him and just as slow and easy when I cut the halter rope. Then I surprised the pony and me both by hittin' the saddle high up on the first jump, givin' out the Absorakee war whoop and drummin' ol' Hoss with m'hat and m'heels. And that sleepy pony jumped pretty near out o' his hide as we clattered off t'ward the rock, back the way we'd comed.

It was like I figgered—the sneaky varmint what trailed us looked for us to cut and run the way we headed, 'stead o' back the way we'd comed.

Howsomever, as ol' Hoss jumped away, I heard the brush pop ahind us and I braced for a bullet what never comed.

It troubled me, though, a-losin' Hawken that way, and as me'n Hoss drug on through the night, the thought crossed m'mind more'n once that I'm gettin' too old for this kind o' thing. We swung away from the crick first chance and headed north, beelinin' for Ishawooa Mesa. I knowed if we could get on top o' the mesa, we'd be lookin' down the gullet o' anyone comin' ahind us. Hoss and me climbed out to the north and swung west along the divide afore skirtin' White Calf Mountain. The day was most gone when we tucked ahind a little rock crop what had a trickle o' water and some short high country grass for Hoss.

He needed it, Hoss did, for he was ganted up and tuckered out. So was this beaver. The past day's work was a little stretchin' for a feller pushin' his three score, ten. But damn! That varmint was still back there somewhar—I could feel it. And afore I frazzled enough t'break, I had some gettin' even t'do. Without Hawken, though, he held most o' the cards. Knowin' that is why I headed for this high, busted-up boulder country on the west flank o' the mountain. If he comed on me'n Hoss here, it'd be mostly short shootin' and I still had m'Walker Colt. After night comed, me'n Hoss could slip down out o' here and build a smart lead, headin' for the Southfork and points beyond. And that's what happened. Now, as I watched the varmint a-trailin' me through the rock patch on Ishawooa's side, the thought hit me that I'd seen him afore. I tuned the glass a mite and racked m'brain, but finally had to allow I never knowed nobody that smart at trailin' and that smart at keepin' cover, what was so young. I thought some on how he'd fooled me at the cliff and how he'd laid out snares that woulda made even ol' Richard proud. Then I thought about m'busted ambush at the big rock and how he'd stoled m'Hawken. "One thing for shore and certain," I said out loud, "it don't s'prise me none as that young coon handled Snake Eyes one on one."

He had Hawken, too, the varmint did. He was a-carryin' it mountain man style, slung over his saddle pommel cross-wise in front o' him. I couldn't see any Winchester, but I knowed he had it and figgered it to be tucked in under his right leg and stickin' to the back whar I couldn't see it. It was the Hawken and how he carried it that made a idea run along in m'mind on how I had to get down off this open mesa and into a dense north slope stand o' small spruce. But then I got to thinkin', that that's what the varmint down below'd expect me t'do. "Shore!" I said. "So far he's out-figgered me ever' time."

So I went back and watched him some more. "He knows I'm a-watchin' him, too," I growled, "else he wouldn't be so plumb careless about how he goes." Then m'mind beginned t'turn. "Yeah, he knows I ain't got Hawken, so he'll pay no never mind 'til he gets into pistol shot." I rolled over and looked east across the gentle, open-top mesa and knowed if push come t'shove, I didn't have a prayer against the varmint, what with him havin' all the long-range firepower. "But that's what he thinks and not what he knows."

So I crawled away t'ward Hoss 'til I knowed the varmint couldn't see me from down below. The way I figgered, I had an hour afore he topped out and I wanted to have m'plan set up afore then.

It was about thirty minutes o' steady ridin' afore I found what I wanted. It was a little sink, like it mighta been made a long time ago by a white bear diggin' out a marmot or a band o' gophers. Wind had blowed away the light dust, and rain broke down the clods in what dirt Ephraim piled up, leavin' only rich loam and a few small rocks. Then snow had catched up in the wallow over the years and made that one little spot a bright place for plants t'grow come spring time. And sure enough, a thick patch o' red injin flower grew in the wallow along with a couple o' elk thistles what Hoss headed for—him bein' plumb addled by the thistle tops, like most every other hoss and all the elk what spends any time in the mountains.

I reined Hoss left, though, 'cause I didn't want no tracks in the grass a-showin' the way to whar I was gonna lay up and wait for my trailin' varmint. I dropped off'n Hoss's back and loosened up the McClellan's cinch enough to slide a handful o' pea-gravel twixt the blanket and his hide. Then I pulled up the cinch tight and he sucked down his back and rolled his eyes back at me, hurt-like.

"Sorry, ol' Hoss," I said as I pulled off a chunk o' rope from the saddle and spliced onto the cut halter rope. Then I threw a injin 'war bridle' 'round m'pony's lower jaw whilst he looked plumb bewildered. And I tied the war bridle t'the front o' the McClellan so's Hoss couldn't get his head down.

"Y'see, Hoss," I says. "I want t'keep you movin' plumb across this mesa. Way I figger it, bein' discombob-ulated will make you find some other place."

With that, I slapped ol' Hoss's hind end with m'hat and he jumped like he was shot. The war bridle and the rocks done the trick so's he was still goin' strong when he topped out o' sight. Meanwhile I was liftin' the grass back into place with each step, on m'sneaky way into Ephraim's marmot hollow.

So there I was, a-layin' 'mongst the paintbrushes ten minutes later, with a sprinklin' o' dirt over me and some greenry stuck around m'buckskins, and layin' on m'hat. Even a eagle would have t'sail close t'see me spread there, and I knowed for shore that I'd out-foxed that out-foxin' varmint what trailed me. M'Walker Colt was a-layin' at m'fingers and the coil o' rope I'd need t'catch the varmint's loose hoss after whatever played out twixt him and me was over was layin' in m'loose hand.

Yep, says I to m'self, *he'll never guess this one and by the time he figures it out, he'll be starin' down six loads of m'Walker and all he'll have is a mite awkward Hawken pointed off in the wrong direction.*

I could hear and feel him a-comin' afore I could see him, so I sighted down the back o' the Walker whilst on came the clip, clop o' his hoss, steady as could be. I was cool as ice. Of a sudden, there he was—the buckskin, that is. But the buckskin wasn't a-carryin' no rider!

Waugh! I seen Blackfeet with scalpin' knives at twelve feet, but I swear the way I seen it this time, I ain't never been in a tighter fix. Here I was, on foot, out in the middle of a big open mesa with a man a-hunting me, not over a hundred yards away. And all's I got is a short-range Walker Colt and two huntin' knives, agin a Hawken and a Winchester—and one helluva smart varmint what knowed how t'use 'em. Wasn't no doubt about it, I was in a turrible fix.

His hoss was still comin' on. He had his bridle reins crossed and tied tight, low down on the saddle so as t'hold his pony's head snugged up to keep him from runnin'. Somethin' caught m'eye 'bout that lash-up, though. Then it hit me. That buckskin couldn't run if he wanted to. *So the varmint wants t'catch that buckskin his own self after this play is over.*

'Bout the time I was wallering that thought over in m'mind, the buckskin spied the two elk thistles I was layin' amongst and headed for 'em.

I laid as still as a snake. *What way the wind?* Then I saw the little puffs o' dust the buckskin kicked up was a-floatin' m'way. Come on! Come on! I silently pleaded. I needn't a-been so sweated. That hoss had his eye only on the two elk thistle tops wavin' high enough off the ground for him t'reach, tied-down bridle, or no.

I shrunk into the ground. Ten feet. Six feet. I couldn't believe the hoss hain't knowed I was there! Three feet. I bolted!

The pony jerked and tried t'run, but was held by his reins for a long blink—then I had him! One sweepin' slit with m'knife and his reins was hangin' in two stubs under his chin and him rarin' t'run.

I'd flung m'knife and had him around the neck, with one leg throwed up and a heel locked around the horn. The big buckskin hit the ground runnin' hard and it was most all I could do t'hang on t'the side and try t'get my bouncin' foot in the bouncin' stirrup.

I didn't have no idea whar the shot would come from, but I 'spected one any minute. Way I figgered it as that buckskin raced across the mesa top, the varmint might put one into his hoss, even was he t'get me. Some comfort. That Hawken could blow a hole through both o' us big enough t'drive a wagon through!

The buckskin beginned t'tire afore he was outta range o' the Hawken, but I never egged him on 'cause the fingers I used t'have—the ones tied up amongst his mane— was all sliced and cut by the bouncin' I took in our injin dash away from the varmint. Besides that, the heel o' m'moccasin was wore off by clingin' t'that horn, as was the blister under it. So when the buckskin slowed to a walk, I 'lowed it and dropped down beside him, still holdin' to his neck and keepin' him twixt me and whar we'd come from. D'rectly, I prized m'fingers loose and grabbed the bit shank o' his bridle.

I knowed I had t'fix up some bridle reins and surely did wish for the rope I left layin' in the grass at Ephraim's wallow. "Wish I had m'Walker, too," I said. "And my flung off knife, and m'hat still a-layin' there, too." Then I shook m'head and said to the blowin', winded buckskin, "I sure hope that friendly varmint and me gets this thing settled purty soon 'cause I ain't got nothin' left t'fight with."

Then I had a thought. I checked the Winchester's saddle boot a-hangin' from the off-side whar I knowed it was. And it was empty like I knowed it would be, too. But, by damn, there was a lariat hangin' from the saddle on the same side as the rifle boot, and I unbuckled it, laid it out, and cut a piece long enough for a set o' closed bridle reins. Then I tied 'em to the bit shanks, all the time a-staring over the saddle, back the way we'd comed.

I never did see the varmint, though I knowed he was back there, a-layin' in the grass and lookin' at me down the barrel o' m'big Hawken. Way I figgered it, he was a-hopin' I'd be plumb dumb enough to swing tall in his saddle— but my mammy never raised no idjit.

Time I fixed up the lariat chunk into bridle reins and shoved m'one and only knife still owned by me back into m'belt sheath, the buckskin was fair blowed and I swung up and clucked him on whilst I hung off the left side o' his saddle.

Five minutes later we was out o' range and I set up tall as I could get m'runt size to go and beginned t'take stock o' m'losses. Then I chuckled and said, "Buckskin hoss, we get down off Ishawooa Mesa to the bottom, why, you can walk thirty feet out o' our way t'eat any thistle tops you see."

We picked up Hoss halfway down the mesa. He'd finally kicked the cinch loose and broke the breast collar strap. But the saddle had wound up wrapped around his hind legs and by the time that'd happened he was too tired to kick no more. He nickered, though, like all was forgived and I took off what was left o' his war bridle and reset the saddle. I saw m'possible sack and blanket roll was goned from the saddle, and sighed. Now that I'd lost them, too, I was as near t'the poor house as a man could be.

I was settin' outside the cabin on a block o' wood the next mornin' a-patchin' m'moccasin when he comed. I'd made a handful of coffee what I found inside and winked off t'sleep for awhilst the night afore. Hoss and the buckskin was hobbled down t'the cottonwoods and workin' plumb hard at fillin' their gaunt. I knowed the varmint was comin' when Hoss th'owed up his head and pointed his ears t'ward the canyon. Shortly, the buckskin did the same and nickered a welcome. I made out like I noticed nothin' 'ceptin' the waterfall splashin' into the pool, and I got busier still on the moccasin.

He took his sweet time comin' in, even then. And I was runnin' out o' something to patch. Then he was there, standin' front o' the wood block and carryin' m'Hawken in one hand and his Winchester in t'other.

"Pot o' coffee's on the stove," I said as I turned the moccasin over, peerin' at it.

He didn't say nothin'—just looked at me.

"Trade you a buckskin hoss for that Hawken," I said.

Ol' Hawken crashed to m'feet as he pushed into the cabin. T'was a poor way t'treat a good gun. D'rectly he comed out with a cup o' coffee and stood in front o' me with his feet spread out, Winchester missin', and left thumb hooked into a belt what had m'knife stuck in it. "What in hell are you doing here, old man?" he finally said in a soft voice what was a lie t'his true blue feelin's.

I studied real hard on m'moccasin t'see if it needed any more fixin'. "Plumb wore a hole in it a-tryin' t'hold on t'your saddlehorn with m'heel." He only glared, so I tried again. "Trade you that saddle for that knife you got stuck in your belt."

Of a sudden that knife whacked to its quiverin' hilt in

the ground twixt m'feet. I could see the varmint's humor wasn't improvin'—not so's a body could tell.

"See you got a little side meat and flour and a sour-dough start in the cabin. Reckon we could have somethin' t'eat?"

I thought I seen a twinkle in them gray eyes. Finally he took a deep breath and said, "Reckon."

Grease was a-runnin' down m'chin and I was moppin' up red-eye gravy with a biscuit when next we beginned t'talk. "Heerd o' you and Snake Eyes doin's in Marquardt Town."

"Who?" says he.

"Snake Eyes. Pansy Bottom's honcho."

He looked bufflered for a minute, then smarts showed in them gray eyes and he nodded while chewin' on a biscuit hisself.

"Wanted t'see who broked Snake Eyes' arm and tooked his gun."

He just looked at me.

"All's I figgered was t'see you afore you seed me."

Still them eyes bored in. I was gettin' tired o' the one-sided palaver.

"No call I could see for you t'take on so, just 'cause somebody got the drop on you."

"No?" he said soft-like.

"It ain't no disgrace t'lose a lookin' match to old Sam Buttercut."

He jerked. "Did you say Sam Buttercut?"

"Your ears don't appear t'lap over, son. That's what I said."

Gray eyes twinkled big this time. "Lucky for Sam Buttercut our game ended when it did, or Sam Buttercut wouldn't have enough left to get the drop on anybody."

I chuckled. "Maybe so; maybe not. But I doubled m'hoss herd whilst t'was goin' on."

He grinned. "I've got to admit, that was some trick,

stealing Buck the way you did. I thought I had you for sure."

"T'was sticky," I said, spearing another biscuit. "I hain't seen a young'un with savvy like yours since I was your age."

He never answered that and I studied on him across the split board table. T'was still nagging me that I'd seen him afore and that warn't possible. He had his head turned a-staring beyond the open door and listenin' like a wild critter. He was darker'n the average white-eye and I figgered he might have some injin blood runnin' loose in him. Dark hair made it look that way, too. Whar had I seen him afore? "Fact o' the matter, don't reckon I seen a feller what could trail so good ever, 'ceptin' Richard."

His head popped around and he snapped, "Who?"

"Richard. He was ..."

"Who?"

I looked back for a long time, then breathed, "He was a friend o' mine. Finest I never had. Best mountain man I never knowed. Taught me ever'thin' I know about the mountains, includin' how t'set snares same as you do. He could trail a piss ant across a mountaintop, too, same as you can, and he was always outguessin' ever'body else, same as you do."

Still he said nothin', just stared at a spot on the cabin wall over m'head.

"Richard even had the same color eyes as you got," I muttered so soft it might've been missed had both of us not had ears for ever'thing down to a needle fallin' from a fir tree. Savvy was in them gray eyes.

"Richard hitched up with the prettiest Blackfeet squaw what ever sewed a moccasin."

We looked at each other for what seemed hours, 'til I asked, "What you goin' t'do about Pansy Bottom and Snake Eyes?"

"Depends on what they do."

"Reckon you'll need some help," says I. "So I'm cuttin' m'self in."

Gray Eyes turned his gray eyes t'ward the door openin' and stared outen it for awhilst. Finally he muttered, "If you're the Sam Buttercut I've heard about, I don't reckon there's anybody better to have on my side."

CHAPTER SIX

"There was trouble in that misnamed hamlet, Lillian." She'd found him sitting on the cookhouse steps. "It was caused by that man who accosted us on the road while I was bringing you and your parents to the ranch. Apparently he wants to destroy the Lazy T Bar."

"How is he trying to destroy your ranch, Ellis?" she asked.

"He says he wants to homestead it—our land! One hundred and sixty acres in a canyon to the south. If we let one of those locusts in, soon there'll be others. Until we have nothing left."

Ellis hadn't shaven and there were bags under his eyes. Lillian suspected he might have drunk more after abruptly leaving her the evening before. But it could also have been the result of little sleep. She asked what kind of trouble there'd been.

"This man whom I had never seen until he accosted us on the road—one whose name I've never heard—just walked up to me at Morton's and threatened me. He said he was taking part of our ranch, whether we liked it or not." Ellis paused before going on. "The man is a killer, I'm afraid. Certainly not one to be taken lightly. He broke Levi's arm for no reason, stealing on him from the rear. I hope you'll understand that we have little recourse but to forcibly expel the intruder from the land. Ellis added, "It will be your land, too, one day."

She asked, "Why don't you notify the proper law enforcement people and let them take care of the unpleasantries?"

He started to laugh, then choked. "Unfortunately there is little law this far from Laramie and Cheyenne. Actually the only law is that which one can enforce oneself. Lack of law enforcement is, no doubt, what this gunman counts on for success. Fortunately the Lazy T Bar is not without its own resources and perhaps a show of force will cause him to tuck his tail and run."

Lillian sat down on the steps beside him and he draped an arm over her shoulders. My only regret, Lillian, is that you will be exposed to this regrettable situation. It is life on the frontier, I suppose. But I had thought to shield you from this type of sordidness."

She reached up to squeeze his hand. "Perhaps I'm made of sterner stuff than you might think," she whispered. "I know, Ellis, that things must be different out here than back home. I'm ready to adjust. If you've considered your alternatives carefully and feel you have but one course of action, then I'll support you to the end."

———•◆•———

The version of the affair in Morton's saloon that August Mathers overheard amongst T Bar hands differed considerably from the one told by Ellis Burroughs. "I cannot reconcile their differences," he told his daughter. "But

I'd not advise asking Ellis for an explanation; not yet, anyway. Instead, we'll simply remain vigilant observers."

It was Ellis himself who offered chance for clarification when he overruled his foreman's wish to march directly on Blood Canyon and forcibly evict the homesteader. "I'll not countenance it, Levi. Not while the Mathers are in residence. Instead, I would first prefer a visit to his enclave in an attempt to dissuade him from his foolishness."

"Then, by damn, I'll have no part of it!" Bunting retorted, voice rising. "There's a time to fight and there's a time to talk. And as far as I'm concerned, there's never no time to talk to nesters."

Ellis held up a hand. "Again, Levi, I do not wish to take precipitate action while the Mathers family is visiting. But I do feel the fact that a nester occupies a piece of our land requires response. Whether that response comes at the muzzle of a gun or through moral dissuasion is hardly relevant. Let me try my way first, but should it prove unsuccessful, then you can utilize your method."

The party chosen by Ellis Burroughs to accompany him on his peace overtures to Blood Canyon was made up of Cletus Wills and Patrick O'Brien, the two Higson brothers, Indian Joe Waters, and Lillian Mathers. The woman had been thrilled by the invitation.

Holding her hands in his, Ellis said, "You'll be properly chaperoned, of course, with a half-dozen of the hands accompanying us." She smiled in a way that dismissed the idea that she needed a chaperone.

"You can learn and understand more about Wyoming ranching during these few days than you'd learn in a year ensconced at the ranch," he said.

———◆———

"Oh look, Ellis," she cried, pointing to her right as they rode side by side through lush, grassy meadows. It was mid-July and the sun stood directly overhead during their first day's ride to Blood Canyon. "Isn't that rock peculiar, sticking up like that, way out in the valley?"

"That's Castle Rock, my dear. They say it was named by one of the earlier fur trappers. It's a landmark readily seen throughout the lower Southfork Valley." Their three packhorses, herded by the Higson brothers, trailed behind. Wills and O'Brien led the party. Waters had disappeared.

Their first night was spent at the Bledsoe line cabin, so named, Ellis told her, for an Englishman who'd previously settled on the site. "The poor man died in an accident when his foot hung in a stirrup and his horse dragged him to death. Terrible thing."

Ellis gallantly gave over the cabin to Lillian, while his hands erected a small canvas tent for him. "But what of the men?" Lillian asked. "Are they to sleep outside? That isn't right."

Ellis laughed. "They always sleep under the stars on their excursions, my dear. They're used to it."

"Well, although I feel guilty, I certainly can't question the propriety of the arrangement."

That night, it rained; buckets. When Ellis knocked and entered the cabin after daylight filtered in, he suggested they remain another day in order to let the men dry their clothing and bedding. Lillian tried her hand at baking biscuits, in order to make amends to the men in their travail. But, though the biscuits turned out well, Ellis thought it better that they continue to distance themselves from his workmen. She acquiesced largely because she'd not felt entirely at ease around the group Ellis had chosen; she could not completely trust Wills and O'Brien, and the Indian made her think of the wolf in *Little Red Riding Hood*. The two Higson brothers seemed better, but even they had an aura of violence hovering over them.

The rain stopped by late afternoon and Lillian felt better for the men. The party set out for the Swenson line cabin early the following morning. That day proved sunny and warm. The rain had freshened the air, providing a crisp clarity that even the rough-cut men admired. The land seemed rife with birds and small mammals—ground squirrels and rockchucks. Deer jumped from their path along the river bottoms and antelope watched from the hills. Elk fed high on the mountainsides where sagebrush turned to bunchgrass. Scattered at random, cattle grazed contentedly along both riverbank and hillside.

They crossed the Southfork shortly after leaving the Bledsoe cabin, riding up the west bank until reaching Ishawooa Creek.

"As you can see, Lillian, our cattle ranges are only sparsely stocked," Ellis explained. "We, here on the Lazy T Bar, are building for the future. When we've completed adequate stocking, we'll have one of the larger herds in Wyoming, and perhaps the most functional ranch in the entire state."

She smiled at his boyish enthusiasm and reached out to touch his arm as they rode stirrup to stirrup amid the rich bottoms. She sensed the easy intimacy fading, however, as their cavalcade approached the Swenson line cabin. As Ellis helped her from the saddle, she asked, "And did this cabin belong to an early settler, too?"

He ignored her while surveying the sky. "It's only mid-afternoon," he said to the men. "I'm wondering if we shouldn't just continue to Blood Canyon and get the distasteful chore over with."

"We might have time," Wills said, also squinting at the sun.

"Hell, there's only one bastard up there," O'Brien said.

"Please!" Ellis Burroughs murmured. "Watch your language. There's a lady present."

O'Brien mumbled an apology and tipped his hat to Lillian.

"Are you sure there's only one man up there?" Lloyd Higson asked. "Hell—beg pardon, ma'am—there could be an army up there."

"Be dark before we got back," the other Higson said, "'specially if any jawboning takes place. Want me to stay here and set up camp while the rest of you go? I can have supper ready when you get back."

"Are you chicken livered?" Wills asked. Both Higsons tensed, stepping apart.

Burroughs quickly intervened. "We'll spend the night here."

O'Brien loosened the girth and unsaddled Lillian's horse. "Cute little bastard, ain't it?" he said, holding her sidesaddle high with one hand.

Ellis ushered the woman inside the line cabin, then returned to his men. Lillian saw him whisper instructions to Indian Joe Waters, but could not hear sufficiently well to understand them. The men talked quietly among themselves for some time, then Ellis returned to the cabin while the Higson boys unloaded the packhorses. Wills and O'Brien unsaddled the remaining horses, hobbled them, and turned them out to graze.

When the rancher politely removed his hat, Lillian asked, "Ellis, do I sense a growing reluctance to confront the trespasser?"

"Not at all. It's just that we must ensure certain protocol."

Just then, Indian Joe trotted his horse from camp. With arms tucked beneath her breasts, Lillian watched him go. "Ellis," she said at last, "I don't know any of the rules—but is it part of proper protocol to send out a spy before an armed party proceeds on a mission of diplomacy?"

The man tossed his head and jammed his hat back in place. "I'm only thinking of what's best for you, my dear. I could never forgive myself if I led you heedlessly into danger." He slammed the door on his way out.

After supper, when she and Ellis were strolling alone along the river, Lillian suggested that just the two of them ride into Blood Canyon to talk to the trespasser. "Don't you think that would be the best way to convince the man of our peaceful intentions?"

"And risk your safety? Don't be absurd."

The following morning, largely because their leader seemed determined to proceed in his own good time, the party was late getting started—a matter that seemed strange to Lillian since they intended returning to the Swenson line cabin after visiting Blood Canyon. Cletus Wills slapped his horse in the face with his hat when the animal resisted the bit, and O'Brien appeared edgy.

Lillian thought the morning's ride beautiful. Wild rose was blooming, its sweet fragrance tantalizing. Here and there small cactus blossomed and a species of Indian paintbrush cast a tinge of red along the lower slopes. Many yellow flowers, none identified by her companions, offered variety to the predominant pinks, reds, and greens.

By late morning, the Southfork Valley of the Stinkingwater narrowed and cliffs towered near the trail, occasionally widening into verdant postage-stamp meadows. Groves of cottonwoods mixed with a few firs and pines stood at the base of small ravines, right and left. She realized none of the men was talking. Then their party entered Blood Canyon. Immense, varicolored walls of red and gray stone towered above them. The trail narrowed to a single track. Ellis Burroughs, riding ahead of Lillian, seemed to shrink in his saddle. And she finally realized these men feared an ambush!

CHAPTER SEVEN

He was a-standin' at the door. "They're comin'," I said from Hoss's back.

"How many?"

"Seven, but one is a woman."

"A woman?"

"Yep. I can tell the diff'rence."

"Where are they?" Gray Eyes asked.

"I seen 'em as they crossed the Ishawooa. Wasn't late, but all the same, I figger they'll spend the night at Swenson's. They're movin' slow and laughin' a lot."

"Is Bunting with 'em?"

I shook my head. "But it's a war party all the same. Leastways four are slingers. And one is a mean-faced half-breed I 'member from Fort Hall."

"I'm a half-breed."

"Do tell? That's more'n I heered afore. B'sides, your face ain't mean; it's just ugly."

"Burroughs there?"

"Yep. Ol' Pansy Bottom. The girl is his'n, way it looks."

Gray Eyes turned to inspect the waterfall. "Well," he says at last, "it's begun. Here's what we'll do...."

———————

The injin comed slow and careful. He didn't come up the ridge neither, but off t'the side a little, and so missed Gray Eyes' near snare by three feet. *Better talk t'the lad 'bout that,* I told m'self silent-like.

I could see flashes o' the injin's face in patches o' moonlight as it filtered through the trees. He packed a long rifle with him, but I couldn't make out what bore it was in the dark. Wasn't no Hawken, though. The injin stopped ever time he tooked a couple o' steps, sniffin' the air and lookin' all around. Then he glided on like a shadow. After awhilst, he moved t'the same limber pine I first crawled to, but he stood up whar I laid down. Course I was there in the daylight and he was there in the dark and knowed he couldn't be saw from down b'low. The injin stood quiet for a minute or two, then moved left t'ward the big pine and the snare that'd jerk him over the cliff.

I was cheerin' him on, knowin' he couldn't see the set in the dark, but damned if'n he never stopped afore he got there and turned back the way he comed. He passed the little pine bush and moved on t'whar the crick dropped over the cliff t'the pool below. I watched him whilst he squatted and tooked a drink, and watched him whilst he raised up and started back. Then I guess he stopped t'look around for whatever t'was he wanted. Somethin' must o' made him happy 'cause he dropped t'his hands and knees ahind the scrub, then went to his belly and made himself comfy. I didn't think much o' his choice o' ambush layups, for he didn't have as good o' fire-field as he would t'the left. And the scrub brush never screened him too good neither.

But it didn't make much difference one way nor t'other when I kicked his rifle over the cliff and stuck the point o' m'Green River knife against his neck.

The Big Dipper made three quarters o' its night swing around the North Star and the moon sunk out o' sight ahind the western ridge. The injin's face warn't so mean no more as Gray Eyes carved loose dirt out from under his fingernails with his toad-sticker. 'Stead o' mean, the Injin could a-been mistook for a paleface in the dark, and white showed clear 'round each big black eyeball.

"Indian Joe Waters," Gray Eyes said as he held up a fingernail in the starlight, studyin' it just as if he could see it. "You're three-quarters Bannock, from over on Henry's Fork and points south. You're wanted down at the falls of the Snake for suspicion of murder and there's some talk about how a fellow fits your description killed a couple of miners over in Elk City. What brings you to Blood Canyon?"

The injin never said nothin', so Gray Eyes tried again. "Prospecting?"

Waters still said nothin'. I could see a darker streak down his neck whar he flapped into m'knife point in surprise when I dropped a knee into the small o' his back at the same time I pointed the knife's business end his way. He sure must a-figgered Gray Eyes and me for easy pigeons. *Whoa now! Not me, he never. Not the way he's a-lookin' plumb spooked my way. He 'members that time down t'Fort Hall, and 'members me, and 'members what I aim t'do about it.*

"Cat got your tongue?" Gray Eyes asked.

He still didn't say nothin', and the white dimmed 'round his eyeballs. He was a-settin' on a wood block, leanin' against the cabin logs. Gray Eyes was a-settin' on t'other wood block d'rectly in front o' the varmint. I was standin' 'longside, so I wrapped m'fingers in the injin's greasy hair and banged his head against the logs to get his attention.

"One thing about it, Joe Waters, with you layin' up on the cliff and four other fighting men with him, your boss isn't planning a social call, is he?"

I rapped his head twice more for to make a good listener out o' him.

"They no fight," he said. He looked up at me, whites shinin' 'round his eyeballs again. "White woman no let fight. Joe make sure boss no get shot from tree. Joe know you no want Joe in Canyon. You turn Joe loose and you don't see Joe no more. Ever.

"Little man, Wills, him bad poison. Fast with gun. So red-headed man. Two brothers plenty tough, but they no shoot from back. Boss carry little gun in belt and 'nother in coat. Knife in boot. You let Joe go, he leave Stinkingwater fast."

"Sam, why don't you take Joe out away from here and see he don't warn the others coming in. Meanwhile, I'll fix things up here to look like nobody's home."

"No, no! Waters pleaded. "Joe 'fraid Gray Eyes and Mountain Spirit Buttercut. He never see Stinkingwater again! Promise!"

I rapped his head again t'shut him up.

As Gray Eyes raised up off'n his pine block he motioned me a little ways away. "Put the fear of God in him and tie him across the trail after Burroughs' bunch has passed. I think the bastard will jump the country. If he does, it might give the rest of 'em something to think about."

Well, t'hell with God—I put the fear o' Sam Buttercut in the skunk. After the riders went by, I strung the injin across the trail, then beat it back t'the cliff top and watched what went on b'low down m'Hawken barrel. It turned out

Gray Eyes warn't a-needin' me....

———•◦•———

At last, the Burroughs party exited Blood Canyon. Lillian gasped. A small canyon fed in from the side; a picturesque cabin sat atop a knoll; a waterfall cascaded from the northwest, over a low cliff, dropping into a pool at its base. Huge cottonwoods ringed the pool on three sides.

"Oh my! Isn't it lovely?" Lillian Mathers asked of anyone listening. No one else seemed to notice as their eyes swept the clifftop, cabin portals, and meadow fringes.

They rode first to the cabin, with Ellis gripping the headstall of Lillian's steed until they'd fallen behind the four T Bar hands. Wills, taking charge though he was the youngest, shouted. There was no reply. Floyd Higson dismounted to knock on the cabin door. Finally he tried the latch, cautiously swinging the door open. After peeking inside, he shook his head at the riders. Ellis and the others relaxed. Lloyd Higson suggested they water their horses at the pool below the waterfall. Ellis suggested eating their noon meal at the pool's edge.

"Yes, you're right, Lillian," Ellis agreed as he leaned against a cottonwood, chewing meditatively on a slice of roast. "It is indeed beautiful. Won't it make a lovely way stop on our way upriver to the Thorofare country?"

Lillian sat by his side, leaning against the same tree. The four T Bar men ranged facing them, with three squatting on their heels and one kneeling. Then the same buckskin-clad stranger who'd attempted talking to them on the road from Marquardt stepped from behind a nearby cottonwood. He carried a shotgun with its twin muzzles ranging along the heels of the four T Bar men.

Both Ellis's and Lillian's eyes widened. Wills started to swing around when the stranger drawled, "Mind if I join the party?" Then he added, "I'll depend on each of you observing good manners for the rest of the afternoon. If you do not, whatever bad manners you do show will be the last of your manners the rest of us will ever see."

"Please, let's all do as he says," Ellis cried, his voice unnaturally high. Wills settled back into place while Floyd Higson and Patrick O'Brien raised their hands shoulder high.

"Always happy to have company, Mr. Burroughs. Is this a social call?"

It was obvious to Lillian that despite the newcomer's mundane words that he was very much in command. She realized then that she must be staring as wide-eyed as Ellis. She glanced at her husband-to-be, then said, "Indeed it is, Mr. uh ..." She let the pause hang for an instant, then proceeded, "It is both a social visit and for business purposes."

"Now you have my attention, ma'am. But why don't we let Mr. Burroughs tell us what the visit is for."

Ellis swallowed, then asked if the two of them could "retire to the cabin in order to privately discuss ..."

"This will do fine," the stranger said, cutting Burroughs off.

When no one else spoke, Lillian said, "We came to persuade you that a homestead here, on Lazy T Bar land, would be inadvisable, Mr. ..." Again she let her question hang. Again he ignored her, continuing to stare at Burroughs.

Ellis cleared his throat, tried to speak; could not. She continued, "As I understand it, Mr. ..." He shook his head and she rushed on. "To allow one homesteader on this ranch may set a precedent for other homesteaders, and might actually lead to many unpleasantries in the future."

She fell silent then, studying him. The man's gray eyes were unsettling. She was stunned to discover that, subconsciously, she must evaluate the newcomer's appearance. *Perhaps a bit too dark-complected, and his nose might be a trifle large. In addition, he's shabbily dressed. But he moved with an almost feline grace when he stepped from his hiding place.* She shuddered to find the man looking at her. He was smiling.

Then the eyes turned flat as he said, without even looking to the side, "Move one more time like that and you're dead, mister."

"For God's sake, Wills!" Ellis shouted. "You want to get us all killed?" Wills again settled into place.

"Not the lady," the stranger said. There was again a touch of humor in his eyes. A revolver swung low on his right thigh. She decided she wanted to know more about this man.

"You do want to avoid future unpleasantries, don't you?" she asked.

"Yes ma'am, I surely do." He'd continued watching her now for several minutes and for some reason she felt weak. "I'm peaceable, and unless I'm bothered, I intend to stay that way." Then he pointed at Ellis Burroughs and said, "So why don't you ask him if I'll be allowed to live up here in this far-off canyon? Ask him if I'll be able to avoid unpleasantries."

She noticed he had a small scar on his chin and another above one eyebrow. She nearly missed the eyebrow scar because a shock of dark hair fell across his forehead. His feet were planted wide-spread, and he wore Indian-style moccasins that looked heavier and more substantial than others she'd seen. His worn buckskin trousers stretched tightly over what appeared to be quite sturdy legs. He swayed ever so slightly as he spoke—in what she suspected was a deceptively lax posture. His hands were rough and calloused, and one knuckle on his right hand was scraped, oozing blood. She blinked. *This man is much more than he appears.*

"... So why don't you ask him what conditions I'm going to stay under?"

Lillian involuntarily broke eye contact to stare at Ellis.

"You see, ma'am," the stranger continued, "I don't make the laws, just abide by 'em. And the law says I can have one hundred and sixty acres of pretty near any government land that I want, as long as I follow some rules. One of those rules is that I must live on the land for a few years. And I must make some improvements. I've made the improvements, as you can see, and I figure to make a whole lot more."

She couldn't help herself. Her eyes swept to the picturesque cabin before returning to rest on the strange man.

"No matter what you might have been told, this land meets the qualifications of available land, ma'am. You see, Mr. Burroughs don't own this land; instead he's just using it until the United States Government finds somebody who wants the land bad enough to want to live on it, trying to scratch a living for himself, and maybe a family off it. And without trying to hog the whole country for himself."

Lillian felt Ellis shifting uncomfortably and couldn't resist doing so herself.

"Well, the government's found somebody who wants this little piece of ground, ma'am. Me. And I think I'll stay right here. I'll stay peaceable, or I'll stay unpeaceable. But I'll stay."

When the man paused for a breath, Ellis Burroughs blurted, "I'll pay you for your improvements. I'll pay whatever you ask!" Wills and O'Brien and the two Higsons stared at him in disgust.

The stranger didn't seem to notice the interruption. "Blood has already flowed on the Stinkingwater, ma'am. The man who once owned a ranch on Ishawooa Creek was shot down in a dusty street in Marquardt when he was too drunk to hold himself upright, let alone hold a gun. The man who done it works for your gentleman friend here."

Lillian twisted to stare at Ellis.

"The fellow on the Ishawooa had a couple of loyal hands who felt obligated to avenge his death. They had more loyalty than ability and they went down in front of a couple of the Lazy T Bar's best. One of those T Bar best squats in front of you right now."

Wills's ears turned red and his cheeks began to flush. Lillian saw him tense and said firmly, "No, Cletus!"

"So you see, ma'am, this land don't rightfully belong to the Lazy T Bar, no matter how you look at it. This particular piece belongs to me now, because I've filed on it and I'll stay on it. I'll live here or I'll die here, ma'am. That choice might not be entirely mine. But I'll tell you, Mr. Burroughs ..." and his eyes left hers at last, to fix on Ellis's pale blue orbs. "...if I die here, there'll be lots of blood other than mine seeping into this dirt."

Ellis swallowed. "I do believe you're mistaken, my good man. We certainly did not come here to talk of war, but of peace. I've offered to buy your improvements. Surely you'd place a value on them and consider relinquishing your claim."

"Surely I wouldn't, Mr. Burroughs," the man said. "Look around. Isn't this one of the prettiest sights you've ever seen? It caught my eye when I was looking for a place to light. I haven't been here long, but it's home. Did you ever have a home, Mr. Burroughs?"

"Of course he did," Lillian broke in.

"No offense, ma'am, but I'm asking your man friend." The shotgun came up to yawn at Ellis's belt buckle. "So tell me, Mr. Burroughs, did you ever have a home?"

"YES!" He was too loud and knew so as soon as it left his mouth. "Of course I had a home. A very nice one, too, I might add."

"Would you sell it?"

"Eh? Sell it? Of course I would—if the price was right."

The shotgun's muzzles dropped and the stranger looked at Lillian. "You see, ma'am, that's the difference between him and me. Some things I have just aren't for sale. *Everything* he has is."

Evidently the gray-eyed stranger considered the conversation at an end, because he said, "All right, you on the end—take your gun out real slow, with the thumb and forefinger. That's right. Be sure you think about what you're doing and don't make any dumb decisions. Now throw that weapon on the ground about three feet in front of you. Very good. Next...."

The other Higson did as he was told and threw his revolver on top of his brother's. Then O'Brien. Then Wills. "Now, Mr. Burroughs, yours."

"Mine? I'm not armed."

"Stand up Burroughs!"

"Now see here ..."

"One last time, Burroughs, stand up!" The shotgun yawned and Ellis scrambled to his feet.

"Now reach very carefully behind your belt buckle and pull the derringer out. That's right, e-e-easy now." Then the man smiled. "Now, just a last piece of advice, Mr. Burroughs—we can take the rest of them off your dead body, or you can add them to the pile. Makes no difference to me. What'll it be?"

Burroughs reached very slowly and carefully into his coat pocket and withdrew another derringer, which was added to the pile.

"Now the knife in your boot." The knife was tossed onto the pile, as were belt knives from the others.

"Very good," the man said. He stared steadily at Lillian for a moment—until she glared back. Finally he asked, "Will you give me your word, ma'am, that you're not armed?"

"And why should I be?"

"Well now, ma'am, it looks to me like coming here on a social call, carrying enough weapons to outfit the Army of Northern Virginia is more the rule than the exception."

"Sir, I did not expect to need a weapon when I came. Do I?"

"I guess that's good enough. Now, all of you, move away from your guns, toward your horses." The man stopped them halfway to the animals, then walked to each steed and removed the saddle guns, making another pile. All except Wills's Winchester; that he leaned against a cottonwood and with a sweeping bow, bade the party mount their steeds.

Lillian was the first in the saddle—without help. While the rest mounted, she asked, "Do you have a name?"

A faint smile touched his lips, but he never replied. Instead he leaned the shotgun against the tree and, in the same motion, swept up the rifle belonging to Wills. Then he laughed aloud and said, "Tell me, Mr. Burroughs, do you always bring a woman along for protection?"

"I will see you in hell, sir," Burroughs ground out, savagely reining his stallion toward the entrance to Blood Canyon.

But the stranger stepped in front of the stallion, catching the bridle and swinging up the rifle muzzle. There was a spell-binding 'click' heard by all. They all also heard the stranger when he said, "If I was you, Mr. Burroughs, I'd go back out the same way you came in. When you do, you can pick up the bushwhacking Indian you sent to gutshoot me."

Lillian couldn't help herself. She turned to look back before her party entered Blood Canyon. The man stood before his cabin with Wills's Winchester in the crook of his left arm. Lillian's face flushed when he raised his right hand in a wave.

CHAPTER EIGHT

The Indian blocked the trail on the Burroughs party's way back through Blood Canyon. The man's arms were outstretched, lashed to pine trees either side with his own lariat, toes barely touching the ground. He watched impassively as Lloyd Higson sliced the rope with a Barlow knife. When he was free, he rubbed his wrists, then wheeled and trotted off down-canyon, toward the Swenson line cabin. Joe Waters, along with the rest of the party, was without weapons.

As the trotting horse party passed the trotting man, Floyd Higson freed one stirrup to allow Waters to swing up. Not a word was uttered by anyone from the time the stranger released the headstall on Ellis Burroughs' stallion until they reached the Swenson cabin.

Upon arrival, the rancher retired to his tent without issuing directions. Lillian stood by uncertainly as the men unsaddled horses. Finally she made her way to the cabin, then to the river. She was the first to see the Indian's saddlehorse come trotting in, stirrups flapping.

Burroughs emerged from his tent upon Lloyd Higson's call to supper. The others watched in silence as the rancher took a tin plate, filled it with stew, tore off a crust of bread, then took a seat on the grass alongside Lillian. "I'm not at all pleased with the way events unfolded today," he said to no one in particular.

"For one thing, it was inexcusable for us to be taken so unawares." He glanced up from his plate to stare directly at Wills and O'Brien. "Apparently, since the man did not meet us with open arms, we assumed he was nowhere to be found." He shook his head, as if in wonder. "How could it be that experienced fighting men—as I assumed you were—did not post a guard? And the Indian ... where's the Indian?"

"Gone," Floyd Higson said.

"Gone? Where did he go? I didn't say he could go, confound it!"

"He just took his horse and bedroll and left," O'Brien said.

"How could he?" the rancher demanded. "He had no horse."

"It came in a few minutes behind us. Had his saddle on, too."

Burroughs' eyes swept the circle, settling at last on Lillian. "We must get you a pocket gun, my dear. If you'd had one, we could have taken advantage of the knave's chivalry."

Her eyes flashed, but she bit her lip.

Cletus Wills leaped to his feet, throwing his plate and spoon to the ground. "What I'd like to know, Boss, is why we're settin' here talkin'. Somebody should be on the wing to the main ranch for a load of guns."

"Perhaps that's where the Indian went."

"Yeah, and maybe I'm my mother's left boot. What I'm talking about, Mister Burroughs, is doin' some settling up with that bastard back yonder. And the sooner I get to it, the better."

"Me, I'd like to know a little more about him, "Lloyd Higson said. "Hell, he can't be alone. If he tied the Indian across the trail behind us and still got to the pond ahead of us, then he's a magician, too. I could see how he could hide while we went to his cabin, then to the lake. But I still don't see how he could've snuck up on us without even our ponies perkin' up."

"He's handled guns, that's for sure," Patrick O'Brien said. "You see how he picked up Wills's Winchester and jacked a shell in one handed?"

Lillian leaped to her feet, striding swiftly into the gathering darkness.

"What we need to do," Floyd Higson suggested, "is find the Indian, ask him how he was taken. When and who by. This yokel is not, by God, alone!"

"I'm not sure he's a yokel, either," his brother murmured.

Wills stomped away, only to return seconds later. When he did, Burroughs decided, "It makes no difference whether one man, or all, ride for help. We'll still have to mount a further attack from headquarters. Besides, we'll need to escort Lillian to safety."

"Good lot of protection we'll be without guns," O'Brien scoffed.

The sun burned overhead, birds sang in the willow brush as Ellis and Lillian rode side by side through deep grass. She'd spoken but a half-dozen words since the previous day when she'd asked the stranger his name, but the rancher seemed too busy with his own thoughts to notice.

"Ellis, was that man right?" she blurted. "About his legal rights and … and about the way you came to own the

Swenson property?"

He glanced at her in surprise. "This is no way to begin our relationship!"

"But we're not *beginning* a relationship, dear. We're trying to maintain one."

"No, the nesting bastard was wrong! At least he soon will be. Lobbyists are hard at work in Washington to repeal the Homestead Act. And as far as Swenson's demise, you received no true picture there, either."

"Does that mean, as the law now stands, that he has a legal claim to that land?"

"Lillian, you must understand this country has only recently been wrested from bloodthirsty savages by courageous and competent ranchers—men with vision and sufficient fortitude to make their visions come true. I am an inheritor of those lusty warriors, none of whom would tolerate a nester on his land."

She reached out to lay a gloved hand on his sleeve. "What of the original owner of the T Bar, Ellis?"

"What? Of Morgan? I purchased the T Bar from a man who'd been broken by the country's hardships. He was paid a more than fair price." The rancher changed the subject before she could ask after Bledsoe, Kittleson, or Marquardt. "I should think it time to set a date for our wedding."

"Not yet," she murmured.

Their cavalcade pulled into the main ranch shortly after nightfall. Levi Bunting and another two hands were absent, riding north to check on cattle grazing the Rattlesnake Hills. Burroughs dispatched a rider after them.

———•—•———

August Mathers stuffed his old crooked-stemmed pipe and gazed thoughtfully at the ceiling while he considered all his daughter told. Mattie Mathers clicked knitting needles and muttered about Burroughs' perfidy. The old man held the pipe by its bowl while he scratched a match alight and let it burn.

"We must remember, things aren't the same out here as back in the East, ladies. It is a raw, new land and ..." (he dropped the match as it burned to his fingers) "... we must remember that Ellis may be right about the law existing only for those strong enough to enforce it.

"I think, too, that he's right about the Homestead Law. Efforts are, indeed, being made to repeal it. But those efforts have, in fact, been going on for decades and are unlikely to succeed. You see, my dears, that law was designed specifically to benefit former soldiers, to bring settlers to the West. And one thing seems quite clear to me—the unknown gentleman you visited is within the law, such as it is. If he is legally correct, then Ellis cannot drive him from the land without stepping outside the law."

Mathers again groped for a match, struck it, and touched flame to his pipe. "Lillian, have your feelings toward Ellis changed since your Blood Canyon journey?"

"I don't know ..." Her face twisted. "Yes," she said. "Yes they have—and they'll continue to change if he goes through with his plan to drive the man from his lawful property." Her forehead smoothed. "Father, it was beautiful. The cabin was all hand constructed of logs taken from the area. The waterfall and the pool and the grove of trees! It was simply beautiful. He seems so determined, too. Such courage. He will fight. I know he will." She paused to consider her own words. "He'll be killed, won't he?"

The fire in her father's pipe died as he studied his daughter. The clicking of her mother's knitting needles stopped.

The following morning, Burroughs sent for Indian Joe

Waters, but Washburn the cook reported the man had disappeared. "He rode into the ranch a good twelve hours before you did, Mr. Burroughs. He was leading his own personal horse—you know, the little bay with the lightning blaze and the four white ..."

"Get on with it, damn you," Burroughs snarled.

"Well, he unsaddled the one he was riding, threw his saddle on his own horse, disappeared into the bunkhouse and came out a few minutes later with the rest of his gear. Last I seen of him was when he swung his horse toward Marquardt. Funny thing, it was. Never said 'boo,' 'howdy,' or 'by your leave' to nobody."

"Get out, Washburn," the younger man muttered, "but on your way, find Wills for me."

Wills pounded from the ranchyard fifteen minutes later, heading for Marquardt. He returned after several hours with a disquieting report, and whiskey on his breath. "He ain't there, Boss. I talked to most ever'body I could find and nobody's seen him. He went around Marquardt, sure enough. I even went down to Corbin's Crossing, but nobody seen 'im there neither."

Burroughs dispatched two other riders with second messages to his foreman, each to sweep in different directions. Then he set the Higsons to selecting twenty of the T Bar's best horses, bringing them in for Schulte to re-set their shoes.

The rancher had seen little of Lillian Mathers since their return from Blood Canyon and talked to her not at all. Though the Mathers family attended dinner formally, Burroughs always seemed busy elsewhere.

Levi Bunting rode into the ranchyard at high noon, three days after the Blood Canyon affair. Lillian appeared at Ellis's elbow as he watched his foreman stride to the ranch house. "Please, Ellis, forget about that one man forty miles away."

He turned his back on her. "I'm not at all disposed to

argue with you about business I have no intention of dropping."

Bunting strode into the office, smirking. "Done it up
brown this time, huh Burroughs?"

The foreman took the swivel chair behind the desk and
called for Wills, then O'Brien, then the Higsons in turn. It
was as if the ranch owner wasn't even in the room.

The men told him of the narrow canyon and the cabin
squatting like a fort atop the little hill. They mentioned the
cliff and the pond and the big cottonwoods growing along
its shore.

"Can we burn the cabin?" Bunting asked.

"There's rifle loops a-plenty in them walls," Lloyd
Higson said.

"What about using a fire wagon?" Burroughs asked,
entering the conversation.

Wills and Lloyd Higson snorted. "If a wagon could be
got up there," said Higson, "why didn't we take one when
we went the first time?"

"Anybody here crazy enough to try pushing a burning
wagon up a hill that's defended by a sharpshooter?" asked
Wills.

Levi asked if there was anything notable about the
nester.

"Soft boots," Floyd Higson said. "And he moved like
he's used to 'em. Snuck up on us like a Indian."

"He is a Indian," O'Brien muttered.

Wills said he'd stake his life the man was more than a
little familiar with a gun. O'Brien agreed.

"How old is he?" Bunting asked.

"Thirty. Perhaps thirty-five," Burroughs replied.

Bunting dismissed the men, then rolled a cigarette with
his one good hand. He struck a match on the chair arm
and touched it to the cigarette. "Now the woman."

"Lillian?" Burroughs asked in surprise. "Why would
you wish to see her?"

Bunting sighed. "Maybe you ain't been around women long enough, Burroughs, but they sometimes got an eye for things most men miss."

When Lillian came into the room, she was accompanied by her father. Bunting asked her if she'd noted anything unusual about the stranger at the nester's place. She said she'd noticed the man appeared determined—and remarkably competent.

"That's not what I meant," Bunting said. "Was there any physical characteristics, such as scars or deformities you might have noticed?"

"Mr. Bunting," she replied, "I will not be a party to a war carried out by you or this ranch against one individual until I discover whether that man is in the wrong." For the first time, she noticed the man's eyes were like those of a snake, half-lidded, unblinking.

"Until then," she continued, "no, I noticed nothing about the man except that he was especially gentle, considering the incentive we gave him to retaliate." She grew angry, switching her flashing eyes to Ellis Burroughs. "Beginning with the Indian sent in ahead with probable orders to shoot on sight, and ending ..."

"Lillian! I must ask ..."

"... with entry of a full-scale war party, equipped to do battle with the Confederate Army!"

"Lillian, that will be quite enough!" Burroughs was angry, too.

She continued to stare at the man she'd journeyed west to marry, as tears welled in her eyes and ran down her cheeks. Then she wheeled and, followed by her silent father, stamped from the room.

Bunting continued to smoke, staring for some time at the doorway through which she'd passed. Then he muttered, "Looks like you might have made a mistake, Mr. Burroughs."

The rancher glared at his foreman. "What is your plan

to alleviate the problem?" he asked.

Bunting pushed to his feet. "Ain't got it clear in my mind, yet. But I'll sleep on it tonight and maybe a plan will come to me."

The next morning, the foreman offered his solution. "The Lazy T Bar isn't the most popular brand in this country," he began. "Everybody's watching what happens in Blood Canyon."

"I know all this," Ellis said. "Get on with it."

Bunting smiled. "This stranger is not exactly an ordinary nester. Way it sounds to me, he's forted up in a place where it's tough to get to him. And the way everybody's watching the outcome here, we can't just send a couple of riflemen up there 'cause we're not sure if he's alone or with somebody. Then, too, it sounds like he knows the land and how to use it." The foreman reached for his coffee; held the cup. "We can't just take a big crew up there to burn the bastard out, neither."

"Why not?"

"Say we do and the rabbit runs for his hole, then holds us off for awhile. That might be the spark needed to get the Marquardt bunch goin'; Judge Kittleson, too. He might be busy with the move to Lander, but he won't be too busy to do us harm. And we'll want to remember he's got friends in the right places, even if you have got his tail under a rock you're standing on."

"But we can't just leave a nester there without doing something!" Ellis cried.

Bunting laughed. "Keep your shirt on, Burroughs. What we need is a reason to get about twenty men in those Blood Canyon hills in a manner where the damn fool can't fight without putting himself outside the law."

"But how?"

"We're going to hold a cattle drive."

"A what? Are you insane?"

Again Bunting laughed. "We're gonna put a herd of

cows into Blood Canyon—and beyond—for the rest of the summer. Way I figure, it'll take about twenty men to put them cows up there, and they'll probably have to stay 'til the herd settles down."

Burroughs' eyes widened. "We'll have men all over those hills!"

"And he won't be able to stay in that cabin all summer. Nor can he watch all of us, scattered as we'll be. When the time is right—who knows? A rifle shot or a match could end our problem."

Ellis Burroughs and Lillian Mathers had one more sharp exchange before the T Bar crew pulled out for the upper Southfork. "Ellis," she said, "you must forego this foolish venture."

His face might have been carved in stone. "I have no intention of inviting the unwashed rabble to invade my land. It's mine, do you hear? *Mine!*

She folded her arms across her breasts. "What has become of you, Ellis? You will be the one outside the law. You're not the boy I've always loved."

"Indeed I'm not. Instead, I'm a man. The business I'm about is a man's business." He gripped her by the shoulders. "I should never have taken you to Blood Canyon. You've been filled with misconceptions by an interloping stranger. Can't you get it through your head that he's out to destroy all we've built? If we leave him, next year there'll be two or three. And the year after, there'll be ten."

"Does the land really belong to the Lazy T Bar, Ellis? Or is it indeed Federal land open to any? And what about poor, unfortunate Swenson? Ellis, I will never be a party to murder, robbery, and violence."

He stared into her depths. "Lillian, you are no longer welcome on this ranch. I'll not expect you to be here when

I return."

Mattie Mathers joyfully clapped her hands when Lillian burst into her parents' room and told them Ellis had ordered them from the ranch. To demonstrate further her eagerness to distance herself from Ellis Burroughs' brand of hospitality, Lillian's mother began struggling with a trunk.

"Father, what will we do?" Lillian cried, sinking a tear-striped face into her hands.

"Well, my dear, it seems apparent that we'll leave the ranch, doesn't it?"

The Mathers family's bags waited on the porch for the buggy to be brought up as Ellis Burroughs rode from the yard at the head of a wagonload of supplies destined for Blood Canyon.

An hour later, the buggy entered the hamlet of Marquardt. "This will be quite far enough, Mr. Washburn," August Mathers said.

"What?" the startled cook replied. "I got orders to take you to Corbin's Crossing."

Mathers chuckled and puffed on his pipe. "I can appreciate the awkwardness of your position, Mr. Washburn. But you can hardly take us to Corbin's Crossing if we refuse to travel past Marquardt, can you?"

The driver reined the team to a halt. "Well, where do you want me to drop you?"

"Does Marquardt have a rooming house?"

"Not that I know of."

"Fine. We'll start one."

CHAPTER NINE

The hoof blight comed a-rootin' through Blood Canyon after August beginned. We seen 'em comin' our way after they passed Castle Rock, but it was hard t'figger just how it was Pansy Bottom and Snake Eyes planned on usin' 'em.

Pansy Bottom hisself was down at the Swenson place on the Ishawooa. He stayed there along with eight others and a big wagonload o' possibles that I helped m'self to some of one night the moon went ahind a black cloud. That wagon got to Swenson's old place a week afore the moo locusts, but warn't none o' the nine that forted up there took no ride into the canyon. Must be they was some skeered o' Gray Eyes, for they stayed so tight t'the cabin that Gen'ral Grant couldn'ta blasted them out with the Cumberland Army. Even seemed like none of 'em even wanted t'come out t'pee. I says to Gray Eyes that I wanted t'plug up the stovepipe some night, but he wouldn't do it, figgerin' instead t'let 'em make a play, no matter what.

The "no matter what" was leastways five hundred cows pushin' and shovin' into Blood Canyon a week or so later. Me'n Gray Eyes watched 'em from the cliff, settin' there chewin' on a grass stem apiece. He wasn't sayin' naught, but a feller could tell by the way his jaw clenched that he was thinkin' powerful thoughts.

We was in the same spot five days later, whilst leastways a dozen o' the shittin' critters was a-standin' under the cabin's eaves for t'fight flies. Warn't nothin' left in the way o' grass anywhar twixt the mouth o' the canyon and the waterfall. Nothin' 'cept dust, and the damn cows a-throwin' that up under their bellies with the front feet whilst they fit the peskys with horns and tails. One big old drumheaded cow had her butt up against the door, a-scratchin' her hind-end back and forth 'til she broked the latch and the door popped open. Them cows bolted away from the suddens, but that old drumhead had her head inside lookin' 'round within ten minutes.

Gray Eyes' jawline went harder. "I could hit her with your Hawken," he said.

"So could I," I allowed whilst chewin' on m'grass stem. "But in time, she'd begin t'stink. B'sides, you're a-workin' on the wrong critter. If you want t'use m'Hawken on Pansy Bottom or Snake Eyes, you have naught t'do but ask."

He just set on, grippin' his jaw tighter and tighter. Cows was a-bellerin' over short rations and daylight was passin' when he climbed to his feet and said, "Sam—let's go fishing."

Well, of all the ideas he coulda had, that one s'prised me the most. "Whar?" I asked.

"How about we try it over to the head of the Yellowstone?"

Two months passed and the new rooming house neared completion. The work had been contracted to 'Dad' Marquardt and his three sons. The logs were cut and skidded from Cedar Mountain to be hewn on site by the elder Marquardt, who was known far and wide for his ability with a broadaxe. Though the Marquardts applied their foremost talents in its construction, the building was unpretentious, even in an unpretentious community. "Mathers' Place," as it was called, consisted of a three roomed forepart, with three additional rooms constructed in a row behind. All three row-rooms were served by outside doors and each contained a tiny fireplace for heat in cold weather. One large room in the main forepart served as combination kitchen, dining room, and sitting room. The other two forepart rooms were sleeping quarters for the Mathers family.

The family moved in by the end of September, followed by a surprise housewarming by the people of the community. In yet another surprise to the new family, Dad Marquardt brought forth a fiddle and the main room was cleared for an impromptu hoedown. Dad proved to be a superb fiddler and the Mathers' Place housewarming lasted 'til the wee hours of the morning.

It was the morning after the hoedown and Dad Marquardt cradled a cup of coffee. As it was common knowledge that the Lazy T Bar had moved a large herd of cattle into the upper Southfork, August Mathers asked about the cattle and their significance. Marquardt snorted and shook his head. "Them cows is only an excuse to get an army of gunmen up there." Then he sighed and added, "I don't hold out a lot of hope for that homesteader. The man had guts, that nobody can deny. But I reckon he bucked a stacked deck."

Lillian bustled past the dining room table carrying a heavy cast iron frying pan. "Why do you refer to him in the past tense?"

Marquardt grinned and shook his head. "He might still be alive, that's right. Leastways they ain't brought the cows back yet. But one man, no matter how big, tough, and mean can't stand against a passel of picked gundogs."

Then the old man leaned back in his chair and eyed the girl's back. "You sweet on him, Miss Mathers. Is that it?"

Her laugh had wind chimes in it as she hung the pan on a wall peg and spun back to stride past her father and his guest. "Perhaps a girl could do worse." She said it lightly and in jest, and Dad Marquardt laughed. But August Mathers sucked quietly on his unlit pipe, studying his daughter as she worked to put the room back to rights.

One night as we laid in camp at a hot spring along Yellowstone Lake, I said to Gray Eyes, "I still think you ought to droved 'em away."

"Sam, they'd have just drifted 'em back."

"Why you so set agin a lead ball twixt the eyes. T'woulda shore solved your problems."

"No it wouldn't. That's what they're hoping we'll do. What are we going to war over? Because a few cows grazed onto a place that had no fences? They'd have the law on their side then, and you've got to know Burroughs has the contacts to get a Marshal in here if it'd be to his advantage."

"That cabin o' yours is fair tore up by now, what with bein' a box stall for the bellerin' bastards. What you aim t'do now?"

"Fish."

I stared into the cracklin' fire for awhilst before sayin', "Your pappy was a peaceable man, but he never woulda stood still for playin' in a no-win game like you're up against."

Gray Eyes peered across the lake, into the night. Finally he went to his soogan. On the way, he said, "I ain't got no pappy."

———————

T'was nearin' first snow when we rode back t'Blood Canyon. There warn't much t'salvage and the infernal moo-locusts was still there. Gray Eyes looked at the tore up insides o' his cabin, turned nose up at the stink, and grabbed a full can o' coal oil the cows ain't ruined, splashin' it on the cabin walls. Then he scratched a match and touched her off.

We watched it burn from the cliff top. It seemed t'pleasure Gray Eyes some when Pansy Bottom's cowboys showed up and beginned scratching heads over how it coulda started. But them same cowboys pushed their cows out o' Blood Canyon that very day.

"Sometimes you're a mite hard t'foller," I said afore the cowboys comed, and whilst the fire crackled b'low.

"How so?" Gray Eyes asked.

"Why'd you burn it?"

"Nobody but you will ever believe I did."

"Now we ain't got no place t'spend the winter."

"The cabin was all but ruined anyway. A wickiup'll suit you fine. Meanwhile nobody in the country'll believe Burroughs and Bunting didn't order it burned."

"They'd a done it nohow."

"Probably. So what have we lost?"

He was right, I could see. But it rankled a old geezer like me for him not to o' fought harder t'keep what was his. I knowed he could fight if he was who I figgered he was. Fact is, I knowed he could fight if he warn't who I figgered he was. *So why don't he fight?*

"The next one won't burn," Gray Eyes said as he

watched the first o' Pansy Bottom's cowboys come foggin' in amongst a cloud o' dust.

"Huh?"

"It'll be built out of rock."

"What will?"

"The next cabin."

I just rolled over and looked at him.

"I'm headed for Billings in the morning to get the mortar makin's. You might hang around here and put up some kind of wickiup after the Burroughs outfit leaves the canyon.

———◦•◦———

It was mid-October and, though still balmy, the days grew shorter. Lillian sat on the front porch of Mathers' Place, staring south. Her potatoes were washed and rinsed and lying starkly in a nearby bowl. Her father sat down by her, stuffed his pipe with fresh tobacco, and followed her southerly gaze. "People around say it's hunting time of year," he mused. "While I've never before hunted, it's something I've always wanted to try my hand at."

She turned her head.

"People also say," he continued, "that there are lots of elk and deer along the Southfork of the Stinkingwater." He lit his pipe. "But I've never been up there before and chances are good I'd not be able to find my way back." He swiveled his head to meet her eyes. "But you, now, you've been up there and perhaps know just the place to see elk."

"Perhaps I do," she murmured.

"What do you say, girl, to joining me on a hunting trip up the Southfork?"

"When do you propose to leave?"

"I should think it'd be best if we waited until morning."

But they were still another day before getting underway. August Mathers rented a packmule and two saddlehorses from Otis Kluster, but there wasn't a woman's sidesaddle in all the community of Marquardt. When Lillian looked in dismay at first her father, then the man's saddle she'd be required to use, her father decided, "You'll just have to ride like a man."

"How can I do that," she asked, "when I'm dressed as a woman?"

"Ain't none of my business," Kluster said, "but was I you, I'd put on a man's clothes. You'll not be the first, and likely not the last."

It took time to round up three pairs of boy-sized denim trousers and an equal number of wool shirts that came close to fitting. By then it was too late in the day to begin their journey, so they put off leaving until the following day.

"Shortest trip they ever took," Kluster said as he unsaddled his horses and mule.

Thus it was that on the third day after August Mathers proposed the trip, Kluster helped with packing what he called the 'panyards,' huge bags hanging from each side of the mule's sawbuck packsaddle. Then the stable owner helped tie down the Mathers' small canvas tent, all the while chuckling over where August and Lillian would "stick an elk, should y'be unlucky enough to get one."

They were on the upper bench, three miles from Mathers' Place, when Lillian first realized her father carried no rifle. He chuckled. "I could never shoot anything. You know that."

Mathers wanted to study Castle Rock more closely, so they forded the Southfork to the western side. "Seems to be some type of igneous intrusion in predominantly sedimentary surrounding deposits."

"I see."

"Notice how the much harder igneous rock has resisted erosional forces wearing away softer sedimentary layering."

"Fascinating."

"Emmelhart first wrote of it in the 1830s. He was a German mining engineer."

"Father."

He swung from his horse to pick up crumbled specimens.

"Father."

"What is it, Lillian?"

"I see dust upriver. Whatever its cause, I believe it's coming our way."

The dust was from a trail herd of Lazy T Bar cattle from the upper Southfork, on its way down to winter pasture. The Mathers' loose-ranging packmule tried to join the trailherd's grazing horse cavvy, but a young cowboy Lillian remembered from the ranch, roped the mule and tailed him to August Mathers' saddlehorse.

"Thank you," Lillian told the cowboy as he swung back atop his pony.

"Oh, that's okay, ma'am. No harm done."

"Are you bringing your cattle home for the winter?" August asked.

"Yep. Good that the weather held, too," the cowboy added.

"And when will you be taking them into the upper Southfork in the spring?"

"Don't expect we'll have to again. Our job's done up there."

August and Lillian exchanged sharp glances. The young cowboy must have noticed, for he began fidgeting with his lariat. Then he looked up and asked, "You folks trophy hunting?"

"No," Lillian snapped. "It seems we're on a burial detail."

After skirting the trailherd, they'd ridden far into the

night, sometimes at a trot, the packmule jogging behind. Lillian was grateful to be riding in a man's saddle, the man's way. They'd stopped for night well above Ishawooa Creek, eating only a hurried cold snack and crawling into their blankets without benefit of a tent or fire.

On their way again at daylight, the little cavalcade rode into Blood Canyon by sunup. Lillian choked back a sob.

The cabin's ashes weren't even smoldering. Nothing was left. The sod roof had fallen in, but hadn't prevented the logs from burning beneath. The waterfall and the pool and the huge cottonwood trees were there, but the starkness of the ashes made the place ugly.

August poked through the remains, then gazed at his daughter. "I find no indication that a human died within."

"Damn them! Damn them all to hell!" she screamed.

"Yes, my dear. I'm afraid that is where they are destined. Meanwhile, take comfort in the fact that your stranger was not inside. If he is as formidable as you say and he'd been inside, they would never have been able to approach closely enough to burn the cabin."

"Perhaps they had already killed him."

"Perhaps. But if so, one should think that young cowboy would have demonstrated more reticence."

"No!" she said. "They could never kill him that easily."

Father and daughter spent that day and the next camped near the waterfall in Blood Canyon. But the area had been so thoroughly overgrazed, and so thoroughly trashed by cloven feet and cowshit, that any sign of an altercation, had there been one, would have disappeared. Lillian and her father even climbed the cliffs above the pool looking for tell-tale evidence: a spent shell case, a place where horses had been tied for a long time. They found nothing.

As they saddled their animals for the return trip, August Mathers gazed pensively at Lillian. "Daughter," he said, "I don't know this unnamed man of yours, but I respect your judgement. Believe me when I say we've not heard the last of him."

———————

The first winter storm hit three days later, just as the Mathers pair passed Castle Rock. They rode directly to Kluster's stable where they could take their horses inside to unload and unsaddle them away from the howling wind. Otis Kluster came to help. By his manner, Lillian could tell the man knew what they knew. She brushed snow from their packs and began methodically to pull clothes, cooking equipment, blankets and such from the packbags. A horse trumpeted and stamped wildly in a back stall.

"Mr. Kluster," she said, "how do you know about what has happened up the Southfork?"

"Miss Mathers, ever'body knows. Mr. Bunting and Mr. Burroughs has told everybody who'll listen. They want it to be a warning to anyone else who plans to settle on the Stinkingwater."

Again a horse trumpeted from the rear. Lillian strode back to stare in the rear stall at Ellis Burroughs' great stallion. She returned to where the men continued to sort out gear. "Where is he?" she whispered.

Kluster made as if to ignore her, but she stomped around him and thrust her nose up near his. "Where is he, I asked, damn you?"

"I ain't in this," the stable owner said.

She smiled. Naturally he'd be bragging in Morton's saloon. She headed for the door, bumping into her father, who carried the packsaddle. "I'm not sure you know what you're about to do," he said.

"Let's both find out," she replied.

He dropped the saddle and held open the door. Somehow the howling, biting snow felt pleasant to Lillian as she began a resolute march.

The outside door banged shut with the wind. Ellis Burroughs sat at a rear table in the dingy saloon. Levi Bunting sat with him, as did saloon keeper Morton and store owner Judson. A hush fell immediately over the noisy throng as she strode the length of the room—just as she'd heard a gray-eyed stranger had twice done. For some reason, she thought of a thousand Philistines and actually wished for the jawbone of an ass.

"You are an ass!" she said.

Ellis Burroughs' mouth fell open. "I … I'm not sure I heard you correctly, Lillian."

"I said you are an ass! Need I say it again? Very well, you are a colossal ass. One of a kind. Tell me, Mr. Burroughs, are you here telling everyone about your twenty men's courageous assault on an unarmed cabin in a lonely outpost of the upper Stinkingwater?"

The rancher blanched.

"Please, Mr. Burroughs, while your epic victory will undoubtedly be told and retold in whatever annals are written about western fortitude and courage, it really will never rank as an assault along with Chapultepec or Little Round Top!"

"Lillian! Are you insane?"

August Mathers laid a hand on his daughter's shoulder and squeezed softly, reassuringly.

"I'm not sure, Mr. Burroughs, what kind of price in wounded or dead your assault on the unarmed cabin cost, but I can assure you it'll be much higher than you ever dreamed."

"Well!" The half-lidded eyes of Levi Bunting glistened as he rose. "The unwashed, little, boy-clad tramp who once aspired to be Mrs. Ellis Burroughs has bared her fangs. Perhaps she needs to be taught that to receive respect, one must first show respect."

"Perhaps," August Mathers murmured, "I should say that in order to chastise her, Mr. Bunting, you must first go through me."

Bunting blinked, then began laughing. He quit when she added, "And I would advise caution. The last time you acted without thinking in this kind of circumstance, all you gained by it was a broken arm."

The T Bar foreman towered over both the girl in baggy trousers and oversized man's shirt and her tottering, white-haired, unarmed, academic father. But they were more than he could handle—the code would not allow them to be shot or beaten.

"Come Father, let's leave these valiant warriors to contemplate their next move on Troy." And they strode from the gaming hall of Marquardt, leaving utter silence in their wake.

CHAPTER TEN

I was out lookin' for fit wickiup brush when the old man and Pansy Bottom's gal rode into the canyon. "They's gonna have t'move Marquardt Town t'Blood Canyon, what with all the pilgrims we're getting up h'yar," I grumbled.

The two of 'em spent a long whilst at the burned-out cabin—longer'n need be if they was just seein' how good was the job Pansy Bottom's cowhands done. I had a good mind t'go tell 'em Gray Eyes burnt it hisself so's maybe they'd go home and leave me in peace. Then damn me if them two pilgrims don't start pokin' 'round ever'whar. What they was lookin' for, I ain't got no idea, but the way they was stickin' their noses into ever'thin', I'm damn glad I never started on the wickiup just yet or they'd a-found it for shore.

They even climbed up the ridge t'the clifftop and I bare had time to beat 'em up there to unhook the snare triggers afore they stuck their feet in 'em. Waugh! That would a-been somethin'—seein' Pansy Bottom's gal go flyin' off that cliff with a two hunnert pound log tied t'her laig!

T'was on that ridge what I heered made me think maybe she and Whitetop ain't what they's cracked up t'be. Dogged iff'n the pair didn't palaver like they was on Gray Eyes' side—made me wonder if there's anythin' a body can count on.

Anyway, after a couple o' days, Pansy Bottom's gal and Whitetop up and rode back t'whar they comed from. Prob'ly had to, for they had no gun to fetch meat. And if they'd a-stayed longer, their hosses and mule would a-starved t'death on the short rations Pansy Bottom's cows left in Blood Canyon.

———•+•———

Neither father nor daughter expected acclaim for their Morton's Saloon confrontation with the 'B-Twins,' as Burroughs and Bunting were sometimes referred to behind their backs. The Mathers family knew the Lazy T Bar was disliked by many settlers in the Big Horn Basin, but they had no idea such dislike bordered on out-and-out hatred.

They learned more of Ellis Burroughs' realm when a rancher named Ashland from the Meeteetse country stopped by. One of his cowboys accompanied him. The cowboy had once worked for the Englishman, Bledsoe. The cowboy—a Mr. Duert—had some harsh things to say about the way Mr. Bledsoe had died.

They learned more of Swenson's and his two cowboys' shootings from Dad Marquardt, who seemed to know even more than he shared.

"Ellis's empire is about to collapse of its own weight, isn't it Father?" Lillian asked.

Mattie glanced at them while stirring a pot at the cook-stove. Meanwhile her husband ground morosely with a pocketknife on his pipe bowl. At last, he shook his head. "I'm afraid not, Lillian. Though Ellis's reputation is in tatters, he has everything else he wants. With Corbin and Ashland gone from Trail Creek, Lazy T Bar stock has access below the gorge of the Stinkingwater. Ellis controls all of the Northfork. With acquisition of both the Kittleson and Marquardt grazing lands on the lower Southfork, and with elimination of competition from Swenson and Bledsoe from above, he controls the entire Southfork. What other people think is of little consideration to men like Ellis and Bunting."

"But what of the law?"

The man took his time filling his pipe. After he'd finished, he said, "Yes, what of the law? Thus far it appears they've not stepped outside the law. Remember, Bunting was exonerated for the Swenson shootings. As well, there is no evidence to support a claim that the Englishman's death was more than an accident."

He began counting on his fingers. "And while Dad Marquardt sold under threat of prosecution of his sons, and swears their innocence, he also admits their case could look bad in a court of law. Corbin and Ashland moved from Trail Creek under only an unspoken threat—certainly incontestable. That leaves Judge Kittleson, and no one knows why he sold. Dad seems to think he was blackmailed about something from his past. But whatever the reason, any legal challenge there would have to come from the Judge himself. And it seems apparent that challenge isn't to be forthcoming or it would've been pursued long ago. So you see, my dear, to this point it cannot be proven that Ellis Burroughs has stepped outside the law in developing his ranch."

"What about Blood Canyon?"

"Quite the same. Can you prove the Lazy T Bar burned the stranger's cabin? No. If you were to ask Ellis, he would say his people had nothing to do with it. Or he would say it caught fire by accident, perhaps from some carelessly handled match. Is the stranger alive or dead? It would be hard to prove he was disposed of by men from the Lazy T Bar when one cannot prove if he lives or lies dead. Yet Ellis's objectives are achieved. There is no unwanted stranger dwelling in Blood Canyon. And no homesteading precedent is established on Lazy T Bar range." He struck a match to his pipe.

Mattie turned from the stove. "Then what will stop him? What can stop him?"

Her husband nodded. "Chapman perhaps. Do you remember, Lillian? Ellis has had words with the Two Dot owner over Sunlight Basin and he might someday overstep himself there. Otto Frank perhaps. The Pitchfork owner is tough, I'm told, and clear-spoken. And don't forget your stranger from Blood Canyon. He might be the one. So far, no one—except Chapman—has stood up to Lazy T Bar ambitions. If it's as you say, Lillian...." The thought was unfinished when there came knocking on their door.

It was Mattie who opened the door, inviting Mr. and Mrs. Kluster, Dad Marquardt, and Mrs. Morton to enter. August helped with their wraps as each stomped snow from boots. After they were seated, Dad said, "We come to talk to Miss Lillian, if we may."

Lillian took a nearby stool.

"Miss Lillian," Dad began, "we think maybe it's time we had a school here in Marquardt. Counting it up, we can think of ten, twelve young'uns what could do with some learning. The way we figure it, of all the folks around the Forks, you're best cut out for the job. We'd appreciate it if you'd listen to the idea."

"Well!" Lillian said, brushing her apron smooth. "This

is something of a surprise. Do you people have a proposal?"

———•——•———

Lillian Mathers became the first schoolmistress of the Marquardt school. Sessions began the day after the beginning of the New Year, 1884, in the main room of Mathers' Place Inn. She received the princely sum of twenty-five dollars per month, to be reduced to twenty dollars when a proper school building could be erected at some unnamed later date. The twelve students ranged in age from eight-year-old Molly Morgan to seventeen-year-old Wilfred Abbot, in size from four feet-one to six feet-three.

Lillian never counted more than nine students in school on any given day. However, she found her new employment challenging and time-consuming. In addition, Lillian's father entered into the educational spirit with zest. And with her mother in the building, discipline was never a problem.

The winter, as it turned out, was, according to most experienced residents, relatively mild. But spring was late to arrive; snowbanks still lay against village buildings as late as the first of April.

———•——•———

Being busy with the children proved a salvation for Lillian Mathers that long winter, especially when she learned how long the arm of Burroughs' disfavor could reach. She discovered it the first time in mid-February when a 'Founders' Day' dance was planned for the people of the surrounding area to celebrate Lincoln's and Washington's Birthdays. The dance was to be held in the little-used barn of the old Marquardt Ranch, just south of town. Dad Marquardt was to provide music. The

Founders' Day Dance was the winter's highest social event, yet Lillian Mathers received no invitations! In a land where men outnumbered women ten to one, no one had sought the presence of the loveliest woman in the Territory. She didn't cry, but her father gritted his teeth and murmured, "Burroughs again."

Marquardt told August the morning before the dance that Levi Bunting had spread the word some weeks before that no eligible male was to give any evidence of designs on Lillian Mathers. The threat, though unsaid, was clear. "I'd buck the sonofabitch, was I not fiddling," Dad said. "But it'd be tantamount to suicide was any of the young bucks to try it."

The afternoon before the dance, several laughing, joking strangers walked from Kluster's Stables over to Mathers Place to schedule rooms. "One of the rooms will be for Affie and me," announced one of them—a large, ruggedly chisled man with gray at his temples. "We'll put twelve boys in the other two. You figure the cost."

Since Lillian had heard of only one 'Affie' in all northwestern Wyoming—Affie Chapman—she supposed the man to be her husband, John Chapman. While she figured the bill, he said, "You gotta purt near be the woman what set Ellis Burroughs and Levi Bunting on their ears in Morgan's saloon. I can see why that New England fop is so took with you. Dogged if you ain't purty enough to consider startin' a war over."

Then he laughed and said, "No, hardly. In Wyoming we only fight wars over grass."

Neither of the two Mathers elders attended the Founder's Day dance, and Lillian refused to go unescorted. They heard later that neither Ellis Burroughs nor Levi Bunting attended, though most of the T Bar cowhands were there.

Over the weeks, Lillian tried to spend as much time as possible with her students so as not to think how lonely she'd become. In moments of solitude, however, she found herself dreaming of a confident stranger with an unsettling gaze and the hint of a smile on his lips.

School ended in May and, in order to stay busy, Lillian offered to give private tutoring free of charge to any who would attend. Three of the younger ones held on for another two weeks, then their visits became so sporadic that she finally dropped the offer.

With so much time on her hands, Lillian asked her father about another trip to Blood Canyon. But everyone August Mathers talked to advised against it. "With a late spring run-off comin', it'd be takin' your life in your hands," Otis Kluster reasoned. "All the fords will be high and muddy. A little rain or a few hot days, and she'll be rampaging. Ain't no place to be caught on the wrong side of."

Upon summer recess, schoolhouse construction began. Lillian helped where she could. Then it was end of June and she heard of a summer dance being planned for mid-July at Otto Frank's Pitchfork Ranch. Since she received nothing more tangible than an admiring glance from potential swains, she assumed the Burroughs quarantine was still in effect. So she gave the coming social no more thought. Then Ellis Burroughs stopped to visit.

Lillian was at the new school hanging curtains she and her mother had made. Though she knew a horse had trotted to the school's new hitchrail, the schoolmistress was tacking up the slender lodgepole curtain rod, stretched to her limit, when the visitor entered.

"Good morning, Lillian," Ellis said from the doorway.

She stiffened, but continued to stretch and tap. Ellis strode to her side and asked, "May I help?"

"Do you ever really *help* anyone, Mr. Burroughs?"

Without replying, he sat down on one of the children's new benches and watched until she finished. The woman's face was crimson and her knuckles white as she turned. He smiled at the way she gripped the tool as a weapon. "Do you hate me so much?"

"Mr. Burroughs, since I've not plumbed the deepest resources of my soul, I haven't the slightest idea *how* much I hate you. But you may rest assured it is a considerable amount."

"What happened to the love we once had, Lillian?"

"It disappeared when you took on the mantle of greed. It disappeared in the ashes of a little cabin in a bloody damned canyon!"

Ellis appeared calm as she railed at him. When she wound down, he said, "He didn't die in the cabin. As far as I know, he's not dead at all."

She gasped, then sought refuge on a second bench. "So you admit you burned it!"

"Not I, Lillian. But unfortunately it may have been one of my men. An accident? Carelessness? Who knows?" The lie came blandly, smoothly, without the slightest hesitation.

"Did you shoot him elsewhere?"

"I said as far as I know, he's alive."

"How do I know that to be true."

"You have my word."

"Ha! Tell me, Ellis, what is a Burroughs word worth?"

He smiled. "We're making some progress. You've just now moved from the formal 'Mr. Burroughs' to calling me 'Ellis'."

"A slip of the tongue. I'll see that it doesn't happen again. In any event, I should think this conversation is approaching an end. Did you have anything else you wanted to say before I go on with my work?"

"Yes, Lillian, I do. I came to ask your hand in marriage."

"You're insane!"

"Yes, we sometimes think that of each other, don't we? But you'll have to admit it would make for an interesting wedded relationship." While she sputtered he added, "Lacking your acceptance of my marriage proposal, I've also come to ask you to accompany me to Otto Frank's mid-summer social at the Pitchfork Ranch."

She stopped sputtering and fell silent. Then she spat, "You're even crazier than I thought if you think I'd so much as accompany you to a dog fight!"

"Listen, Lillian. We've had our confrontation in Morton's Saloon. Despite that, you are the only woman I've ever considered seriously. I realize we've had our differences and I realize you cannot reconcile yourself to the methods used to build the Lazy T Bar into the cattle empire it is. But it's the truth when I tell you I know nothing of any illegal actions that assisted in establishing it. If there have been...."

"What of Blood Canyon and a burned cabin?"

"I'll give you that much if it'll make you feel better. But Lillian, at least understand that the mere burning of an abandoned homesteader cabin is a policy that any cattleman in Wyoming Territory would have pursued. As for the occupant, the man was not there, Lillian. And according to my men, he'd not been there since you and I talked to him."

Ellis seemed sincere. She thought of Dad Marquardt and felt guilty when the notion flitted through her mind that perhaps his sons really were cattle thieves. And Kittleson did sell, did he not? The Englishman and Swenson? It is possible Ellis had nothing to do with either of their tragedies. And did not Corbin and Ashland simply move of their own volition?

"I really would like to change, Lillian. The Lazy T Bar

is as large as I'd ever hoped it would be. From here on out, my only concern will be for holding what we have. Levi is even now down in the new County Seat in Lander, filing 'Desert' and 'Timber' claims. And some of our most trustworthy men are filing remaining homestead leases that will neatly consolidate Lazy T Bar holdings into an effective land block that will preclude future problems between us and homesteaders. Believe me when I tell you I'm especially vigilant in seeing that everything we're doing now is scrupulously beyond reproach. And I give you my word it will remain so."

He paused while she plumbed the depths of what appeared to be earnest blue eyes. She thought of what her father had said about Ellis the probability that Ellis bore no more guilt from building his ranch than most Wyoming cattlemen. Then she thought of Levi Bunting.

"Lillian, the problems between you and me remain. I want to mend that. I know I haven't been what you'd like me to be and I truly will try to be more the man you'd want. I am sorry, Lillian. Will you forgive me? Will you accompany me to the Pitchfork social? It can be the first step towards a future together."

When she was tardy with a reply, he added, "You do want us to have a future together, do you not?"

He was handsome. Oh, he was handsome. She thought of their childhood years together and how she'd once deeply loved him. Then she recalled how lonely she'd been for the past year. She mulled over what Ellis had said about his future plans and wondered if Levi Bunting would agree. "What about Levi Bunting?" she blurted.

The question seemed to catch Ellis by surprise. "What about him?"

"I don't like him!"

Ellis's blue eyes shifted to the window by Lillian's head, then returned. "Neither do I, Lillian. But to give the devil his due, at the present time, the Lazy T Bar would be helpless to outside attack without him. One must remember this is a wild, new land. Our individual rights are subject to our individual ability to defend those rights. I'm sure you know I'm no bare-knuckle fighter. Levi Bunting is the knife edge of Lazy T Bar defenses."

She leaned her head back against the log wall, still staring at Ellis, and remembering her father's assertion that the law was pretty much up to each individual to enforce.

Ellis misinterpreted her stare because he said, "Look, Lillian, let's strike an accord. I will dismiss Levi Bunting the very moment I can be assured the Lazy T Bar can survive without him."

"I wonder what Levi Bunting would say if he heard you say that?"

"The devil take him!" Ellis said. "Forget about the marriage proposal just now. Will you accompany me to Meeteetse? We'll stay as houseguests of Otto Frank. We'll take the buggy through Oregon Basin. Have you been there?"

She shook her head, bewildered that she could even be thinking of accepting his invitation.

"I thought not. If we leave very early in the morning, it's a simple one-day drive—around thirty miles. However, travel is fast from the Sage Creek road on. Your mother and father will certainly want to accompany us, and they'll be most welcome. You know I've always thought most highly of them."

"One moment, Mr. Burroughs."

"Make that Ellis, then I'll accept the interruption."

"What about this supposed 'quarantine' you've had me under since last Christmas? I think it's fair to tell you I resent interference in my personal life."

Ellis smiled. "I'm guilty," he said. "I determined, even after the Morgan's Saloon affair, that I'd not give you up without a fight. Lillian, I'll leave no stone unturned until you're mine."

She glared at him, but it was difficult not to laugh at his seriousness.

"Will you go with me to Meeteetse and the Pitchfork?"

"Perhaps."

"Perhaps?"

"Yes."

CHAPTER ELEVEN

A wickiup ain't the easiest thing t'build on the Southfork o' the Stinkingwater when there's a real shortage o' good brush on account o' too many cows over too long a time. But when Gray Eyes showed up some days into his Billings' trip with a couple o' buffler robes t'go over the top, what I'd th'owed up cozened up some.

He comed in near sunup one mornin' after snow flied, a-trailin' a bunch o' packhorses a-snortin' and a-blowin' in the cold and loaded with most near ever'thin' a body could use t'spend a easy winter. There was a passel o' things a body wouldn't want, too, like mortar makin's, but Gray Eyes seemed happy with 'em, so's I didn't mind.

I did look at them hosses, though, and asked him if we needed to keep eyes peeled for the high sheriff. He laughed and said he had a bill o' sale for each and every one. With that, I shook my head, never havin' knowed anybody with bullion enough to *buy* that many ponies.

Next, I wondered how we was gonna keep them hosses

up in Blood Canyon through the winter. But after we off-loaded 'em and pulled off their saddles, he said for me t'ride herd on 'em whilst he got a little sleep. Way he told it, when next it comed night he planned on us drivin' our hoss herd t'winter pasture down on Pansy Bottom's place.

Sounded plumb simple. Them lower foothills did lay snow-free most o' the winter 'cause o' the wind.

We rode the biggest two new ones back t'Blood Canyon and Gray Eyes hooked 'em into a harness he'd brunged from Billings and set t'work a-buildin' a makeshift sled. A couple o' days later he was a-sleddin' rocks from Blood Canyon cliffs for his new cabin.

He worked at it, Gray Eyes did, from daylight to dark. When the weather warmed up and the snow was too rotten for sleddin', he was out pickin' over rocks from the nearest cliffs, carryin' or rollin' or tuggin' the ones he figgered would do for his wants to a pile near the trail.

I watched him for awhilst, then dogged iff'n I didn't find m'self wantin' t'help. I fought that loco notion for awhilst, then went t'pile some rocks m'self.

Gray Eyes figgered we had near enough rocks by the time deep cold set in and he tooked the two gaunted-up harness hosses what warn't winterin' too good on cottonwood limbs, down t'join t'others what was winterin' with Pansy Bottom's hosses. After he got back, he set t'work on a set o' snowshoes for him and one for me.

During the deep cold o' January, he climbed out o' the Blood Canyon bottom on them shoes, over the ridge t'the east, and set t'work cuttin' roof poles for his cabin. They was good poles, too, long and straight; a body could see that when I helped drag 'em from whar he'd brung 'em off the ridge. He finished gettin' 'em by middle o' February and set right to work peelin' 'em with a draw knife. That job took awhilst, for though he didn't have so many poles, the bark never slipped none neither.

By the near side o' March he said he was ready to start

105

layin' stone quick as the river ice went out so's he could get some sand for mixin' mortar. Soon as the ground thawed, he set his foundation so solid dynamite wouldn't budge it. It was only then that the rascal quit workin' all day hours and most o' the night and turned into purty good comp'ny.

I recollect one night after it shoulda turned spring, winter blowed back in. The wind was howlin' and tiny bits o' snow was a-blowin' off Montany prairies right into our wickiup. The fire in the middle war blowin' fitful and its smoke was makin' the rounds. Gray Eyes lit up one o' his rare seegars and I'd just touched a coal to m'pipe. I could barely make him out in the poor firelight a-leanin' against a pile o' packsaddles.

"What you reckon Pansy Bottom and Snake Eyes'll do when they find a cabin in Blood Canyon again?" I asked.

"I don't know, Sam."

"Reckon they'll shove them moo-locusts up here again?"

"Could be."

"Air ye gonna fight 'em this time?"

He tooked a long time t'answer, drawin' deep on his seegar and lettin' it all out afore he did. "I don't suppose. Not like you mean, anyway."

"That means cows'll be in your new cabin afore spring's out," I said. "Don't reckon we'll want t'winter in that cabin next winter neither. Maybe we'd best keep the wickiup."

He never said nothin', but I seen the palaver warn't a-goin' his way. So I lit into him agin, sayin' I couldn't see takin' Pansy Bottom a-layin' down. He just set quiet, not stickin' up for hisself like I figgered he should.

"I knowed you ain't skeered," I said. "Shore as hell, the law ain't gonna come down hard on a man what tries t'keep Pansy Bottom from drivin' a bunch o' cows into his bedstid. I just happen t'think it better t'stop him afore he gets through the Canyon."

Gray Eyes sighed, then said, "Can't, Sam. It's not legal."

I snorted. "Dammit, boy, it's like I say. Either we stop 'em or they'll ruin your new cabin afore spring's out."

He sighed again.

"Afore spring's out...." I repeated slowly. "Spring's out. Spring...." Though I didn't look, I could feel his eyes on me.

"Yep," I says, "Ol' Richard woulda never set still for nothin' like you're a-doin'. Like I said afore, he was a peaceable man, but there was limits. He was some mountain man, Richard was. Taught me all I knowed. Last I seen o' Richard t'was over in Medicine River country in Montany, whar the plains peters out agin the mountains. He'd hooked up, Richard had, with maybe the purtiest Blackfeet squaw a feller never did see. That was 'bout eighteen-fifty. And they had a papoose what tooked after his mother in looks—'ceptin' for the eyes. Them eyes was Richard's—sorta the color of high, thin clouds on a otherwise bright day.

"Last I heered o' Richard was when DeMott told me him and his squaw was shot down when a bunch o' soldiers butchered a injin camp on the Musselshell."

Them gray eyes kept on a-borin' into mine whilst I stayed with the tale, though I cain't say I really saw 'em. His seegar end glowed red when he pulled on it, though, and he nudged the sticks 'round the wickiup fire with his toe.

"Well, story has it that Richard's papoose was growed and a-workin' for the army when his pappy went under. Story says the lad went loco after he heered what happened and hunted down the soldier major what ordered the massacree."

The seegar end glowed red again.

"Lessee, now, that woulda been ten, twelve years ago. What you reckon happened t'Richard's papoose? Way I heered it, they never did ketch him and he just dropped plumb from sight."

Gray Eyes still didn't say nothin'. After awhilst he got up and went outside in the blowin', driftin' snow and he never comed in for a long time. When he did finally stoop into the wickiup, I told him, "Richard's papoose, when I seen him on the Medicine River and tucked a finger under his chin, was named Jethro."

Gray Eyes never even turned his face m'way in the flickerin' light as he crawled under his buffler robe. "I ain't got no pappy," was all he said.

———◦•◦———

Gray Eyes had laid stone afore, it appeared t'me. He war so good at it that I had t'bust m'butt some harder'n I wanted to just t'keep mortar mixed ahead o' him. That cabin beginned t'take shape soon's the snow melted off the bottoms, and by the first o' June its walls were all up stout enough to hold off a mountain howitzer. But the big s'prise was how the doorway was staggered offset, and too narrow for a cow t'get into, and all the rifle loops, and how the window openings was heavy shuttered t'make like a fort. It was hell for stout and tighter'n a week-long drunk.

The roof poles was up a week or so after the walls and we made up a injin travois t'pull in sod from the low side o' Blood Canyon, whar the cow brutes hain't pulled all the grass out by the roots like they had up t'our place.

We took time out t'round up and bring in our hoss cavvy in May. Gray Eyes was right. They'd wintered real good with Pansy Bottom's herd and we warn't missin' a one. We pushed 'em on top o' Ishawooa Mesa, whar Gray Eyes and me had got friendly near a year afore. T'was near the first o' June when we left 'em there. And we bringed Hoss and Gray Eyes' buckskin down t'Blood Canyon whar a little grass was a-startin' t'pop up, even after the hoofed locusts tore it up last summer.

"I've got to take a little trip, Sam," Gray Eyes said t'me one day around the end o' June. "I'm going down to the county seat. Should be back in a couple of weeks. Way spring run-off is now, I don't think we'll see anyone for awhile, so why don't you go catch some fish?"

That sounded right proper t'me, so when Gray Eyes left, I snooped in onto the hoss herd on Ishawooa Mesa, figgerin' t'head on t'some o' the divide lakes twixt there and the Thorofare country. But bein' as my t'baccy was a mite low, I dropped into Marquardt Town for a little dab. It was there whar I heered about a big doin's at the Pitchfork place out o' Meeteetse what was comin' up in a week and I done me a smart lot o' thinkin'. Way I figgered it, if Gray Eyes was to Evanston, or Cheyenne, or Laramie—wherever was the county seat—he'd likely comed back t'Blood Canyon through the Greybull country and Boulder Basin. Leastways, if he could get over the top account o' snow he would. Way it seemed t'me, if he comed that way, he'd pass near the Pitchfork and it'd likely be 'bout the time o' the big doin's. Hmmm. Iff'n he stopped at the doin's, and iff'n anybody follered him....

"Shoot," I says to Hoss, "why don't we go fishin' over t'Boulder Basin?" Hoss flicked his ears. "Fish are bitin' better there than over t'the Thorofare nohow."

CHAPTER TWELVE

Ellis Burroughs and Lillian Mathers were alone during their long drive to Otto Frank's Pitchfork Ranch. Mrs. Mathers absolutely refused to ride in a buggy with Ellis Burroughs and no amount of reasoning made the slightest difference. August Mathers chose not to enter the ensuing argument between mother and daughter, but he listened. Finally he knocked out his pipe and said, "Lillian, I think it best if your mother and I stayed home and minded the inn. Who knows? Travel may pick up any day now."

"That's ridiculous!" Lillian exclaimed. "Mathers' Place hasn't had a guest in a week, Father. You know that!"

But August Mathers only shook his head.

They disapproved, Lillian knew. She'd explained the entire schoolhouse meeting with Ellis from start to finish, not neglecting Ellis's promise to rein in Levi Bunting. Her mother merely sniffed, but her father was more thoughtful.

Ellis arrived at daylight on the appointed morning, driving a team of beautiful high-stepping bays. "Good morning, sir," Ellis said when August Mathers met him at the door. "I regret that you and Mrs. Mathers are unable to accompany us. It looks like a grand day for a drive, doesn't it? The Pitchfork get together should prove to be an exciting event. Most of the people from around the area should be there. Are you sure you're unable to ..."

"Good morning, Ellis," August interrupted. "Please step inside. Lillian will be ready in a moment." She hurried in a few minutes later with an early morning wrap over her shoulder and an overnight valise in hand.

Ellis took the valise and as he stepped through the door, Lillian kissed her father and whispered, "I'm not afraid, but I wish you and mother were going."

His smile was wan. "We won't rest easy until you're safely home."

The drive to Otto Frank's ranch was indeed long. As the sun rose it began to bake the land and Ellis helped her from her outer wrap. "Why do they call it Oregon Basin?" she asked, eyeing the sagebrush-filled land.

"Something to do with a bull from an Oregon trail herd," Ellis said, holding the reins loosely and following her gaze. "Apparently the bull wandered away and could not be found. It was assumed, so it's said, that he would starve to death during the winter. But instead, the bull was found fat and healthy in the spring. That's when people began to understand the dynamic nature of this land as cattle country."

"It's not as pretty as the Southfork, is it?" she asked.

"No, but such grass as is here is surprisingly nutritious. I wouldn't mind establishing the Lazy T Bar over here."

Her head snapped around and she said, voice rising, "I thought your ranch was big enough!"

"Oh it is," he chuckled. "But chances are it'll either be us or Otto Frank who expands here. Frank is terribly ambitious, you know."

"Aren't there several ranches between Mr. Frank's

Pitchfork and here? Ashland, for instance? Or Wyler? And for that matter, aren't there some between here and the Lazy T Bar?"

Ellis pulled in the buggy and set the brake. "Please, Lillian, let's not talk of ranching or cattle or cowboys for the next few days. Instead, let's talk just of you and me and the way we'd like it to be."

Her smile was weak, but when he slipped his hand into hers and squeezed, she returned the pressure. Then he picked up the reins, threw off the brake, and clucked to the obedient bays. But as the buggy rolled across Oregon Basin, she wondered if this region was destined to be included in some future Burroughs Empire.

They ate their noon meal as they crossed the Sage Creek Divide: thick beef slices and sourdough biscuits, potato salad, lettuce and radishes and baby carrots from the T Bar cook's garden. A jug of lemonade was behind the seat. She was surprised at how hungry she'd become, but when Ellis said it'd been seven hours since he'd eaten, she realized she'd not even bothered with breakfast.

Otto Frank turned out to be a rotund little German who bustled about the Pitchfork ranchyard like a vaudeville stage director. He shook hands with Ellis and bowed low over Lillian's hand. She could swear there was a glint in the little man's eyes as he straightened, but he turned away saying, "I'll take the team to unhitch and feed them." Then he shouted, "Joe!"

When a tall, skinny, teenage boy hurried in response, Frank said, "Vill you take Mr. Burroughs und Miss Mathers to their quarters? Mr. Burroughs vill stay in Dryden's cabin; Miss Mathers is to take an extra room at the house."

The boy took Lillian's valise and told Ellis, "Hang

there 'til I get back."

As she stared out her room's single window at the happy, bustling, ranchyard activities, she could not help but compare its vibrance to the depressing atmosphere prevalent at the Lazy T Bar.

———————

The dance was well-attended. Half the people living in Marquardt and its surrounding countryside were there, as well as a few from more distant places. John Chapman arrived with his ever-smiling wife and a half-dozen Two Dot cowhands. Dad Marquardt was already on hand on a raised musician's platform, tuning up for the evening.

Otto Frank provided the refreshments, including outside liquids for those who found the punchbowl too tame. She recognized Cletus Wills and Patrick O'Brien from the Lazy T Bar. And what was the huge blacksmith's name? Smith? No. Schultz? Not quite. Schulte? That's it, Schulte. She glanced over the crowd, ticking off the ones she knew, listening to the music and watching the first dancers onto the floor. Then she became conscious of how other people seemed to turn away as she and Ellis approached. A man broke away from a cluster of cowboys and strode toward them. She stiffened.

"Good evening, Levi," Ellis said. "I hope you have good news."

"Good for the most part," Levi Bunting replied, staring at Lillian with half-closed eyes. "It's good to see you again, Miss Mathers. I hope your drive to the Pitchfork was comfortable."

"It was, Mr. Bunting. May I say I'm surprised to see you here. I'd heard you were in Lander."

The unblinking eyes swept for a moment to Ellis, then returned to Lillian. "Yes, I was. But it was planned for my return through Pitchfork. Actually I arranged to meet Mr.

Burroughs here."

"Was the land office amenable to our filings, Levi?" Ellis asked.

"Like I said, for the most part. They're a little green yet at that new courthouse, but we helped 'em learn about desert and timber land claims." Thus far, the foreman had not unfixed his unblinking, half-lidded eyes from Lillian, though he talked to Burroughs. "And there wasn't any problem with the boys filing homestead claims, especially with 'em being there. There is one fly in the ointment, though."

"What is that?" Ellis asked.

"We never got a chance to file on that Blood Canyon chunk."

"I don't understand. Didn't you explain to them that it had been abandoned? We have every right to file on it— as has anyone else. It's just a matter of who is first. If that arrogant sodbuster hasn't lived there for more than six months, he has legally abandoned it. Did you tell them that?"

"The land is his, Mr. Burroughs."

Ellis shook his head, plainly annoyed. "His? What do you mean, 'his'?"

"He paid it off. He was in a week before we got there."

"I don't understand. The Homestead Law doesn't allow early proving."

The Homestead Act ain't in it," Bunting growled. "He went the Pre-emption route. The bastard had already been to the Evanston Land Office and paid his dollar and a quarter an acre for one hundred and sixty acres at Blood Canyon. Then he rode to Lander and filed the Pre-emption with the Fremont County Clerk. We don't get title to Blood Canyon."

"Impossible!" Ellis exploded, voice rising. "I never heard of such a thing!"

Others in the hall turned their heads and craned their

necks. Burroughs and Bunting ignored them.

"Jay Christ, Burroughs, the Pre-emption Act is nearly fifty years old. It's how Morgan acquired title to our ranch headquarters, and Kittleson picked up title to his headquarters land. It's seldom used by the unwashed multitudes, though, 'cause most of 'em ain't got a pot to piss in, let alone two hundred dollars."

Lillian stood by Ellis Burroughs, swiveling her head from the rancher to his foreman, gleaning a great deal about her 'new' Ellis Burroughs.

"What do we do now?" Ellis demanded. "Who is this man?"

"The deed of record shows 'Jacob Weatherby'. I never heard of him and neither has anyone else I've talked to."

A little shiver of joy coursed through Lillian. She had his name!

"One thing about it, Burroughs," Bunting continued, "he's not just any nester. When he came up with two hundred dollars and the knowhow to use the Pre-emption Act, he passed from being ordinary and dangerous to being just plain dangerous."

"What do we do now?" the rancher again demanded.

"One thing's certain. He's got to go, one way or another."

"Damn, damn, damn," Burroughs muttered, then seemed to notice Lillian. He took her arm and guided her toward some empty chairs along one barn wall.

"You were right, Ellis dear," she said, smiling up at him. "He's not dead."

"He won't be alive for long now, though. No one—especially not him—can get away with stealing my land!"

She stopped abruptly, still some distance from the chairs. Squares whirled around them, keeping time to the music and the caller. "So the 'new' Ellis Burroughs had a quite short life. What happened, sir, to the legitimate pursuits of the Lazy T Bar?" Her voice, too, was rising. Again heads turned. "Does it so thwart you, Mr. Burroughs, to see just one person have a little piece of inoffensive land in all the Stinkingwater? Or does the Burroughs Empire have to gobble up every last little spadeful of brown dirt in Wyoming?"

Ellis pulled her arm, but she jerked it away and stamped her foot. "So this is how you keep your word, Mr. Burroughs! Will it be a bullet in the back this time? Or will you engineer his death by dragging him behind a half-broke horse?"

Ellis wheeled away. With face flushed and veins throbbing at the temples, he stomped to the door. Equally angered, she made her way to an empty chair, oblivious of curious glances from swirling couples.

And that's where she remained for two hours, sitting rigidly, alone, assuming the Burroughs quarantine was not only still in effect, but had probably been reinforced.

Ellis returned to stand beside Levi Bunting, across the hall from Lillian. *If this is a test of wills,* she thought, *then by all the Gods that made me, I'm game!*

"May I have this dance?"

She looked up and gasped at the nicest pair of gray eyes she'd seen in a year. She recovered quickly, however, fluttered her hand and said, "I don't know, sir, my card is nearly full. Do you have a name?"

He smiled. "You have a one-track mind."

She rose and curtsied. "And you, sir, have a nasty habit of avoiding the question."

As the man she now knew as Jacob Weatherby led her onto the floor, she glanced at Ellis Burroughs, saw the rancher whisper into his foreman's ear, saw Levi Bunting smile and stride away.

The dance was a square, with Mr. Duert doing the calling. But even as Lillian Mathers formed up with her partner, the music turned to a waltz. As chance had it, she faced the fiddler's platform, saw Mr. Duert turn with a startled expression, and noticed Dad Marquardt point at her and her partner with his chin.

"I'm a little rusty," Jethro Spring said, holding her at arm's length and stumbling into a distant cousin of a waltz.

"Rusty you might be, but you're also insane."

"Are you worth the trouble?" he replied.

"You still haven't told me your name."

"Why don't you just call me Rusty?"

"All right," she said. "I'll call you Rusty Weatherby."

Gray eyes fleetingly met hers, then switched to the barn's doorway. "Word travels fast," he murmured.

She followed his gaze. Levi Bunting strode through the door followed by the huge T Bar blacksmith. Schulte smiled and rubbed his hands.

"I saw the cabin," she said. "Father and I rode to the Southfork in October. We were hunting. We chanced by your home. I'm sorry."

The blacksmith started across the floor.

Gray eyes again swept across her face. "Yes, I know you were there. Elk hunting, too? Without a rifle between you?"

Schulte threaded his way between the swirling couples. Lillian felt herself guided away, across the floor.

"How could you have known we carried no rifle?"

The man Weatherby smiled, warily eyeing the black-smith who pursued them relentlessly. "We may not have much time left, Miss Mathers—meaning things might come to a head soon. I do want you to know before we're interrupted that I appreciate your concern." With that, he stopped and made to shove her behind him, turning to face the approaching blacksmith.

"Nice music," John Chapman said as he and Affie glid-ed between him and the ham-fisted Schulte. The black-smith tried to step around, but the smooth-dancing Chapman couple glided in front of him. He started the other way, but found the Chapmans moving in that direction, also. Again he started around. Again John and Affie Chapman blocked him.

The blacksmith stopped and reached out for John Chapman.

"I wouldn't," said a nearby Chapman cowboy who danced with a pretty Meeteetse lady. Another Two Dot couple sidled up, and other Two Dot hands drifted individually onto the floor.

Then rotund little Otto Frank was there, smiling. He tilted his head up to the red-faced Burroughs blacksmith. "I am sorry, Mr. Schulte, but I must ask you to leave der dance floor. Only those what has girls to dance mit are allowed out here."

Several unescorted Pitchfork men drifted up to stand around Otto Frank and await the blacksmith's decision. Schulte wheeled and plowed straight through the crowd, disappearing through the double doors into the inky night.

"Shall we continue?" Jethro Spring—the man she knew as Jacob Weatherby—asked.

Dad Marquardt's grin was ear to ear and his fiddle music became inspired. Otto Frank led his Pitchfork hands from the dance floor and the Two Dot cowboys without partners remained in the building, leaning indolently against a wall.

"You're so infuriating," she said after they'd continued dancing for several minutes.

"Why?"

"I asked how you could've known Father and I visited your cabin? And how you could've known we were unarmed? You didn't reply."

He smiled and said nothing.

"And why not tell me your name is Jacob Weatherby?"

"Are you sure it is?"

"I heard it only tonight, from a mutual acquaintance of ours ..." She paused, unable even to try keeping the disgust from her voice. "... that 'Jacob Weatherby' is on the deed to your Blood Canyon property."

"But are you sure it's my real name?"

"What then, pray tell, is your name?"

Again he smiled—glistening white teeth in a bronzed and weathered face. Her brow furrowed as she studied him, saw the beginning gray flecks in his otherwise dark hair. *Not altogether handsome, perhaps even forbidding, but somehow comforting,* she thought. *And though he's certainly not an accomplished dancer, he glides easily enough.* "You are a strange man, Mr. Weatherby," she said at last.

"What's wrong with Rusty?"

"Nothing. I shall call you Rusty, if you'll call me Lillian in return."

"A deal."

They moved among the gliding couples as if the floor was theirs alone. "Do you know what I wish?" she said.

Again he smiled, this time an even greater transformation. "No ma'am. I don't know what you wish."

"I wish this one single dance would go on all night."

"It already has gone on a long time, seems to me," he mused.

Several more minutes went by. She asked, "Didn't you consider the risk you were taking by coming here?"

"I figured once a year wasn't too much to see you."

This time it was she who smiled. "You've not exactly worn out your welcome. My father never considers any of my swains serious until he meets them."

"We might have to correct that little oversight."

"My parents—both of them—really are dear people. Tell me about yours."

His voice was flat and suddenly very hard. "They're dead."

"I ... I'm sorry."

"Why should you be sorry? You had nothing to do with it."

"To do with it? I don't understand. Rusty?"

His step faltered, then he picked it up. "No, I'm sure you don't," he said at last. "And chances are, you never will."

She puzzled over his word choices. Her hand lay along his side, just above the belt. His flannel shirt was new, but she could feel the warmth of his ribs through it. A soft leather boot brushed her foot and she glanced down.

"Sorry," he said. "I told you I was rusty, but the truth is I've never had time to learn much about dancing." Sweat glistened on his forehead and trickled down one cheek. He wore an expensive scarlet silk neckerchief at his throat, and his hair was neatly trimmed.

"Quite all right, sir," she murmured, wishing she could lay her head on that neckerchief.

"Did I pass inspection?"

"Mmmm."

"Lillian."

"Oh, I'm sorry. I was lost in thought. What was it you said?"

"I asked if I passed inspection?"

"Say it again."

His brow wrinkled, but he said, "I asked if I ..."

"Not that. My name. You said my name."

"Lillian?"

"Yes, that's it. Now say it again."

"Lillian."

"I like the way you say it." Here she paused, ending the moment.

"Do you plan to rebuild your cabin?"

"It's rebuilt."

"What?" She was the one who faltered then. He grasped her more closely and they continued on.

"You must do something about those ears. I repeat myself too often."

"How could you have rebuilt so soon?"

"Didn't. Spent all winter at it."

"All winter? That's impossible! My friends tell me one cannot survive winter in the upper Southfork, let alone carry out a cabin raising."

Jethro Spring merely smiled.

She studied him for a few moments, then said, "I hope you didn't cut those beautiful cottonwood trees for cabin timbers."

"They're still there. I need those to be able to creep upon unsuspecting maidens. All us lecherous nesters are that way."

She smiled. The music was tantalizing.

"Actually, Lillian, I built this cabin out of stone." He smiled. "It'll be a little tougher for just any old cattleman to burn—by accident."

She surrendered to the mood, leaning into him, then snapped back to reality. "Really, didn't you think it dangerous to come here tonight? I have reason to believe you have enemies who are planning to kill you."

"They might need help."

She squeezed his hand. "Please be careful." Sweat flowed freely down his face; she felt clammy beneath her dress. "Where is your gun?" she asked, suddenly noticing he carried none.

"Checked at the door. Everyone has to do the same."

"Ellis Burroughs checked none of his."

"That figures." Then he said, "This is a long dance. Doesn't it seem long to you?"

It did indeed. She glanced around. Only a few others were dancing; the rest had stopped from exhaustion. Ellis Burroughs had disappeared, but an unblinking Levi Bunting stood by the door, arms folded, left foot propped against the wall behind him.

Still, Dad Marquardt sawed benignly on, his fiddle music switching from one waltz to another; his infectious grin following just the two of them.

"I'll go back through Boulder Basin," he said. "It's a

rugged drop down into the Southfork, but it's a dandy ride across a high tundra plateau—after you get on top. The trip up from this side is easy. I'll beat 'em back. And no bullet along the way."

"Take me with you," she whispered.

He stumbled again.

"Take me with you," she whispered more fiercely.

"I can't do that, Lillian."

"Don't be a fool. Of course you can. I can ride anywhere you can. The Boulder Basin Trail isn't too much for this lady!"

"That's not what I meant, Lillian. There'll be trouble in Blood Canyon again. I don't reckon you should be involved in it. Besides, I don't want to rush us."

"Rush us? Rush us! Rusty Jacob Weatherby, or whatever your name is, you jackass! It's been over a year since I first—and last—saw you. Is that what you call 'rushing it'?" She hurried on before he could answer. "Listen, you idiot—I ... I love you."

He pulled her into his arms, right there in the middle of Otto Frank's barn floor and held her tight. "All I can tell you, ma'am, is I'm certain to see you before another year is up." Then he broke their embrace and led her to her chair as the music wound down and stopped.

"Thank you Lillian," Jethro Spring said, bowing over her hand. Then he wheeled and started for the door.

"Nice evening, isn't it, Mr. Bunting?" the man known as Jacob Weatherby asked as he waited for his holstered Colt.

Lillian followed. As she reached the door, Levi Bunting reached out a restraining arm and she hiked her dress and kicked him hard—and high. The arm fell away.

It was a bright moonlit night. A lantern hanging over the barn door and another over the refreshment stand gave additional light. A man walked toward Jethro Spring. He led a buckskin horse.

"I brunged you yer horse, Mr. Nester Bastard," a grinning Isaac Schulte said....

CHAPTER THIRTEEN

Jethro Spring still carried his holstered Colt in his hand. He knew he could flip off the leather thong holding the weapon in place and jerk it out. But a glance told him the blacksmith was unarmed, so he tossed his gunbelt aside and hit Isaac Schulte with all his might!

Though blood spurted from the big man's nose, his grin stayed in place as he dropped the buckskin's leadrope and reached for the smaller man. Jethro moved right, slapping the blacksmith's groping ham-like hands away and hitting the bigger man at the base of his neck. At the same time, Jethro stabbed a left into Schulte's kidney and another right to his ear.

The blacksmith roared and swept a backhand left in a wide arc that passed above the smaller man's bobbing head. It was coming back to Jethro now—the years he spent as a middleweight prizefighter, the training in Oriental fighting he received from a Chinese friend. As Schulte paused in confusion, Jethro closed, driving a knee into the big man's groin and a head under his chin, hammering Schulte's mouth closed with a clatter of teeth.

Then the two men parted. A handful of Jethro's shirt was left in the blacksmith's fist. The big man's eyes narrowed to slits as he wiped snot and blood from his nose. Only the two men's rasping breaths broke the silence.

Jethro smiled, recalling Sailor Dan Grimes and the way he'd beaten the near indestructible "Sailor Man" by blinding him with his own gore. Quickly the smaller man glided back to the attack, feinting another kick at the big man's groin. When Schulte dropped his hands in protection, Jethro hit him with a right and left combination above both beetle-browed eyes.

He moved aside as Schulte charged, but a flailing right broke through his defenses and staggered Jethro. Surprisingly agile, the blacksmith wheeled to continue the attack, but a striking moccasin boot connected with his pivot knee and the bigger man staggered. It was enough for the younger man to land rat-a-tat blows on Schulte's eyebrows. Blood seeped down from the left, into the man's eye. He paused, wiped blood and cursed.

A crowd of men—and one woman—closed around the two. Lillian saw Ellis Burroughs and slid up to him, brushing him with her shoulder. He seemed not to notice, standing with his mouth open and eyes shining like a cat watching wounded mice.

Again Schulte charged. Again the lighter man spun away, landing a series of light blows over his opponent's right eye. Then Cletus Wills slapped Jethro's nervous buckskin with his hat and the horse bolted between the combatants. Schulte reflexively swung at the buckskin causing the horse to shy into Jethro, staggering him. Schulte was on him in a moment, swinging wildly, breaking through the smaller man's defenses, driving him back and down.

"Oh, Ellis," Lillian said, moving against the rancher.

Without taking his eyes off the combatants, the rancher slid an arm around her shoulders. She took his belt buckle in one of her hands.

Schulte began kicking the scrambling Jethro Spring; Ellis pulled Lillian tight in his excitement.

Somehow the smaller man eluded most of the kicks as the blacksmith wiped blood from his streaming eyebrows with both hands. Then he located Jethro on his hands and knees, gasping for breath. With a roar, the big brute charged, but Jethro threw himself into the blacksmith's churning legs and Schulte struck the ground with a thud.

By the time Schulte regained his feet and cleared his eyes, the smaller man was up, standing near Ellis and Lillian. Only the sleeves of his shirt were left, connected by a thin strip across his shoulders. Great welts were rising on his chest and back. His face was cut and bruised and a trickle of blood was on his lips. But when Schulte charged again, the smaller man had his speed back and great spurts of blood shot from the blacksmith's brows.

Soon, Schulte could only stand and roar like an enraged bear while the smaller man roamed around him at will, striking a kidney here, measuring an ear there, nimbly kicking groin or knee, or once even, the blacksmith's head. Suddenly Schulte sat down, still upright, still roaring.

Ellis Burroughs squeezed Lillian and she squeezed him in return as Jethro shuffled around and around the blacksmith, finally delivering a wicked kick behind his ear. The giant toppled over and lay still.

Ellis Burroughs exhaled and drew his arm from Lillian's shoulders. She released him.

Jethro Spring stared around him with glazed eyes, sucking great gasps of air. At last he turned and began to limp through the silent crowd.

One man detached from the group; the half-lidded eyes of Levi Bunting glistened in the moonlight. "One moment, Mr. Weatherby," he commanded. He held a revolver.

The battered warrior pivoted, holding out open hands. "I'm not armed, Bunting."

"But I am," Lillian said, thrusting Ellis Burroughs' tiny belt-buckle derringer against the small of Levi Bunting's back. There was an ominous click in the sudden hush as she eared the hammer back.

"Lillian!" Ellis gasped from behind her. "Now see here, that's mine. You have no right ..."

She thumped the little weapon's barrel against Bunting's backbone for good measure and snarled, "Shut up, Ellis."

To Bunting, she said, "I'm an impetuous woman and I've got this hot damned urge to shoot you."

Bunting dropped his revolver.

"You can go now, Mr. Weatherby," the woman said. But he was already gone.

Levi Bunting stood stiffly until the last sounds of a buckskin horse trotting into the night diminished. Then he turned ever so slowly, his unblinking eyes fixed on the tiny derringer. Ellis appeared at Lillian's side, holding out his hand for the gun. She murmured to them both. "I could save the entire world a lot of trouble if I killed you two now." And she pulled the trigger.

The dirt leaped between Levi Bunting's boots. He jumped and blinked and his arm shot out to slap her.

Then Otto Frank and John Chapman and quite a few other men were there. One of them had Bunting by the collar, twisting it. Pointing to the plank where a jug perched, Frank announced, "Refreshments there is. I suggest we men retire to those refreshments und let what women are here get refreshed themselves."

The cowboy holding Bunting's collar twisted tighter. Then Lillian saw the knife another held against the T Bar man's ribs. Ellis Burroughs was white. Two men stood so close to him that he could barely gasp, "Yes! Refreshments. That does sound delightful."

The entire troop of men moved en masse to the refreshment table, some stepping over Isaac Schulte, still lying in a fetal position, blood leaking from his nose, mouth, eyebrows, and one ear. Still gripped in one of the blacksmith's massive fists was a scarlet silk neckerchief. Lillian stooped to slip the neckerchief loose, then used it to dry her tears as she sought refuge in the darkness.

She bumped into a horse that was tethered to a box elder. Through flooding tears, she saw it was a big dapple gray, still saddled, with a bridle hanging from the horn. "Do you know the way to Boulder Basin, Big Fellow?" she asked softly and thought he said yes. Slipping the bridle from the horn, she held it out. The gray was well trained, reaching out to take the bit with an open mouth.

She dropped the derringer down the bodice of her dress, untied the gray's halter rope and, using the saddle strings to pull herself up, crawled up and into an unusually big man's saddle. The gray plodded away from the Pitchfork Ranch, stirrups the woman could not reach, slapping with each passing step....

CHAPTER FOURTEEN

Come time for the doin's at the Pitchfork, I quit fishin' and dropped down t'the Greybull side to look for sign o' Gray Eyes. Fish warn't bitin' real good nohow, so it warn't no pull to quit. I knowed Gray Eyes wouldn't leave no wagon tracks for a blind jasper t'follow, so's I looked plumb hard t'make shore he ain't a-passed. Near as I could tell, that warn't the case, so I set t'watchin' down canyon to the east.

He comed slow and a feller didn't need no eyeglass t'see he was a-hurtin'. Howsomever, with a eyeglass t'was plumb easy t'see why he was a-hurtin'. He slumped in the saddle and his face looked like he'd cozened up nigh on to a badger whilst he was in his hole and backed against a corner. One eye was black and he was holdin' an arm against his side like he had a broken rib or maybe two. He had no hat, nor shirt, and blood was matted up in his hair.

Hurt as he was, he still looked t'his backtrail now and again, stoppin' his buckskin and turnin' the hoss so's the man hisself wouldn't have t'twist in the saddle.

"Now maybe you'll be mad enough t'fight Pansy Bottom," I muttered to m'self.

Meanwhile I set t'watchin' his backtrail better'n he could do.

———•-•———

The sun was into its down'ard slide when I seed the next rider a-comin'. That'un rode a big gray hoss, but even far off, somethin' warn't right about that rider. Comin' closer on, I could see it was a female—the very same one what comed up t'Blood Canyon twice. She looked funny, settin' up on that big gray what was big enough t'carry three or four o'her. She had on a dress what'd frazzle the eyeballs off'n most fellers her age and it was hiked plumb near t'her waist so's she could straddle the saddle sensible-like. With her dress whar it was, her laigs blossomed pink, and they warn't knobby-kneed a-tall, like some I seen.

So I studied on them laigs awhilst.

That saddle she was a-ridin' was way big for her leetle butt and the stirrups hung near a foot b'low her toes. That saddle warn't hers, shore enough. And likely not the gray, neither.

A feller'd have t'be dimwitted if he didn't think she follered Gray Eyes. He'd be dimwitteder still if he thought she had a chance in God's green earth of ever catchin' him. So I set back t'watchin' both their backtrails. Leastways I set t'watchin' for varmints after them pink laigs turned a corner, out o' sight.

After dark I picketed Hoss in a little patch o' grass, then, in case somebody follered up it in the middle o' the night, I moved down next t'the trail. By mid-afternoon the next day, I gived up on anybody else a-comin' and figgered t'head on back t'Blood Canyon and see what Gray Eyes was up to.

So I saddled Hoss and let him drink a bellyful from a little spring. Then we rode a ways and I looked at the back-trail country one more time afore we'uns headed upriver.

The tracks was easy t'foller. I'd looked at the buck-skin's marks for over a year now and could spot them any-whar. And them washtub prints o' the big gray stood out like a bloody tongue. Since thar warn't no other hoss tracks on the Greybull, 'ceptin' m'own, them tracks could be follered at a high lope—and Hoss was ready t'move.

Plain as day, the bigfoot gray missed the turn t'Boulder Basin. What warn't so plain was whar Gray Eyes went and that's prob'ly the reason the gal missed it. I studied on the trail fork whilst Hoss kept tryin' t'turn t'ward Boulder Basin and home. He was a-prancin' around, th'owin' his head and blowin' his nose. But directly I started him on up the Greybull, a-headed after the gray. Way I figgered it, them pink laigs was purtier than Gray Eyes' black eye.

It was near on t'dark when me'n Hoss comed on t'whar she spent the night afore. Right along the trail it was, and plumb easy t'see. She'd fetched no fire—prob'ly didn't know how—and it looked like she'd laid out under a brush pile. Must not a-slept much neither, way she'd rolled and set up, then laid down and rolled some more. Her hoss never got no graze neither, for she'd tied him to a tree what he'd stomped and pawed all the dirt away from the roots 'cause he was hungry.

I got t'thinkin' how we was headin' into the high country and how cold it got come night. Then I thought about that dress o' hers and how it'd frazzle a feller's eyes and maybe keep him warm enough to keep her cozy. But without a feller for her to cozy up to, whar would she be? Light was fadin' though, so me'n Hoss got plumb serious 'bout night trailin', figgerin' to catch her afore she got in t'more pickle. But after whilst, me'n Hoss quit, bellyin' down for the night 'cause Pink Laigs and the gray hoss's tracks beginned t'sashay back and forth and I figgered they was as lost as they could be—which meant the chance me'n Hoss could lose 'em in the night. On top o' that, both him and me was tired.

We was up and follerin' 'em at daylight howsomever. Hoss'd got a fair bellyful o' bunchgrass whilst on his picket rope, and he was movin' strong. Problem was, them tracks was wanderin' worse than ever. Trackin' turned harder when they hit off on a rocky bench. And soon it was mid-mornin' and we ain't catched 'em yet.

Finally we spotted the big gray in a little basin b'low us. Looked like he was feedin' peaceable-like, so we worked our way down t'him and he was glad t'see another pony, a-whinnyin' and a-snortin' and a-carryin' on. But the gal warn't around.

The gray was still packin' his saddle, but didn't have nothin' on his head. No bridle, no halter, no nothin'.

Took some doin' t'git back t'whar the gal turned him loose. I could see whar she'd tied him up the night afore and whar he'd pawed up roots 'cause he was so hungry. She musta felt sorry for him after awhilst and tooked off his bridle so's he could graze. She shoulda knowed better than t'turn a hoss loose t'graze on a rocky ridgetop what's got no grass.

It didn't look like Pink Laigs likely slept much this night neither, for I never did see whar she laid down. I knowed it to be cold in this high country come night for we passed a couple o' snowbanks off t'the northeast. Likely the wind was a-blowin', too, 'cause she first set down on the south side o' a big boulder, then moved t'other side. Too, she'd pulled up and broke off what grass and flower stems she could find and tried t'cover up with 'em. Stupid woman, I thought. *They's a perfectly good blanket under that saddle what's on the gray.* Likely she was afraid t'pull the saddle 'cause she figgered she might not get back on the big critter.

Way it looked t'me, I had t'find Pink Laigs afore

t'night or she might not make it. The sun said t'was mid-afternoon.

I didn't find her afore dark—trackin' is tough when a body follers somebody what don't know whar they's goin. But I did find the heel o' one o' her dancin' slippers, and I picked up the gray's bridle whar she dropped it whilst crawlin' up a snowbank. I held the bridle in m'hand and eyed her tracks across the snow. There was a dab o' blood in the right hand track. I allowed as how the way snow was meltin', the gal was maybe a hour ahead o' me. But dark was a-comin' on fast and she'd broked over a ridge and headed into a timbered canyon. I didn't know if I could find her in the timber in the dark. But neither did I know if she'd be alive come mornin'.

First grass I comed to, I picketed both hosses, pullin' the saddles and stackin' 'em against a rock. Then I rolled up both saddle blankets and tied 'em with a chunk o' rawhide, picked up m'Hawken and started dark trailin'.

She was only a quarter-mile away. I was on her afore I seen her. Well, almost on her—she shines from some distance away. She was sprawled out on the ground, layin', way it looked, right whar she fell. Them pink laigs was shinin' in the moonlight whar her dress'd hiked up as she went down. She only had one slipper on—t'other had popped off in the shuffle and laid up by her knees. Her hair was flung out and tangled worser than any injin squaw I never seed.

I bent over and felt a pulse what was faint and had a beat like a hoss with a limp. As near as I could tell in the moonlight, Pink Laigs' dress was not in fine fettle neither, bein' ripped and ragged. So I undid the blankets and laid one out on t'ground. Then I lifted Pink Laigs to it. She never woked up when I did neither, but she kinda sighed and her breathin' comed a little more steady soon as I laid t'other blanket over top o' her. Then I fetched a fire.

I had the fire goin' good and it war warmin' the

sleepin' Pink Laigs right smart when I hiked back to m'saddle and tooked up a can and some ground coffee. The ponies was feedin' right smart when I passed 'em, not even raisin' a head t'see if I aimed t'let 'em be.

I figgered if I went downhill far enough, I'd strike water and I was right without goin' too blamed far. Pink Laigs was still a-layin' whar I left her when I got back. I put the coffee on t'boil afore I checked her again. She stirred a little when I fingered the pulse along her neck, but she settled right down soon's I moved away. She was sleepin' so good I allowed as how I wouldn't wake her just for hot coffee, and I drunk the potful m'self. Then I built up the fire, went back t'the saddles and brung m'saddlebags and possibles sack down t'the gal. I put on another pot o' coffee t'boil, slicin' some chunks o' jerky into it. Next I salted it a mite and dumped in some wild onions I'd pulled back down the Greybull whilst I watched for Gray Eyes and whoever comed behind. Then I went t'sleep.

It was breakin' day when I poked up the fire and went t'see about the hosses. Both of 'em was standin' content, but I moved their picket ropes nohow t'give 'em a crack at some new grass. After that I set Hawken down and pulled up a couple more wild onions, then drifted back t'the sleepin' gal. Only she warn't sleepin'. Instead, she was settin' with her back to a tree, wrapped in both saddle blankets. As I walked in a-carryin' the onions and Hawken, the top blanket dropped away and the snout o' a little derringer gun poked out at me. "Who are you?" Pink Laigs demanded.

I heered a tiny 'click' as the hammer was eared back. "Sam Buttercut," I said as mild-like as I could make it muster.

"Where did you come from?"

"Originally from No'th Caroliny, but more recent from Montany and points no'th, south, and west."

"What are you doing here?"

"Well, for starters, I'm a-tryin' t'save your life. But if that leetle gun goes off and if it hits whar it's aimin', both o' us will die 'cause you'll kill me and you ain't got a chance in hell o' gittin' out on your own."

That put her t'thinkin'. D'rectly she said, "It's not loaded anyway."

"Well ma'am, whether it's loaded or not, I'd look on it as a personal favor could you point it someplace else'n m'belly button."

She drawed her hand and the derringer back under the hoss blanket, then drawed the blanket tighter around her.

"Are ye cold?" I asked.

"I'm better, thank you."

I moved slow and easy to a tree and leaned Hawken for I didn't know for shore if the little gun really warn't loaded, nor whar it pointed from under them saddle blankets. Then I broked the two new onions into the pot o' last night's bouillon coffee whilst the gal watched big-eyed and alert as I handed it to her. "It'll be hot, so be careful. Don't drink it too fast neither if it's like I think and you ain't et in three, four days."

She tooked it usin' blanket folds twixt her hands and the pot, and sipped only a little to beginned with whilst I rustled some more wood. After I comed back, I sliced me a bite o' jerky and watched her polish off the stew. "I'm indebted to you, Mr. Buttercut," she said, settin' down the pot. "I believe I owe you my life."

I never said nothin' 'til I comed back t'the fire with a fresh pot o' water and stuck it on t'boil with more coffee, meat and onions. After it heated awhilst, I asked, "What is a woman doin' up here t'the head o' the Greybull?"

She stared at me. She was a purty gal, now that I was up close. Her eyes was on the greenish side o' hazel, some might call it, and her hair was heavy and wavy and long, with a brush o' rust color in it. A few freckles popped out 'round a pert little turned-up nose and her face was oval-like, a-taperin' down to a cute dimpled chin. She had dark eyebrows as heavy as a pair o' caterpillars, and long eyelashes, and full lips, and laugh wrinkles at the corners of her wide mouth. Her brow was furrowed now, drawin' attention back t'her over-big round eyes.

"I guess I've been a very foolish woman," she said at last.

I broked up a few more tree limbs and poked 'em into the fire. "That didn't answer m'question."

"I ... I planned to go to the Southfork of the Stinkingwater. I planned to go through Boulder Basin."

"Why?"

Her big eyes shut down for a long time as she rested her head on arms what was laid across drawed-up knees. Then she opened them eyes real big and said, "Because I'm a foolish woman."

"Even foolish women have reasons."

I could see she was gettin' riled at the question. She tossed her head a little and some o' her hair fell across the forehead and more onto her left shoulder. Though I couldn't see nought but her head above the blankets, I knowed the rest o' her was fine doin's, havin' studied on her a good bit in last night's firelight.

"I'm not sure I have to answer all your prying questions," she finally said.

"Yeah, you do."

"I beg your pardon! May I ask why, *Mister* Buttercut?"

"It's okay by me, ma'am," I said as I handed her some more coffee stew. "Truth o' the matter is that you ain't a-gettin' out o' here 'thout me. For one thing, you ain't even got a hoss, and nobody walks out o' here lessen they knows whar they's a-goin'."

I could see that'd hit her twixt the eyes 'cause she cooled down a mite whilst her eyes studied on me over the stewpot top. "What difference does whatever reason I may have to go to the Sinkingwater make to you?"

"Meanin' no disrespeck, ma'am, but I air the one askin' the questions."

"If you must know, I was following someone."

"Why?"

"Well, I never!"

It was clear she was plumb set on gettin' het up, but the way I figgered it, I ought t'know why she was a-follerin' Gray Eyes. "Why?" I asked again.

"I don't have to answer your questions!" she cried as she flung the undrunk pot o' fixin's t'the side and th'owed off her hoss blankets. Problem was, she got up a mite too quick and had t'grab the tree she'd leaned against. Then she got a grip on herself and th'owed a mean look my way afore she started off downhill—away from the hosses.

She cut a right smart sight, too, she did, a-marchin' off down that hill in a ripped-up dancin' dress, and purt-near ruined dancin' slippers what had only one heel twixt the two of 'em. She stumbled once afore she disappeared, and fell t'her knees. Then she was goned.

I built up the fire and fetched another pot o' water for a fresh batch o' stew. Afore it was done, she comed back. She was wobblin' when she fetched up t'her blankets and flopped down. I never looked up from the stew.

"I ... I was following a man. I think he was going to the Southfork of the ... Stinkingwater ... through Boulder Basin."

"Why was you a-follerin' him?"

She hitched one blanket around her pink laigs and finally laid out on her side. She was a-breathin' hard and she had some trouble takin' her eyes off the stew pot as it bubbled away. Then her eyes dulled and just afore she passed off t'sleep, she mumbled, "Because I love him."

I kilt the deer in mid-afternoon. It was a small doe that

stopped t'look back. She shoulda went on over the hill and t'hell with what me and Hoss was. Pink Laigs was awake when I dropped the carcass by the fire. She was propped up, sippin' on the last pot o' stew. "I didn't know you had a horse, Mr. Buttercut," she said, eyeballin' Hoss.

"A feller'd have t'be loco t'travel this country without a hoss, ma'am. Meanin' no offense o'course."

She studied on me some whilst I skinned and carved the deer. "Why did you have to know my reason for wanting to go to the Southfork of the Stinkingwater, and to go through Boulder Basin?"

I never bothered t'answer. She wouldn't eat none o' the liver raw, even when I told her it'd make her muscles jump up and down. So I cooked it in pieces what I propped up against the fire on sticks. She ate them 'bout as fast as I could warm 'em. Then she follered that up with spit-fired backstrap 'til it was comin' out her ears.

"Ohh," she said as I handed her another chunk o' backstrap, "I'm stuffed. I don't believe I could possibly eat another bite."

Then she laid down and went t'sleep. She slept all the rest o' that day, all night through, and part o' the next day. When she woked up, she was hungry again and quick polished off the rest o' the backstrap. I gived her a drink o' coffee from the pot and she asked whar was I gettin' the water from.

I told her down the hill a ways.

"I must look a fright," she said as she dragged fingers through her hair.

I didn't think so, but didn't say nothin'.

"Is the water so far I might not make it, Mr. Buttercut?"

"Reckon you could do it, ma'am, was I t'show you whar t'was."

"Would you? I feel I must clean up as best I can."

I drunk off the rest o' m'coffee and raised up to

m'hind laigs. She was none too steady when we started, but stoutened up some afore we got down t'the water, 'specially after I knocked off her one slipper heel t'level her up with t'other side. T'was a small spring flowin' out o' the ground and travelin' a few feet afore it sunk again. The water itself was pure and cold enough to put goose pimples on a rifle barrel. I dipped up another pot o' water and stood there a-waitin' for her t'wash up so's we could go back t'the fire.

"Ahem. Well, Mr. Buttercut, I wonder if you could leave me now and allow me to freshen up a bit?"

"Are ye shore you can find your way back t'the fire, ma'am?"

"Oh yes, thank you. Even if I shan't, you'll be within earshot."

I didn't get the total drift o' her lingo, but it come plain she didn't want me there. So I skipped back up to our blankets and the fire, poked up the blaze and put on the pot o' coffee water. Then I leaned back against a tree and wondered more about Pink Laigs 'freshening up.'

When she comed back, she looked better, I'll give her that. The smudges were goned off her face and hands and arms. Her hair was tied around the wad o' it with a white ribbon that, on closer lookin', was prob'ly a strip tore from some underdress. Anyway, that ribbon held her hair to the back and didn't let it spread out front what was so fetchin'. She'd shuffled her dress n' things so's no two rips nor holes matched up t'show her real self—a big loss, the way I figgered it. But overall she looked better. Her face beamed and her skin was gettin' back a healthy color. On top o' that, them laugh wrinkles was plain as day in her smilin' face as she set down on her blanket.

"There, you see, Mr. Buttercut, I can find my way back."

I grunted as I chewed on a deer rib.

"You mentioned taking me to the Stinkingwater. When

shall we be able to start? I feel quite strong now. Perhaps by taking turns riding your horse, I'll be able to travel, don't you think?"

She held one wore-out slipper out for me t'look at. Its strap was broke and a hole showed through the sole what was 'bout to come off, too.

"Surely I'll be strong enough by tomorrow, Mr. Buttercut." When I didn't say nothin', she asked in a tiny little peep, "When will you be ready to start for the Stinkingwater, Mr. Buttercut?"

"Ready right now, iff'n you'll quit your everlastin' chatter." I pitched the rib bone aside and climbed t'my feet. She wobbled up and I kicked out the fire, then picked up the coffee pot and possibles sack and handed 'em to her. After that I grabbed the saddle blankets and the last venison hock, and went for the horses.

"Oh!" she said as we comed in sight o' the grazin' ponies. "You found my lost horse!"

"T'warn't him that was lost, ma'am."

As I pulled up the saddle cinch on the gray, I told her, "Somebody ought t'show you how t'pick a hoss and saddle when you go t'buy one, Pink Laigs," I said, "for neither of 'em fits you."

"My name is Lillian," she said, kinda stiff like. "Not, as you say it, 'Pink Laigs'."

She had some trouble gettin' into the saddle, so I helped her. Right away it was clear what was the matter. She was tryin' t'ride sidesaddle. I was put out and said, "Pink Laigs, we'uns got some tough country t'travel through and you'd better get used t'ridin' spread-saddle like you was a-doin' on the way up h'yar."

She sucked in her breath, but she swung her right laig over the horn so's she set astride. Her dress hiked to above her knees. "That's how come I call you Pink Laigs," I said.

She sniffed and set her purty nose a mite higher.

We follered the ridgeline back and late that afternoon,

dropped back t'the Greybull and t'the camp whar she'd laid out her first night. "Why, I remember this spot," she said.

I pulled the saddles and staked out the ponies in deep grass. She'd got into m'possibles sack and dug out the pot and filled it with water. Then she went out gatherin' some sticks for a fire. Whilst I fetched a blaze, she went out for more sticks.

Later that evenin', as we set starin' into the distance, chewin' on roasted venison quarter, she said, "You saw me following Mr. Weatherby, didn't you?"

"Follerin' who?" I asked.

"Mr. Weatherby."

"Who's Mr. Weatherby?"

"His name is Jacob Weatherby."

"It is, eh?" I thought, *Well, well. Jacob ain't too far from Jethro, and Spring usually does have some Weather.*

"What do you call him, Mr. Buttercut?"

I th'owed a piece o' gristle into the fire and dragged the back o' m'hand across m'mouth. "Gray Eyes," I said at last.

"Gray Eyes," she mused. "Gray Eyes—I like that. It's not quite as expressive as 'Pink Laigs', but somehow I like it better than Rusty or Jacob or Mr. Weatherby."

We was both quiet then, lost in our own thoughts. The night darkened and she drawed her saddle blanket up around her against the cold. A coyote yipped from top o' a distant hill.

"Do you know him, Mr. Buttercut?"

"Yep," I says as I rolled into m'saddle blanket.

The fire died and that same coyote howled off farther away. Then a trembly voice comed out o' the dark. "Do you like him, Mr. Buttercut?"

"Yep," I answered. *Damn talky woman,* I thought to m'self.

———•—•———

"Looks like we eat jerky t'night," I told the woman the following morning while saddling her gray horse, "lessen we get clear over into the Southfork afore dark."

"Oh, will we?"

"Tain't likely."

"I have faith in you, Mr. Buttercut." Then she giggled and added, "I really don't have any choice, do I?"

"Nope," I said. "You cain't ride on down the Greybull t'the Pitchfork. They hang hoss thieves in that country."

We'd been ridin' for a peck o' hours and the sun commenced to beat down strong. We'd turned an hour ago whar Gray Eyes did, a-headed west t'wards Boulder Basin. But for the last ten minutes somethin' was a-raggin' the small hairs on the back o' m'neck that up ahead warn't as right as it should be. I checked m'Hawken's prime and looked back at the gal what follered. Then I swung m'eyes up ahead. We was climbin' steady and would break out to the high country in another few minutes. The game trail we follered switchbacked up onto a steep ridge. Once we got t'the top, we'd sidehill around and into Boulder Basin. Then it'd be downhill the rest o' the way into the Stinkingwater. Still, somethin' warn't right and I didn't know what it t'was. So I stopped Hoss whilst I eyeballed up ahead.

"Is something wrong, Mr. Buttercut?" Pink Laigs asked.

"Just blowin' the ponies."

"Oh, fine." Hoss was sweatin' plenty on his neck and flanks and under his tail, but the big gray hoss didn't know he was carryin' nothin' despite the fact the gal and that big saddle weighed more'n me and my dinky McClellan. We started on.

Half a hour later we was under the top o' the boulder-scattered ridge and my unease had growed 'til I commenced t'think them boulders was heads o' Sittin' Bull and half the Sioux nation peekin' down at us. But dogged iff'n I could figger *why* I figgered the way I figgered. The trail we follered sashayed on up the side o' the ridge and passed twixt a couple o' big rock outcrops. And I didn't like it. So I blowed the hosses again whilst I studied on them outcrops 'til I could hear Pink Laigs a-fidgetin' ahind me. I told her we'uns was gonna make a dash up a game trail ahind us and for her t'stay right on m'tail.

She looked puzzled, but she was pure heart. "Whatever you think best, Mr. Buttercut."

Suddenly I wheeled Hoss onto the game trail, a-diggin' in m'heels, and a-hollerin' "Hi-i-yah!", and he jumped and bolted up the steep trail, scramblin' for all he was worth, with Pink Laigs and the big gray thunderin' right ahind.

It was a punishin' ride. As we neared the top, both hosses was lathered and blowin' like it was their last. But the game trail was toppin' out, curvin' around and passin' twixt a big rock and a little stand o' three-foot-tall limber pines. It was twixt the rock and the limber pines whar I stopped t'gived the ponies another blow—and got the jolt o' m'life t'find a white-haired old feller settin' a bay hoss in the shade o' the rock! Just as I swung m'Hawken barrel, Pink Laigs squealed, "Father!"

'Bout that time a man raised up out o' the limber pines. He was t'my right and a tad ahind me. He carried a Winchester in his hand and it was pointin' m'way. "Sam, Sam," Gray Eyes said, "whatever am I going to do with you?"

"And Mr. Weatherby!" Pink Laigs squealed again.

Gray Eyes had a grin so wide it looked like his ears might topple in. "Now I'm one up on you," he said t'me.

"Hell," I cried, "I didn't even know the game was in play!"

Chapter Fifteen

Pink Laigs an' Whitetop hugged and kissed, and Pink Laigs come t'hold Gray Eyes' hands in her own and they both stood like they was rooted. Whitetop comed over t'me and held out a hand and says, "I'm August Mathers. Mr. Weatherby said your name is Sam Buttercut."

"I are Sam Buttercut, right enough. And 'how do' to you."

Then Gray Eyes led us down the hill t'Boulder Basin, up t'this lake, and over t'this boulder whar he said, "This'll do for a campsite." He rolled away a couple o' smaller rocks and dug out a cache o' beans and coffee in jars. T'was also pots and pans in the cache that he'd stashed God knows when.

Later, he takes me aside and says, "Sam, I know you have some fishline and hooks. Why don't you and Mr. Mathers go catch us a mess of fish for supper?"

I didn't tell him I'd tried this lake the week afore, whilst waitin' for him t'come through here on his way home, and how I'd like near starved t'death on what fish I didn't catch. I didn't tell him 'cause I could see he was set on me goin' fishin' and takin' Whitetop with me. So, me'n Whitetop went a-fishin'.

He's a right pert feller, that Whitetop. He caught on that cutthroats was a-spawnin' in the outlet creek and he shore knowed how t'catch 'em. On account o' that me'n Whitetop was back in a finger-span o' sun time and Gray Eyes was surprised … and maybe a mite peeved.

That night, 'round the fire, we'uns told how me'n Pink Laigs got together. I seen Whitetop's eyebrows raise when I called his gal 'Pink Laigs' the first time. But he soon was chucklin', too, along with Gray Eyes and the gal.

"And how is it, Mr. Weatherby," Pink Laigs asked, "that you are also known as 'Gray Eyes'?"

His head snapped around t'look at me. "Is that what this old rascal calls me?"

"Didn't you know?"

"No. Come to think of it, I can't ever remember Sam calling me anything."

"I like it better," she said, "than Rusty, or Jacob or Mr. Weatherby."

"Okay, Pink Laigs," he replied. "You call me Gray Eyes and I'll call you Pink Laigs."

Me'n Whitetop both heard the whole story of the Pitchfork fight for the first time. "The way Pink Laigs tells it," I says, "Pansy Bottom and Snake Eyes ain't exactly the most pop'lar folks in the Territory." I had to stop right there and explain who Pansy Bottom was. And as soon as I did, Whitetop and Pink Laigs needed no help with Snake Eyes.

Gray Eyes explained that while neither Chapman nor Frank was afraid o' the Lazy T Bar, they warn't lookin' for no fight with 'em neither—unless the Stinkin'water outfit crowded their grass.

Whitetop turned to Gray Eyes' problem. "Lillian and I

are forever indebted to you and Mr. Buttercut for your efforts in our behalf, but I've taken you away from your homestead far too long. In light of what happened at the Pitchfork, I can assure you Burroughs and Bunting will retaliate. I would estimate the time frame for retaliation is about right—and here we sit!"

"Here we sit," Gray Eyes mused. "And here we'll sit for another day, so Lillian can rest more. After that, we'll mosey down to the Stinkingwater. I know her mother'll be anxious. The 'Rock House' isn't nearly so important."

"'Rock House'," I said, rolling it around m'tongue. "It's a good name. Danged iff'n it ain't."

I rode out the next mornin'. Way it looked t'me was Gray Eyes and Pink Laigs was bound t'enjoy their camp-out. But I'd done mixed too much mortar and packed too many rocks for that Rock House to leave Pansy Bottom's cowhands time to get into mischief.

I pulled up t'the Rock House near on t'dark. Warn't nobody in there. Nor on the cliffs up above. Nor acrost the Southfork, a-hidin' in willow brush. I see tracks whar two ponies had been rode up through Blood Canyon plumb recent, though.

I met our bunch as they comed down out o' Boulder Basin t'the Stinkin'water the next afternoon, and we moved down the river to b'low the mouth o' the Ishawooa. Pink Laigs didn't like the idee, for she wanted t'see the Rock House, but Gray Eyes put the kibosh on that by tellin' 'em they'd be in easy ridin' distance o' home, come tomorrow.

We waved goodby t'Whitetop and Pink Laigs early the next mornin', watchin' 'til they disappeared around a river bend. Then Gray Eyes turned t'me. "All right, Sam, let's have it."

"There's a supply wagon and half a dozen hands holed up at Swenson's cabin," I said. "And there's a big herd o' cow critters a-movin' this way, accordin' t'the dust down-river."

"How long do we have?" His mouth was pinched, and a vein pulsed at his temple.

"Well, iff'n they ain't a-plannin' t'move 'em too fast, I reckon it'll take 'em three, four days t'drift into Blood Canyon."

Gray Eyes stared off into space for a whilst, then he said, "Let's pick up our horses on top of the Ishawooa and ride on back to Blood Canyon."

And all he said on the whole ride to Ishawooa Mesa and back t'the Rock House was, "Things are drying up. Hasn't rained now for two months or more, seems to me like."

The next day we pushed the hoss band way up the Southfork, above Blood Canyon and a fur piece b'yond. That night a gentle breeze beginned t'blow from the north and we burned ever' stick o' grass from the Ishawooa, clean through Blood Canyon and past the Rock House.

Way we done it was startin' at the river, one t'each side, and pullin' burnin' greasewood ahind our hosses at a high lope, across the valley o' the Stinkin'water. Like Gray Eyes said, it never rained in all o' two months and the country was plumb dry.

We could see cowboys turnin' out t'fight the fire after we'd strung our fire line from side to side acrost the valley. But they was all comin' from the Swenson place and they was all ahind the fire, with no chance t'get in front.

The Rock House stood, o' course, and so did the cottonwoods up by the lake, and the trees on the ridge above, 'cause the rock cliffs kept the fire from the trees above 'em, and the ground whar the cow critters had teared it up the year afore still hadn't growed enough grass t'burn a hot fire 'round Gray Eyes' trees. But it was enough t'keep the burn a-goin' through the canyon, and when it got t'better doin's above, it took off and never stopped 'til it reached most near the Eastfork, way on upriver.

Like I said, there warn't no stick o' grass left on the upper Stinkin'water for 'em t'drive their cows to. And with no cows in the upper Stinkin'water, there warn't no reason for Pansy Bottom and Snake Eyes t'have no gun-totin' cowhands up there neither. Shucks, it was beginnin' t'look like it might be lonesome in Blood Canyon this summer. Black, too.

But lonesome and black was better than the cow yard it was last year.

———

They comed three days after the fire. There was near twenty o' 'em and it looked like a mean war party. Gray Eyes said they was out more for show than serious, though. He said if they was serious, they wouldn't come through our canyon all in a bunch, Snake Eyes in the lead.

We'd seen 'em comin' even afore they got t'Blood Canyon. Gray Eyes got up from the hill whar he laid and said he'd wait for 'em in the Rock House whilst I waited up t'the cliff. That suited me fine, bein' as I ain't no inside man nohow. When I left, I says to Gray Eyes, "Iffn the shootin' do start, don't pay no never mind t'Snake Eyes—he'll be the first one dead."

As Pansy Bottom's bunch pulled up in front o' the Rock House door, I laid down m'eyeglass and picked up the Hawken. Then I tooked a fine bead on the lead rider and tightened up a mite on the trigger. Some o' their hosses kept stompin' around, but they was their riders and Gray Eyes' problem. My job was to keep a bead on the snake-eyed varmint—and his big roan stood real still.

After awhilst, I took t'wonderin', was the shootin' to start, who might I set ol' Hawken to next. 'Bout then the snake-eyed varmint I had m'bead set on took to flutterin'. I raised one eye up over the Hawken barrel to better see. Ever'body down b'low was a-starin' back toward Blood Canyon whar a whitetopped old man and a gal ridin' straddle-legged comed a-ridin' like they was headed for a social. I laid down m'Hawken and picked up m'eyeglass. Waugh! She's shore purty!

Then the whole wad o' Pansy Bottom's cowhands up and rode out, cuttin' a wide swath t'ward Blood Canyon and forcin' Whitetop and Pink Laigs aside. I had a notion t'knock the dust from under Snake Eyes' hoss for that. But I got up and knocked pine needles off'n me instead.

By the time I got down off'n the clifftop, Whitetop was sayin' he and Pink Laigs talked it over and figgered t'come up t'Blood Canyon for a week or two, knowin' that Pansy Bottom and Snake Eyes wouldn't dare move against us iff'n the Mathers two was hangin' around. Way Whitetop figgered, it would give us some breathin' room afore they had t'go back down t'Marquardt Town.

Gray Eyes said, "Horsefeed, Mr. Mathers. There's no horsefeed left around here. Surely you can see that. Otis Kluster won't be too thrilled when you bring back starved horses to his stable."

But Whitetop drew on his pipe and stuck out his chin. "Come now, Mr. Weatherby. You and Sam are surely not horseless, so why not put our horses with yours and let us camp by the cottonwoods?"

Then Pink Laigs laid a hand on Gray Eyes' arm and Whitetop turned to me and said, "Sam, I'd like to put up our tent down in the cottonwoods by the pool. I trust you'll be kind enough to give me a hand."

That evenin', while we sipped on a cup o' coffee, Pink Laigs said, "We know you and Sam must have set the fire. Was there no other way?"

Gray Eyes chewed on a pine twig and stared at the eastern skyline. "Couldn't see any," he said at last.

"But it looks so awful. All this black."

I butted in. "It's a sight better'n the dust n' cowpiles that was left here last year."

"It'll grow back, Lillian," Gray Eyes said. "By next year, it'll be even more lush and green than it ever was."

"But not the trees," she said.

"No. The trees will take longer."

"But there ain't none o' Pansy Bottom's gunhands in the hills neither," I chunked in.

Whitetop said, "Strategically speaking, Sam is right, Lillian. Now that Lazy T Bar cattle cannot graze the upper Stinkingwater, there is no legitimate reason for Burroughs or Bunting to have T Bar cowboys up here. One must remember, they had wanted to drive Mr. Weatherby out while maintaining the specter of legality."

"And now they'll have to find another way," Gray Eyes murmured.

"Yes," Whitetop said. "I suspect we were witnesses to that 'other way' earlier today; obviously intimidation, perhaps more. I fear, Mr. Weatherby, that your altercation is about to move into a more violent arena."

Pink Laigs asked, "What will they do next?"

Gray Eyes shook his head. "What do you think, Sam?"

"Bushwhacker," I said right out. "They's ought to be gittin' it clear purty soon that you ain't a-runnin'. A bushwhacker'd be clean and simple."

"Surely ..." Pink Laigs beginned.

I cut her off. "Shore as God made little apples, they ain't gonna charge in here like they did today iff'n they was serious. Why somebody could get hurt—and that somebody might be one o' them."

"What Sam says sounds right," Whitetop said. "But can you defend against a lone gunman who chooses the time and place?"

"The place ain't theirs to choose 'cause Blood Canyon is our stompin' grounds."

"And," Whitetop continued, passing his 'baccy pouch on over t'me, "the time really isn't theirs, either, since Mr. Weatherby is becoming a symbol of resistance they cannot long ignore."

"But the question was," Pink Laigs busted in, "can you defend against such an attack?"

"Pink Laigs," I said, "theys bushwhacker'll be under sod long afore Gray Eyes is."

CHAPTER SIXTEEN

It was the day after Pink Laigs and her daddy rode in t'the middle of our to-do with Snake Eyes and his T Bar bunch that Gray Eyes led the four o' us up t'Ishawooa Mesa and found Pansy Bottom's cows had beat us up there. It was the first time I noticed ol' Richard's son a-losin' it.

Whitetop was a-studyin' the rocks all the way up the mesa. He'd stop now'n then, pull a little hammer out o' his saddle roll, and break off a piece o' rock. Then he'd turn it over a bunch o' times afore he th'owed it down and went t'look for another rock.

"This is fascinating country, Sam," he'd say over and over again. "Both igneous and sedimentary layering—isn't that fascinating?"

"Nope. Not to me it ain't," I told him. But that never dampered him a-tall.

I was ridin' ahind, pullin' the packhoss, and Whitetop had stopped t'dig at another rock while I waited. I was a-lookin' at Gray Eyes and Pink Laigs when they topped out and I sees Gray Eyes settin' there and starin' like he didn't like what he seed. After me'n Whitetop rode on up, I found out what it was that Gray Eyes stared at—cows. They'uns was all over the mesa.

We figgered t'camp by the a little pond just inside the mesa's south point. But the water had been muddied up by cow critters and we stopped only long enough t'gived our thirsty ponies a drink afore we started for someplace else.

Not long after we left the muddy pool, Whitetop whoaed his hoss an' got off t'look closer at a big rock what he said musta been carried by a glacier t'whar it laid. "You see, Sam," he said, "how this rock's edges are rounded more than the others we've seen? That speaks glacier. So do these striations." He was a-pointin' t'somethin' I couldn't see. "With striations like these on a glacier-carried rock, it has to mean this rock was once part of a cliff. Isn't that quite interesting?"

Since I couldn't say as I knowed what the Sam Hill he was talkin' about, I let him ramble on.

"Now this appears to be some sort of limestone. And it appears to be full of brachiopods." Ol' Whitetop was a-lookin' t'the back o' the big rock and tappin' away with his hammer. D'rectly he stepped over t'my hoss and handed up a piece o' rock with a big shell stuck in it. "See, Sam, you're looking at a form of life existing in a sea that covered this land millions of years ago."

"Wait just a hour, you ol' fraud," I told him as I turned the stone with the shell stuck in it over and over again. "There shore as hell warn't no ocean or sea or whatever you calls it, here on top o' these mountains. I been a-listenin' t'your chatter all day and you ain't said nothin' I knowed enough about t'call you on it. But a ocean o'er these mountains? Ha!

Even so, I took the rock and whispered, "The shell is right int'restin' though. Durned iff'n it ain't."

"You're right, Sam," he said. "The sea never covered these mountain peaks when that shell was deposited. But the shell is here in your hands—and, as you say, it's interesting. Therefore, the only explanation must be that these mountains weren't here when it was deposited. They were, in fact, formed later. What do you think of that?"

I just looked at him and the brackio-whatever, and turned it over an' over in m'fingers. "Whitetop," says I, "you shore are workin' hard at makin' things more complicated than they need t'be."

Gray Eyes rode back t'us then and reckoned we'd best go on back t'the Rock House.

"That's disappointing," Whitetop said as he handed Gray Eyes another chunk o' shell rock. "I've just found an interesting specimen here, Mr. Weatherby. I believe we might be able to trace this one specimen back to its source. Do you see how this glacially transported rock is only slightly rounded? It couldn't have come far. If we could trace it to its origin, the layering of sediment might contain yet more illuminating fossils."

Whitetop sorta wilted when Gray Eyes shooked his head and handed the rock back. "We'd better get along now, Mr. Mathers. Dark will be coming on before we know it, and it's a long way back to usable water—now that Burroughs' damned cows have fouled the only good source up here."

Gray Eyes was right—night was comin' on when we come t'the little high country trickle flowin' through a grassy meadow. Cows warn't here yet, but they was a-driftin' our way and this meadow and crick was shore t'be cut up and ruined in a few days.

We didn't see it then, though. The next day we pulled out for Blood Canyon and the Rock House.

The two o' us—Gray Eyes and m'self—spent half a day checkin' out the Canyon afore we let Whitetop an' Pink Laigs ride in. After we met and figgered there warn't no rifle barrel poked at us, I rode back t'bring in t'others whilst Gray Eyes set to cookin' supper.

The next day, Whitetop an' Pink Laigs left t'go back t'home. Gray Eyes was still a-broodin' over Pansy Bottom's cows a-ruinin' Ishawooa Mesa an' he warn't what I'd call fit comp'ny for man nor beast. Gray Eyes an' me left for the Ishawooa soon as Pink Laigs and her daddy cleared the Canyon.

They warn't no grass left and hungry cows were bellerin' their fool heads off and pullin' up what roots was left. Gray Eyes set his hoss a long time and looked at the muddy pool what nothin' could drink outen of. Our little stream was nothin' but mud, too. And the grass whar we grazed our ponies was all gone. I reckoned the Pansy Bottom bunch musta drifted a thousand head onto the mesa t'hit the place so hard.

Me'n Gray Eyes kept a-movin' west 'til we dropped into the basin o' the next crick and camped for the night. I took care o' our hosses whilst a broodin' Gray Eyes started cookin'. T'was while we was eatin' that he speaked for the first time in four hours.

"I could poison that waterhole, Sam. It's the only water for at least half the Mesa. I could poison the water and maybe it'd get through to the bastards if buzzards picked the bones of half their damned cows."

I stared at Gray Eyes whilst gnawin' on a chunk o' bannock, then sopped up gravy with what was left. I didn't like what was happenin' t'the mesa neither, but it warn't hittin' me as hard as it was the feller 'cross the fire. "Whyn't you take a gun t'Pansy Bottom an' Snake Eyes an' be done with it?" I said at last. "I don't hold with takin' it out on some poor, dumb cow brute what ne'er had no choice whar they et." I knowed, and he knowed, too, that the cows warn't at fault. I studied Gray Eyes some more, thinkin' that I didn't like what I saw happenin' t'him, what with hate of a sudden icin' over his eyes. So all I said as I got up t'change picket pins was, "I never did know nobody low enough t'pizen a waterhole."

Gray Eyes hain't moved a-tall when I hied back t'camp. He was starin' into the fire like he didn't care iff'n a rifle slug comed in from the dark. Wal, I cared an' I drug m'blanket away from the fire and laid out with one eye open 'til the fire died down an' he got up and moved his soogan a ways outen the dark.

We cautioned back t'Blood Canyon two days later, comin' in down the stream whar me'n Gray Eyes beginned our friendlies. We left Hoss an' Buck in a little meadow and hung our saddles in a tree. Again, we spent most o' one day lookin' for what we both knowed was a-comin'. Then we gave it up and had supper. After we et, I told Gray Eyes that I was feelin' it in m'bones that Pansy Bottom's bush-whacker was a-sneakin' up on us, and that I'd be sleepin' out for awhilst. When all he did was nod, I added, "Tain't no use in both o' us bein' gunned down just to be accom-modatin' t'Pansy Bottom."

He grinned, then poured up some water for the dishes.

The bushwhacker was slow; nigh on t'two weeks later afore he comed. He warn't no good a-tall, though he did come from upriver, 'stead o' from downriver whar I looked for him most. He rode his pony way too close t'the Rock House, an' never tried t'hide his boot tracks 'til he got mite-near into rifle range. Don't reckon he figgered us for makin' much o' a check out a ways. He died thinkin' that way—warn't special-bright that one. Fact is, he was so dumb, he went for his belt gun when I pressed m'knife point agin his neck. Likely, anybody that dumb wouldn'ta had answers t'Gray Eyes' questions, nohow.

But that dumb bushwhacker warn't the last one sent out agin Gray Eyes that fall. I was the last one....

I rode up the Southfork a-lookin' to our pony herd what we hain't seen since the fire. After I looked 'em over, I got t'castin' around t'see whar I was. Near as I could tell, it warn't more'n five miles on up t'the top o' Stinkin'water Pass, and but maybe twenty on down t'the Dubois Post whar I hain't a-been for a coon's age. "What the hell," I said to m'self. "I been on a dry long enough. 'Sides, I got some money jinglin' in m'pocket now."

It was whilst I wet m'whistle at the post for three days when the barman I'd friendlied up with early-on offered me the job o' riddin' the cattle country o' a pesky nester up on the Stinkin'water. He said there'd be some money in it, so's I jumped at the chance t'do m'duty—and for the chance t'get ahold o' the two double eagles he spinned on the bartop for me t'take on the work.

The barman varmint told me there'd be three more double eagles "on completion of the job" and he commenced t'tell about a place up the Southfork called Blood Canyon. We talked for the rest o' that night and the varmint bought most o' m'whiskey. Some time in the middle o' all our fun he reckoned I might have some competition, what with a gent already a week or two ahead o' me. But he said they'd pay the first one who brunged in the nester's scalp.

Wal, I th'owed a fit when I found out about the other feller what was hired t'do m'work and I asked how I was s'posed t'know this other feller iff'n I seed him? The barman varmint said that'd be easy—my competition had red hair. He also said he figgered a ol' mountain man like m'self had savvy enough t'get the job done whar maybe his first choice warn't that bright.

So, I was a-whistlin' when I left the Dubois Post the next mornin', headin' north and west toward the

Stinkin'water. I had reason t'whistle, even though m'head was about near t'blow its top. The bushwhacker's neck I'd split near the Rock House had hair most the color o' the blood seepin' into his shirt collar. And I had me three gold eagles a-rattlin' together in m'possibles sack. T'top it off, the whole damn three-day drunk at Dubois never took but one o' the two eagles I found in the red-haired feller's pockets.

On the way back I drifted our ponies near down t'the edge o' the burn at the Eastfork. What with it bein' into September, me'n Gray Eyes might be wantin' t'put 'em on winter pasture afore long.

—•+•—

"At least we know why the red-haired bushwhacker came down the Southfork," Jethro Spring said when Sam told him about being hired at Dubois to rub out 'a pesky Stinkingwater nester'. "And we also know how far afield Burroughs and Bunting will go to keep any bushwhacker taint from their own ranch."

"Way I figger it," Sam said, "we'uns are safe through the fall and winter, whilst Pansy Bottom an' Snake Eyes give their hired 'whackers' time to work."

Jethro agreed enough so's he used the time to round-trip our horse string to Billings for a load of barbed wire and winter supplies. And when he comed back in early October, he spent the last days afore winter snows cuttin' fire-killed juniper trees for corner posts for the Blood Canyon place, then diggin' postholes and settin' them afore freeze-up. With snow still holdin' off and warm chinook winds blowin' out of the Yellowstone, me and him cut several cord of fire-killed jackpine and fir for our winter's wood supply.

With August Mathers serving as go-between, Jethro worked out a deal to winter their stock at Corbin's place on the lower Stinkingwater. And during the first real snow of the winter, Sam took out their horse string, returning on a single draft animal.

That first snow was a big one, followed by several days of bitter cold. But Sam and Jethro relaxed in comfort before their tiny Rock House fireplace and the cast iron cookstove brought in from Billings.

The deep snow and bitter cold was tough on the draft animal, however, and Jethro took him out in early December. He returned on foot, knocking furtively at Mathers' Place like a thief, after dark. "It's inconvenient," he told the Mathers family, "but there's a gain by Burroughs and Bunting not knowing if I'm alive or dead."

Then he told of the red-haired bushwhacker's accident, and Sam's subsequent employment "to put me under."

Lillian's mother especially enjoyed the story. There was little doubt—though she'd never met the little man—that Sam was her hero. Also of little doubt was the fact that the woman had only contempt for Ellis Burroughs.

"And you'll travel back to Blood Canyon without a horse?" August Mathers asked. "Is that practical?"

Jethro nodded. "The snow starts getting deep around Bledsoe Creek and it's over a horse's knees at the mouth of the Ishawooa. I'll have to snowshoe from Bledsoe's, I'm sure."

"That means you don't anticipate anyone else getting up there this winter?"

"They'd have to be tough."

"Does that mean I won't see you again before spring?" Lillian cried. "There is to be a mid-winter dance again."

"It's better if I remain out of sight and have Burroughs and Bunting wondering, than to show up and remove all doubt."

"Can you not come visiting, Mr. Weatherby?" Lillian's mother asked. "Surely you can come safely to Mathers' Place, just as you have now."

Lillian's father chuckled. "Of course you're right, Mattie. But I don't think you realize what a walk it is down from Blood Canyon to Marquardt."

"But an entire winter!" Lillian pouted.

Jethro thought she'd never been more beautiful. She wore a ruffled dress of flower pattern design and full-length sleeves. Obviously she wore several petticoats, probably for winter warmth. Her slippers poked from beneath her dress hem and the dress was gathered at an extraordinarily slender waist. He wanted to see if his hands would encircle that waist.

"All right," he murmured. "I'll return on the evening of the first day of March. Sam might come, too. We'll arrive after dark and stay out of sight."

"Why not come for Christmas?" Lillian asked.

He grinned. "March first."

<hr/>

Lillian was the most beautiful girl he'd ever known, Jethro reflected as he trudged through deepening snow near Bledsoe Creek. He carried his Winchester in his right hand and still had his snowshoes strapped to his back as he neared the T Bar line cabin.

He passed through Burroughs' wintering horse herd only a little distance out of Marquardt, noting that T Bar cowboys had moved the herd down because of the severe early winter. *It's a good thing Sam and I don't have our ponies mixed up in the T Bar bunch this winter,* he thought. *Some cowboy would've spotted Buck and asked questions.*

Then they would've picked out the rest and put two and two together.

No one had been at the Bledsoe cabin for weeks, but it was stocked with provisions and plenty of dry wood. He found a candle and scratched a match to it. Then he shrugged the snowshoes from his back and stood them outside in the snow. He lit a fire, sliced some bacon from the slab given him by Mattie Mathers, and opened up a can of pork and beans from the cabin's shelves. While mixing flour and water for bannock bread, he thought about other girls he'd known. None were like Lillian. There were a few girls, of course; no healthy man ever aged over thirty without crossing a woman's path now and again—ladies of the night, say, easily found in most dusty cowtowns of size in the West, or in riverfront dives from Fort Benton to New Orleans.

He shook his head. There was that six month deal with the Cherokee witch down in Indian Territory, when he was running for his life. *How long ago? God, how time marches on. Mustn't think of her. What was her name? Whispering Leaf. Mustn't think of her. Too much like Ma. But she wasn't like her. Not at all like Ma. Ma was pure and quiet and there.*

But Whispering Leaf had saved his life when soldiers nearly had him. *Figured I was hers for life, too. Wanted me to kill for her. If I hadn't been so young and naive, it probably wouldn't have taken me six months to figure out I wasn't her slave.*

He thought again of Lillian and smiled. He'd known other nice girls, too. But none matched her in class. None with near the sand and spunk she'd shown. And none, either bad or good, who could match her for looks or build. He thought of the church organist in Fort Worth, and the one whose mother owned a dress shop in St. Paul. He recalled Oregon City and the little blond waitress who didn't have too much wrong with her except that, at twenty-four, he was fiddle-footed and didn't like the rain.

Thoughts of Susan McSween made their way into his mind and a slow, crooked-mouthed grin spread over Jethro's dark face. He thought he'd shoved the woman aside forever, but there she was, the New Mexico temptress, with her coquettish smile and manipulating ways. No doubt about it, Susan McSween had taken him for a ride and he'd loved every minute of it. And when she told him to go to hell, he'd even enjoyed that trip!

Naturally, thoughts of Susan McSween took his mind back to Lincoln County, New Mexico Territory, where most of the girls came from Spanish stock—sloe-eyed and dark-haired and … Oh Ma! Pa! *Why? Why?*

The sonofabitch paid for killing you. I want you to know that. He paid for it! And he died slow.

Damn it, man, the bread's burning! Forget the past. You're living in the present and the bread's burning. What the hell, the bacon was done ten minutes ago and the beans is scorched and the bread burned. So, eat the cold bacon and scorched beans and burned bread. Wash it down with plenty of hot coffee and have more beans for breakfast. And for God's sake, quit feeling sorry for yourself. You're alive and have been for a dozen years or more, while that Major's been in the grave all that time. Most of the world's forgotten about it by now. Go out, hell, and live a normal life. He paid for it. And you've paid for it because he paid for it.

Jethro, spoon poised over the can of pork and beans, shook his head once again. *What the hell is a normal life? Damn it, nobody cares what happened at a dusty army post in Dakota Territory more than a decade ago. You've paid yours, surely. It's over. You can lead a normal life. That is, you can lead a normal life in every way except fall in love with the most wonderful, beautiful, intelligent girl you've ever known.*

You've got a price on your head, you know!

It was snowing hard when Jethro snowshoed from the Bledsoe cabin the following morning. The powdery blanket remained soft and fluffy, with slow traveling all the way to Blood Canyon.

"Did you have a good time in the settlements?" came the voice from the darkness as he shuffled up to the Rock House two days after leaving Bledsoe's.

"Snow's getting deep, ain't it, Sam?"

"It might be a real winter," the little man replied.

It wasn't, though. The chinook came before Christmas, although the warm winds hardly touched above Blood Canyon. Above the canyon, all the chinook did was settle the snow and put a crust on when it turned cold. Down below, the hillsides opened up around Bledsoe Creek and Sam said he could glass horses grazing there when he 'shoed' outside in early February to take a look.

The little man also said it looked like someone had ridden a horse up to the Swenson place, and tried to get above. "But he gived up afore he got halfway 'tween there and Blood Canyon. I'd say it looks like we'uns are as safe as if we was in the Papal Palace, leastwise 'til spring."

Jethro worked most days at cutting and snaking in posts for the fence he planned to build in the spring. Most of the posts were fire-charred, making it hell-for-dirty work. The man might've not stayed clean, but he never took time to get bored.

Sam never helped with the posts, nor later with the fence. "Agin nature," was all he'd say about Jethro's fence plans. But the little man did most of the scouting and cooking, and when they ran low on meat in late January, he snowshoed below Blood Canyon and brought back a young doe.

"You know," Jethro said, "I'm not sure how many years you got on you, you old rascal. But when you came in carrying that Hawken in one hand and holding that doe slung over your shoulders with the other, I figured you for young."

The fenceposts piled up until, in mid-February, Jethro called it enough. Then he set to whittling off the burnt bark with a hatchet because a drawknife was worthless on the fire-killed posts. It was work that went slow.

Along toward the end of February, the two men were sitting inside the Rock House eating one of Sam's good venison stews when Jethro said, "You know, Sam, I'm getting damned tired of your cooking."

The old trapper never looked up, contenting himself with saying, "Wal, there's the stove."

"Yeah, but I think maybe I'm getting tired of eating across the table from anybody as ugly as you, too."

Still Sam never riled. "You ain't no ravin' beauty yourself. What'd you expect, Lily Langtree?"

"That'd be nice," Jethro said. "But no. Better table manners perhaps?" He grinned, seeing he wasn't getting under Sam's skin.

The old man raised his head. "What's your plan, son? How do you figger t'improve on what you got?"

"I thought I'd visit the settlements. Absorb a little culture. Tuck in a napkin. Hold a teaspoon. Maybe exchange pleasantries instead of belches."

The little man nodded, knowing his partner was thinking of Lillian Mathers. "Reckon you could do with a little culture—you only been with me whar you could absorb some for lessen two years."

"You want to go with me?"

"When d'we leave?"

"We're expected for supper March first. That'll be the night after next. We'll have to leave in the morning."

Sam nodded. "Then you better wash the dishes, so's t'get your fingernails clean."

CHAPTER SEVENTEEN

Sam and Jethro set out before daylight, gliding easily on their snowshoes atop the crusted white blanket. They moved to the east side of the Southfork below Blood Canyon, crossing on ice. Then they climbed out of the Southfork bottoms and set a course for Bledsoe's, figuring to arrive there after dark. They made such good time on the crusted snow, however, that the sun was still climbing when they were across the river from the mouth of the Ishawooa. Shortly after, the snow began to soften before the warming sun, but by then they'd started hitting the first of several snow-free slopes and their speed continued.

There were lots of fresh horse tracks around Bledsoe Creek, both in the frozen snow of the bottoms, and in the muddy, thawing hillsides. None of the tracks appeared to be of shod horses, however, and seemed to be wandering like grazing creatures would. Just before coming in sight of the cabin, Sam and Jethro spooked a band of wintering T Bar ponies that were standing droopy-eyed among the cottonwoods. Most of them ran only a short distance, then turned wild-eyed and snorty, play-acting as if they would run again. But a few of the animals the men surprised never ran at all.

It had been a while since anyone had been in the cabin, though the place had been used since Jethro last visited. The sun was about to sink behind the western mountains as the two men unstrapped their snowshoes. "We made good time today, Sam," Jethro said as he shook the ash grate on the little cookstove and laid kindling wood. "We'll have to be careful tomorrow or we'll hit civilization before dark. I expect we won't have to use snowshoes at all for the last leg, the way the weather's holding. What do you think?"

Sam stood in the doorway, drumming the doorsill with his fingernails and looking thoughtful. "Whyn't we go down t'night?" he blurted.

"Because I'm tired," Jethro replied. "We've walked better than twenty miles already today. I don't feel like walking another twenty tonight."

"Warn't talkin' 'bout walkin'," he said, still drumming the doorsill.

Jethro straightened from peering at the fire he'd just kindled. His eyes caught Sam's and held them. "Why not?" he mused.

Jethro had the coffee done and venison steaks fried by the time Sam tied up two T Bar horses to the hitching rack outside. The red-eye gravy was a tad thin, but both men wolfed it and the steaks down, topping them off with cup after cup of steaming black coffee.

After the meal, Jethro cleansed any sign of their presence from the cabin while Sam cached their snowshoes. Then Jethro blew out the candle and closed the cabin door, stepping into the darkness, Sam had already tied a couple of 'Injun' bridles for their new riding horses.

"Reckon this is better'n walkin' any day," Sam said.

Jethro nodded, murmuring, "Sam, you might turn out all right," as he jumped astride a fat bay mare.

"Glad you seen m'worth," the old man replied as he led an equally fat gelding to a cottonwood stump. From there, it was an easy step atop the horse for the tired old scout.

The two gentle cowponies were slow of gait, but their riders took consolation in the fact that riding bareback was much warmer than if they'd had saddles to sit. Sam chose wisely, too, for the two fat old plugs were more comfortable to straddle than if they were skinny, with sharp backbones. Jethro and Sam turned the two T Bar steeds loose a couple of miles from Marquardt, leaving them to make up their minds whether to drift to their home ranch, or mosey back to the wintering horse band.

There was still an hour or two until daylight. The temperature had dropped well below freezing during the clear night. Sam wore an old Hudson's Bay blanket-coat he'd carried rolled up over his shoulder while hoofing it to Bledsoe's. Jethro wore a heavy, red-plaid wool mackinaw. Still, the cold seeped in.

The first coal-oil lamp flared in Mathers' Place at six-thirty a.m. Sam said, "Hit air the purtiest sight I never did see." The men waited a few minutes before knocking.

When Mrs. Mathers opened the door a crack to peer out, Jethro, said, "I know we're a little early for supper, but it is March first." The door swung open as both visitors made for the stove. Only after his teeth stopped chattering did Jethro introduce Sam to Mrs. Mathers.

Soon the Mathers family and their guests sat down to a breakfast of biscuits and ham and eggs. Then Lillian left for her schoolhouse, suggesting that she might close its doors early because of Sam's and Gray Eyes' arrival. August

Mathers led their exhausted guests to one of the Mathers' Place cabins.

Jethro awoke shortly after noon, using water from a kettle bubbling on the top of their heating stove to bathe and shave. Sam's eyes popped open once, then the old man snored again.

Lillian was back from the school when Jethro entered the kitchen. Her hands were covered with flour from the dough she kneaded. A lock of rich auburn hair had fallen across her forehead and a dab of white flour spotted one cheek. She wore a fetching tiny apron over a long plaid skirt and white blouse. With wrists on hips, she reached to peck him on the cheek. Her mother, working nearby, did not seem to notice. August Mathers, also seemingly oblivious, rocked as he read a three-week-old Denver Post. Jethro felt his face flush. Lillian giggled.

August Mathers laid his paper aside. Jethro politely listened to him, but his mind was on the women and his eyes were for Lillian alone. She finished kneading her dough and set it near the stove to rise. Then she and her mother started on what looked like crusts for several pies.

"… and I guess it's fair to say I'm fascinated by the geology of this country," Lillian's father said. "Do you know I once set out to become a mining engineer?"

Jethro shook his head.

"But of course you don't. I actually hold an engineering degree, but became wrapped up in manufacturing."

Jethro nodded. Lillian worked the kneaded pie dough flat with a rolling pin. He admired the way her blouse puffed out at the shoulders while the sleeves were tight and white.

"No regrets, Mr. Weatherby. I've led an interesting and challenging life that has seldom been boring. But the two years we've lived here in Wyoming has re-stimulated my too-long dormant interest in geology …"

Whoops! That's not pies Lillian's working on. Not if

that's a cookie cutter in her hand. Mrs. Mathers must be working on the pies.

Lillian turned and smiled through even white teeth. *It's almost as if she sensed I was staring at her. Isn't she beautiful?*

"Take, for instance," August Mathers continued, "that rock on Ishawooa Mesa—do you remember the one I took the bracheopods from?"

Jethro didn't, but he nodded.

"Should I call you Jacob?" August asked. "I do believe I've heard Lillian call you Rusty."

"Sure, fine. Whatever. I like Gray Eyes, too."

"Do you?" Lillian asked, turning from her cookie dough.

"Makes no difference to me," Jethro said, shrugging.

"It does to me, Gray Eyes," she said, gliding to the bench where he sat, peering down into his bottomless eyes, "because I like Gray Eyes too. It fits."

"For you, I'd answer to anything."

She smiled and wheeled back to her cookies.

It was as if August Mathers had a one track mind. "I'm not sure you appreciate the importance of that fossil-filled, glacial rock. I've been doing some reading and unless I'm mistaken, those bracheopods came from the Mississippian era. If the rock originated from cliffs—and I think it did because of residue from calcitic-formed stalactites still clinging to it demonstrates that a cave existed. If so, there may be rock layering above it that could be higher yet in the stratigraphic column. We may find fish skeletons, or even—God help us—if we get into Cretaceous rocks, much larger skeletons."

Jethro had taken a pencil stub and a notepad from his shirtpocket. 'B-R-A-K-E-O-P-O-D,' he wrote. "What does that mean?"

"I beg your pardon?"

"Oh, never mind." Jethro tucked the notepad and pencil away as his eyes returned to the girl.

Suddenly there came a knocking at the front door. Lillian and her mother froze. August Mathers motioned with his pipe and Jethro ducked into a curtain-shrouded bedroom, obviously Lillian's. A silken robe lay neatly folded on the bed and a flannel nightdress lay alongside. He couldn't take his eyes from them. Then he heard August Mathers say, "Why Sam! My goodness man, come inside. You needn't knock."

"Hain't spent a whole helluva lot o' time in wickiups with two doors, Whitetop," Sam said. "Warn't sure which door t'use." As always, he carried his Hawken.

After Sam had taken a place on the bench beside Jethro, August Mathers said, "Tell me about your winter."

Jethro told of his plans for the fence and how far the idea had progressed. Sam told of his discovery of the single set of horse tracks revealing that someone tried without success to reach Blood Canyon.

Lillian interrupted twice with batches of hot cookies that melted in their mouths.

Jethro also told of the early, heavy snowfalls; how warming weather had burned off a lot of it, particularly below the Ishawooa. "There's still quite a bit of snow at the Rock House, and it's packed almost hard enough for an elk to walk on."

"Most down t'Swenson's old place," Sam added.

"Did you have the dance in February, as you thought?" Jethro asked Lillian.

She beamed. "Yes. And you'll never guess what happened!"

"What?"

"Ellis Burroughs' quarantine collapsed." When Sam and Jethro looked puzzled, she said, "You don't know about the Burroughs quarantine?"

When Jethro shook his head, Lillian told of her first experience with the Founder's Day Dance, and how Dad Marquardt told of Levi Bunting's threat to any man daring enough to escort Lillian Mathers to anything, for any occasion. "Obviously the quarantine was still in effect at Otto Frank's Pitchfork dance after my spat with Ellis."

Jethro's expression was one of bemusement but he said nothing. She continued, "You broke the quarantine when you asked me to dance. And you got away with it."

"Not entirely," he said. "I had a couple of cracked ribs and some teeth kicked loose. I might've backed off if I'd known about the quarantine. But news don't travel well above the Ishawooa."

Lillian laughed gaily. "I don't believe you."

"Well," Sam broke in, "I can tell you he never looked good a-tall when he rode by me. Iff'n he was the winner, I shore'd like t'see what the loser looked like."

Lillian sobered. "I didn't mean about Mr. Weath ... Gray Eyes being hurt. I meant about the quarantine making any difference to him."

"Has anyone heard how the blacksmith came out?" Jethro asked.

"Mr. Schulte was laid up for awhile, as I understand it," August Mathers said. "I also understand he's not as bellicose as previously, having somewhat more respect for his fellow man."

Jethro fumbled for his notepad. "What does 'bellicose' mean?"

The other four people in the room craned their necks to see the notepad as he wrote B-E-L-I-C-O-S-E.

Lillian murmured, "It's spelled with two 'ells'."

"Bellicose means angry and 'pushing', eager to fight," August Mathers explained. Then he asked, "May I see your notepad, Mr. Weatherby?" When Jethro handed it to him, the old man leafed through it, murmuring, "Extraordinary!"

"It's an attempt at improving his vocabulary, isn't it, Father?" Lillian asked.

"Indeed it is," the elder Mathers said, handing the

notepad back. "And it's quite comprehensive, too. May I ask how long you've been engaged in this practice, Mr. Weatherby?"

Jethro shook his head. "Ever since I became curious enough to listen, I guess." Then he added, "I didn't want to hurt him. But he was big. And he was mean."

It was Lillian who grasped it first. "You're back to the blacksmith now, aren't you?"

"May I ask how you developed your fighting dexterity?" August asked. "Marquardt told me you displayed some bareknuckle traits of English pugilistic tradition. But he also said you utilized some other moves he'd never seen before."

Mr. Mathers, Mrs. Mathers, and Lillian all waited expectantly, while Sam sat slumped on his bench, with his back against an interior wall, eyes focusing on a spot over Jethro's head, as if he didn't care. The younger man sensed Sam's mood was one of high-expectancy.

How can I tell how it was to fight like a savage in every river-rat camp along the Mississippi just to stay alive, where only the strong survive. How a day came when another steve-dore offered to teach me how to feint and parry and bob and weave and jab and cross and punch from the shoulder. Before, it'd all been roundhouse swings, but after Joe Barry took me under his wing I became a fighting machine. From St. Louis to San Francisco, St. Paul to St. Petersburg, I'd become 'Kid Barry.'

Can I tell them, after Joe Barry died screaming from a cancerous blight in a Seattle hotel, about the fight in Portland where the invincible Kid Barry went up against a local Chinese fighting hero in a rules-off fight where the winner took all? How can I tell them that a cocky, bare-knuckle fighting sensation smelled easy money and grabbed for a bundle he missed by a mile?

Can I tell them about my aged Chinese opponent and how, at first, I felt sorry for him? Can I tell them of my humiliation? How his movements were like wisping smoke? Can I talk about how his punches were delivered by his fingertips, or by the side of his hand or the heel of his foot? Can I tell them how the fight wore on, hour after hour; how at the end I was driven only by stubborn pride and an ebbing fighting spirit? Can I tell how, after two hours, only pity remained in my inscrutable opponent's eyes?

It was Ling San Ho who took me to his own home. How could I tell them that? How could I tell them about the months spent in Ling San's serene household? And then to have it all end with a race riot on a Colorado railroad right-of-way!

Mrs. Mathers raised the globe on an oil lamp and struck a match. Jethro finally mumbled, "I reckon I just learned to fight here and there, that's all."

They took places around the supper table in a subdued mood. Then Jethro asked Lillian, "You mentioned earlier about the Burroughs quarantine being broken at your latest shindig."

She squealed. "Tom Marquardt asked me to accompany him."

"Great! Which one is he?"

"He's Dad's eldest son. The dance was, of course, held in the Marquardt barn."

"Which brings up a point," Mr. Mathers said. "Ellis Burroughs wanted to have the Founder's Day Dance at the Lazy T Bar, but virtually everyone throughout the Stinkingwater opted for Dad's barn. It was a distinct slap in the face for Burroughs."

"It's good that folks are losing their fear of the T-Bar," Jethro said.

"Exactly!" August said. "And it's how to improve on that trend that we wish to discuss with you tonight."

Jethro had no chance to ask what Mr. Mathers meant as Mattie passed her chicken pot pie. The pie was helped along with side dishes of mashed potatoes and gravy, canned beets, and sauerkraut taken from a big crock in the cellar. There was hot bread and plenty of butter, and scalding coffee—all one could eat and drink.

"So Tom Marquardt took you to the dance," Jethro later mused. "Was there any trouble?"

Lillian's eyes sparkled. "I'm sure Pansy Bottom and Snake Eyes"—she paused to smile at Sam— "didn't like it. But each of the Marquardt brothers danced with me. So did Mr. Corbin from the stage post, and Mr. Kluster from the stable. And one of John Chapman's cowboys. I had a grand time. The only way it could've been better was if you'd been there."

"Resistance to Burroughs' autocratic ways is building, Mr. Weatherby," August Mathers said. "And of a certainty, you've become a symbol of that resistance, though your appearances are altogether too rare. In fact," he went on when Jethro failed to comment, "I'd like to discuss that very thing—resistance to Burroughs—if I'd not be intruding."

Jethro stopped spooning a second helping of pot pie. "Certainly, sir. Please continue."

"As you know, there was little resistance to Burroughs and his ambitious ways for the first three or four years after he came to this country. The litany of his expansion is an unbroken series of successes throughout that period. I could name them all, but you are perhaps more familiar than I. At any rate, the Burroughs Empire expanded markedly, at the expense of many small ranchers and farmers within this area. None successfully resisted him, though some tried. Without going into the legality of his actions, suffice to say the will to fight Burroughs' intentions was lost. Perhaps Judge Kittleson's defeat so disheartened the survivors they dared fight no longer. If a Territorial Judge cannot resist Burroughs' designs, how can a small rancher with a wife, a few children, and fewer cows?

"Then you came along. They've seen how one hard-working, determined man can thwart ... ah ... Pansy

Bottom." There was a smile and a quick glance at Sam. "Frankly, what Lillian says is true. The breaking of Burroughs' quarantine is a manifestation of the strengthening of collective backbones. Do I paint a true picture?"

Jethro thought he saw where this discussion was headed. "Probably," he muttered.

A hush fell over the room, broken only when August Mathers continued. "Mr. Weatherby, there is a deliberate attempt by anti-Burroughs elements in this region to organize. They're undertaking their resistance with eyes wide-open. They know there is a certain amount of risk in what they're doing, yet they're willing to assume that risk with one proviso...."

"And that is?" Jethro asked with a heavy heart.

"They need your participation, sir."

Here it is, Jethro thought. *How many of these unequal fights in someone else's interest must I go through? Good God! It was easy enough to see a fight was coming when I decided to take a homestead here on the Stinkingwater. But, at least, for once in my life, I'd be fighting for ME, instead of for someone else. I'm tired. I don't want to fight someone else's battles. Leave me alone! Let me fight my own battle, in my own way, for my own interest!*

"I'm not much of a joiner," Jethro said, glancing at Lillian. He was surprised at her widening eyes. Her father's shoulders slumped.

Mrs. Mathers reached for the coffee pot as August Mathers reasoned, "Without you, they may not succeed. Without them, you may not succeed."

The silence became heavier. Mr. Mathers started to say more, then smiled in embarrassment and shrugged, returning to his half-finished plate.

"We have hot apple pie, Mr. Buttercut," Lillian's mother said.

"Ain't had none o' that, ma'am, for thutty, forty years. Might as well try a dab an' see iff'n it's still fittin'."

"Perhaps I don't understand, Mr. Weatherby," Lillian murmured.

"Gray Eyes."

Her smile was brief. "You are traveling at night, not wanting anyone to see you here, are you not? You want Snake Eyes Bunting to wonder whether you are alive or dead, do you not? In fact, you'd like him to think you dead so he and Ellis Burroughs won't attempt your demise in another manner. Is that not correct?"

Jethro nodded. "I just want to be left alone."

"Yet you are so confident of success, you can dismiss the coordinated assistance of others with similar dreams?"

There was no change in his expression.

"Pie air good," said Sam. "Fact is, the whole damn meal was larrupin'!"

"Mr. Weatherby ..."

"Gray Eyes."

"Gray Eyes," Lillian continued, "you and Sam might be terribly competent. Oh, I know you are. You may in fact be the most competent two men in the world. You certainly are the most competent I've ever known. But you are two! Did you hear me? I said 'two'! There are sixteen men at the Lazy T Bar right now, counting Burroughs and Bunting—and that is the winter crew. For the summer, the number will be nearer thirty. That's thirty men in three months. Is it that those numbers mean nothing to you?"

He continued to stare at Lillian, but he said, "I'll try a piece of that pie, Mrs. Mathers. One thing I learned a long time ago is if Sam compliments the cook, the food is outstanding."

But he was thinking: *It was Lincoln County, New Mexico Territory, back in '77, when I took a job with the young rancher, John Tunstall. Tunstall was an Englishman who hooked up with the lawyer, Alexander McSween, in a Lincoln trading company to challenge the crooked, cheating 'Santa Fe Ring.' Tunstall, of course, turned out to be too innocent to play against the 'Ring's' money, military, and political power. And McSween proved too impetuous. But both turned to me to lead their followers, while reserving strategic decisions to themselves.*

And how about Colorado? A tear actually trickled down his face when he thought of the little Swede, Gunnar Einarssen, whose stubbornness led to his death, despite Jethro's best efforts to keep him alive against the merciless machinations of the corporate giant, Amalgamated Minerals & Mining.

Tunstall and McSween and Billy the Kid and Gunnar are all dead. For what? Now these people want me to pull their chestnuts from the fire for them when all I want is to be left alone.

"Sam was right, Mrs. Mathers," Jethro said as he finished the pie. "Everything was delicious. I can't remember how long it's been since I've had a meal near its equal."

"I can," Sam said. "Never."

Jethro fixed August and Lillian with a direct gaze. "Look, I came here to the Stinkingwater to live my life in the way I'd like to live it: peacefully. I see no reason to be afraid of Bunting and Burroughs. I don't need help. Why do I need to get involved?"

"Why don't you ride down here in the daylight?" asked Lillian.

"Yes, we'd be glad to have you and Mr. Buttercut visit anytime, day or night," Mrs. Mathers added.

"You're a damn fool," Sam said, staring at Jethro.

Another awkward silence fell. Finally August Mathers said, "Discounting the advantages to you individually, the fact remains these other people have dared resist Ellis Burroughs largely because of the example you've set. While you may be, as you say, invulnerable to Burroughs— and I have serious reservations about that—these other people have no such sense of invulnerability. You are a symbol to them, Mr. Weatherby, and whether you believe it or not, or choose to accept it or not, they have honored you by praying you'll participate. I'm certain, if they'd had the remotest idea you'd not feel honored enough to participate, they'd never dared to make their first move.

"By their first move," Jethro asked, "do you mean inviting Lillian to a dance? Isn't that rather melodramatic? Can you really believe Burroughs or Bunting will take action against Tom Marquardt simply because he escorted Lillian to a dance held in the Marquardt barn itself?"

"I can indeed, Mr. Weatherby. I think it was a remarkable act of courage on young Tom's part. Even if I am being overly dramatic, you should remember to think like young Marquardt; he at least believes he exercised courage. And isn't that the real test? Perhaps you forget that I know the Burroughs people well. Don't you realize he'll see the breaking of the Burroughs quarantine as an act of defiance? Its importance is as a symbol. Whatever else they are, Ellis Burroughs and Levi Bunting are not fools. They realize that to be contested over small things will inevitably lead to being contested over big things."

"Are you telling me Tom Marquardt's life is at stake just because he invited Lillian to a dance?"

August Mathers shook his head. "I don't know. Bunting is an unknown quantity and Wyoming is a wild new land. But it's not just Tom Marquardt, you know. Others participated in defying the quarantine. Joe and Billy—Tom's brothers—danced with her, too, as did Corbin and Kluster. Believe me, Mr. Weatherby, it was a calculated act of defiance on each individual's part. And that defiance did not escape Burroughs' attention."

Jethro stroked his chin. "Didn't you say a couple of Two Dot cowboys danced with Lillian?"

"One did," Mathers replied. "I think we can assume from that cowboy's actions that John Chapman is at least sympathetic."

Lillian spoke so softly Jethro had to strain to hear.

"They need your help, Gray Eyes. They need your quiet confidence and your native intelligence. They've not known before how to resist until you demonstrated how to do it within the law."

Jethro surrendered. "What would you have me do?"

"Talk to Dad Marquardt," August said immediately. "He knows we've been in contact, and he asked for an opportunity to see you."

Lillian leaned over to cover Jethro's hand with one of her own, while Sam stared off into space and scratched his ribs. "Okay, I can talk to the man if you'd like. But I think it's fair to warn you I'm not likely to change my mind."

Jethro was forking the last of a second helping of Mattie Mathers' delicious pie when he thought to ask if it would be difficult to see Dad Marquardt while he and Sam were down for this visit.

"I don't think so," August Mathers replied, exchanging glances with Lillian. "We're expecting him around seven this evening."

CHAPTER EIGHTEEN

"**D**on't I know you?" Dad Marquardt said, looking at Sam. "Ain't I seen you before?"

"Reckon your memory's a-slippin' with age, you ol' coot," Sam said. "I 'member you a-right. You allus did get least two-thirds o' whatever whiskey was around t'drink."

"Why, pon my soul. It's Sam Buttercut, ain't it? Whatever in hell are you doin' back to the Stinkingwater?"

After Sam and Marquardt had finished their backslapping, Jethro was introduced.

Dad Marquardt proved a genial old man with a flowing white beard and a fringe of hair rimming a bald spot. His blue eyes sparkled and held steady. "It's a good night for a walk," he said as he shrugged from a mackinaw coat identical to Jethro's. "Looks like the weather is holding, August. Maybe it'll be an early spring after all."

The newcomer inquired politely about winter in Blood Canyon, asking about the snow depth there. Then he mentioned their mid-February Founder's Day Dance. "We missed you boy. Wasn't near as much excitement at this one as at Pitchfork last summer."

Jethro's smile was thin. "It's time I thanked you for the long dance there, Mr. Marquardt. But I think it's fair to tell that my feet were wore off to my knees by the time it finished."

Marquardt's laugh rattled the house. "You didn't look to me like you was too stove up come leavin' time. That was entertainment we don't get when you're not around."

There was other small talk. Then Marquardt turned to the reason he wished to talk with Jethro. "I reckon August has told you of the Burroughs resistance plan he come up with?"

Jethro glanced at Lillian's father, who seemed preoccupied with stuffing his pipe.

"He's right, I know," Marquardt continued. "But when a feller gets as old as me, he just wants to fight shy of trouble the rest of his life. I reckon Bunting woulda run us clear out of the country, me'n the boys, if you and the Mathers family hadn't come along. I just wished we'da got together when Burroughs first bought out Morgan. You remember, Sam? Hell, it was clear right after that what the bastard was goin' to do. If we'da fought 'em then, it woulda been all over early. But hell no! Each and every one figgered he wouldn't come after us."

The old man paused, then shook his head and went on, "But the hell with what was; we're here to talk about what is. We need to figger out a plan for throwin' a rope around their cavvy, don't we?"

Jethro took a deep breath. "Mr. Marquardt, I didn't say I was 'in'. Aren't you jumping the gun by asking me for an action plan?"

Marquardt glanced at August Mathers, then asked, "But you will be, won't you, boy?"

Jethro shrugged. "What is it you're trying to do? Who are you? When you talk about resisting Burroughs, how far are you willing to go? Are you planning to drive him from the country? Kill him? Win your land back? Does Chapman and Frank know about this? How about Ashland? Corbin? Wyler? Potter? Demis? Have you talked to a lawyer? Are you intending to stay within the law? Or are you prepared to move outside the law if Burroughs does?"

Marquardt's eyes dropped to his feet. "I don't know as we got all the answers yet."

"Well, Mr. Marquardt, they're all questions I'll need answered before you can count on me. And if one of them—just one—isn't answered right, you needn't ask again."

Dad Marquardt's blue eyes turned hard. "I guess I figgered everybody with somethin' to gain by buckin' Burroughs would want in. Did they tell you what my son Tom did by takin' Miss Lillian to the dance? Did they tell you that the three boys drawed straws to see which one would stick his neck on the line? Did they tell you that near a half-dozen folks talked about how we'd buck Burroughs and decided to begin it at the dance? Do you know how much guts it took, knowin' that most everybody who bucked Burroughs before is a-layin' in a cold grave right now? Have you got any idea that you're the only man whatever bucked Burroughs and Bunting on the whole Stinkingwater and lived to tell about it? Then you tell me you don't know yet whether you're in. My boy's life is on the line and …"

"Shhh!" Lillian's urgent whisper interrupted. They all heard the horses trotting up to the Mathers' Place hitchrail.

August Mathers pointed to Lillian's bedroom. Just as he did, Sam stuck his head from behind the curtain and muttered, "Pansy Bottom! Him and that gunslinger he had when Pink Laigs and him was up in Blood Canyon."

Dad Marquardt and Jethro joined Sam in the bedroom. Sam and Jethro took places on either side of the

window, Sam with his Hawken. They saw Ellis Burroughs and Cletus Wills leave the hitchrail and stride toward the house. Jethro reached to Sam's belt and pulled the little man's Green River knife, cursing to himself that he'd not brought his Colt, and that he'd left his Winchester in his room. Dad Marquardt appeared unarmed and Jethro doubted if there was a gun in the entire Mathers household. *Thank God for Sam and his Hawken.*

Loud knocking came from the front door. Jethro tiptoed to the curtain where a slit of light ran across Lillian's bedroom and onto a mirror near Sam. Marquardt never moved. But Jethro noted there was no fear on the old fiddler's face.

They heard August Mathers open the front door. "Good evening Ellis. What brings you out on such a night?"

"I have a matter of importance I'd like to discuss with you, sir, if you're not too busy."

"I can't imagine what we'd have to discuss, Ellis. Can't it wait?"

"I'm afraid not, sir."

"Well then, I hope it will be brief. Won't you come in—alone?"

Mrs. Mathers snorted from the main room's far side. "If you are inviting that man in here, I won't stay."

"Oh Mother!" Lillian cried as her mother slammed the back door.

Burroughs said to the man behind him, "Please stay with the horses, Wills." As he entered, he smiled. "Now I know where Lillian gets her feisty spirit."

As Lillian's father closed the door, he asked, "What is it we can do for you?"

"Um, may I take off my coat?"

Lillian snapped, "Whatever you came to discuss can't possibly take that long."

"Please forgive us," her father said. "Would you take

off your coat, Ellis? And make yourself comfortable."

Jethro leaned over to peer through the curtain slit as Burroughs unbuttoned his long velvet coat and slid a silk scarf from his neck. As he shrugged from the coat, Jethro checked the newcomer's belt buckle. There was an indent in his shirt that indicated the derringer was behind the buckle. Burroughs carelessly draped the coat, his hat, and the scarf over a bench and proceeded to the room's best chair—August Mathers' rocker. "The matter I wish to discuss with you concerns Lillian's and your attitude."

Lillian and August, still standing, glanced at each other.

Ellis smiled. "May I say, Lillian, that you appear quite fetching in your attire?"

"You can say anything you wish, Mr. Burroughs. However, it remains a question whether I'll accept anything you say at face value."

He laughed. "You will, my dear."

August Mathers studied his pipe as he said, "Perhaps I do not understand your allusion to our 'attitude'. Would you be kind enough to explain?"

"Of course," said the blonde-haired man. "I can enumerate many examples of how you've disappointed me. Do you wish to hear them all?"

"Perhaps it would be best."

Burroughs raised an index finger and ticked it with the forefinger of his other hand, counting. "Number one, you left the Lazy T Bar rather precipitously two years ago."

"You threw us out!" Lillian exploded. "You told us we were no longer welcome at your ranch because we opposed your attempt to force Mr. Weatherby from his rightful land."

Burroughs smiled. He raised a second finger. "I must say I was somewhat disappointed when my cook told me you'd insisted on traveling only as far as the Marquardt hamlet, instead of quitting the Stinkingwater, as I'd suggested."

Lillian glanced at her father who said nothing while crossing his arms and staring down at Burroughs. She jerked back to the newcomer and said, "It's a free country as yet, Mr. Burroughs."

Again a smile flitted across his face and he raised a third finger. "Three, the regrettable altercation in Morton's saloon. Obviously I didn't relish that occurrence, but I chose to exercise considerable forbearance despite the provocation."

Lillian lapsed into a silence to match her father's.

"Four," Ellis Burroughs counted. "Lillian's behavior at the Pitchfork. Let's call them four, five, six, and seven—there were several, actually: her explosion over a discussion between my foreman and myself, her taking up with that Blood Canyon outlaw, her stealing my weapon, and her threatening gestures toward my foreman. Each action was an embarrassment to me and I'm afraid I do not remember them fondly."

"My, my," Lillian said softly, "isn't that just too bad?"

"Hear me out, my dear. Number eight, the two of you riding into Blood Canyon to save your outlaw friend after he'd threatened my crew."

"Yes, Mr. Weatherby certainly posed a danger to your posse," said August Mathers, "standing alone, and in the doorway of his own home."

"Number nine," Burroughs resumed. "I hear rumors that the entire Mathers family has taken up with this outlaw. That is not, Mr. Mathers, a rumor I like, even if it is academic."

"Get out, you pig!" Lillian Mathers demanded. "Get out!"

"Oh, but I'm not finished. I have still another."

"Please continue, Mr. Burroughs," Lillian's father said. "Finish what you have to say, then do as Lillian says and leave."

"Ten, I do not appreciate the intended embarrassment

at last month's dance. It didn't work, but I failed to appreciate it, nevertheless."

Lillian's eyes blazed, but August Mathers softly said, "I'm sure you never came here merely to recount your supposed humiliations, Ellis. Just what is it you want?"

"It's not so much what I want, Mr. Mathers," replied the blonde man, his voice edged with steel, "as what I'll get. Until the dance, I suppose I thought common sense would eventually prevail and that you people would see the error of your ways. Really, I thought of you, Mr. Mathers, as being misled by a willful, headstrong girl and that you'd soon correct her character deficiencies. However, the dance was the last straw. That was when it became obvious to me that you and your misguided wife are openly supportive of Lillian's willfulness and might, in fact, encourage it."

"And if I do?" August Mathers murmured.

"And do you support a coalition trying to tear apart the Lazy T Bar?" the younger man snarled. "That was apparent at the dance also."

"Is that all, Mr. Burroughs?" Mathers asked. "No, wait—what about this so-called outlaw in Blood Canyon? I've heard he took out a Pre-emption Claim on his land. What do you propose to do about the man now that he owns the land outright?"

Burroughs leaned forward. "I believe we can discount that man, Mr. Mathers. I've received information that he is no longer with us."

"Ha!" Lillian exclaimed.

Her father shot her a sharp look. "Do you mean he's dead?"

"Suffice to say he's no longer with us."

"But how could you know?" August Mathers persisted.

"One of my men visited up there in January."

"Might he merely have been away from his cabin for a short period?"

"Mr. Mathers, I said the man is no longer of any consequence."

Jethro glanced across Lillian's bedroom at Sam. The little man's snaggle-toothed grin split his face.

August Mathers nodded slowly to himself. "Ellis," he said, "you mentioned something—I believe 'a coalition against you,' was it? Could you tell me more about it? Do you mean ..."

"I didn't come here to discuss me, Mathers," Burroughs snapped.

"... the simple fact that my daughter chose to dance with another?"

Burroughs leaned back in the rocking chair, drumming his fingers on the arm. "You were a valued employee of my father. Once a destitute competitor, you were rescued through my father's benevolence. Though my father owed you nothing, he valued our family's friendship enough to offer you an excellent position as a vice-president in the Burroughs' enterprising—and solvent—Empire. I might add that while your service to my father was not distinguished by any particular brilliance, at least you exercised a certain degree of loyalty. Because of that loyalty, and because of that loyalty alone, my father granted you a generous pension."

Lillian murmured, "Are you about to say what I think you are?"

Ellis Burroughs ignored her. "Let's not delude ourselves, Mr. Mathers. We both know your existence here in northwestern Wyoming is directly dependent upon my father's benevolence. Certainly you cannot exist on the seedy rewards of this hovel," he suggested as he looked around him with a deliberate sneer.

"Spit it out, you swine!" Lillian ground out.

"In good time, my dear." Burroughs' chair squeaked as he rocked back. "After the dance I asked myself if the loyalty pension of August Mathers was deserved if, in fact,

August Mathers' loyalty was no longer so clear." Burroughs voice softened to a whisper. "So I sent a telegram. I trust you'll appreciate the fact that the telegram had to be sent from Billings and returned to the same hamlet. The transfer to and from there had to be made via stagecoach. That accounts for the lapse of time between the dance and now."

Jethro again peered through the curtain. He was in time to see Burroughs pull a folded sheet of flimsy paper from his shirtpocket. "Would you care to read what the reply telegram from my father's corporate treasurer says?"

August Mathers spoke as quietly as Burroughs. "Why don't you read it so we can all hear, Pansy Bottom?"

"I beg your pardon! Do you mean me?" he asked, scarcely waiting for a reply. "Lillian can read over your shoulder, no doubt. I'd much prefer you read it." He extended the yellow flimsy, but Mathers refused to take it. Burroughs sighed. "Very well, it reads:

> TO: ELLIS BURROUGHS - PRESIDENT
>   BURROUGHS STOCK & CATTLE COMPANY
>   MARQUARDT, WYOMING TERRITORY
>   FEBRUARY 20, 1884
>
> FROM: MASON T GOUGH
>   CORPORATE TREASURER
>   BURROUGHS ENTERPRISES
>   14 FIFTH AVENUE
>   NEW YORK, NEW YORK
>
> REGARDS YOUR ENQUIRY AUGUST MATHERS PENSION STOP   PENSION SUBJECT TO DISCRETION OF CORPORATE OFFICE STOP CORPORATE OFFICE APPROVES TRANSFER AUTHORITY TO ELLIS BURROUGHS STOP   PLEASE ADVISE STOP END OF MESSAGE.

Silence reigned in the room. Lillian softly said, "You've sunk to a new low tonight, weasel. You may leave now."

Jethro's hand clutched Sam's Green River knife. He knew he could reach Burroughs before the man could pull his hideout derringer, and Sam could handle Wills with his Hawken. Then Sam glided to the dresser and with a finger dipped into a jar of Lillian's lip clay, scribbled 'NO!' in the gleam of light shining on the mirror.

"Are you quite through, Ellis?" August Mathers murmured.

"Almost. I think it fair to tell you I sent a two-word reply. It simply said, 'STOP PENSION'. Now I'd like to get to the heart of this discussion, sir. I will, in the future, expect more favorable accountability on your part—and on yours, too, Lillian. As soon as I see a tangible example of that, I will authorize the resumption of your pension. If that favorable accountability is exemplary, who knows, I might even authorize an increase."

August Mathers sighed. "Thank you for your warning, Mr. Burroughs. I'm sure we'll discuss it. Now if you'll excuse us...."

"Certainly, sir," Burroughs said, rising. "I surely didn't mean to inconvenience you in any way." Burroughs strode to his coat. "I hope you'll note I never demanded you leave the Territory. You see, I still hope to win Lillian's hand in marriage."

———————

The two horses trotted toward Morton's saloon. Then the Mathers' Place back door opened and banged shut.

"It smells in here," Mattie Mathers said loudly enough, it seemed, for the entire community of Marquardt to hear. "Are you both going to just stand there? We have guests in the house." She began stoking the fire.

Lillian's bed creaked as Dad Marquardt pushed to his

feet. Jethro held the curtain aside and as Sam passed through the bedroom doorway, the gray-eyed man reversed the Green River knife and passed it, handle first, to him.

August Mathers stood as before, head down, facing the rocking chair. Anger made Lillian's face distorted and hard. Her eyes challenged Jethro as he trailed Marquardt and Sam into the room.

Sam broke the uneasy silence by asking, "D'you have any o' that apple pie left, ma'am? I plumb forgot iff'n it was any good a-tall."

August Mathers turned to his guests and said, "Let's all sit up to the table and have coffee and pie." After everyone had taken a seat, Mr. Mathers asked, "All right, now where were we?"

Dad Marquardt cleared his throat. "August I have to know; are you still in?"

Lillian's father laid down his fork and placed both hands on the table. "Yes, I believe so. I've made decisions in the past for the benefit of my family. It's possible some of those decisions were ill-advised. In essence, I may have compromised ideals for security. I hope not. But perhaps. At least the dividing line between ideals and security has never been as sharply drawn as in this case. "Also"—Mathers choked off a laugh— "it has never before been put as crudely as tonight. Ellis Burroughs has much to learn if he ever hopes to match his father's subtlety."

Lillian pushed back her chair and hugged her father. "We have my teaching salary. We'll do fine. I know we will."

August Mathers placed a hand over his daughter's fingers.

"Then the next thing to do," Jethro said, "would be to figure out who can be counted on over the long haul."

Sam and Lillian smiled. Dad Marquardt cocked his head. "Are you in now?" he asked.

"If what we just saw and heard was not some sort of a

stage performance, then I'm in."

Everyone else waited for Jethro to lay out their course. He knew it was going to happen. Just like in New Mexico. Just like with the Chinese on the railroad line. Just like with Gunnar and his mine on Fall Creek. *The mantle has fallen to me. I knew it would. All I ever wanted by coming to the Stinkingwater was to walk away from the bullshit while I had life and health and a little gold from a generous little Swede who died because he wouldn't give and wouldn't run. That's what I wanted to do—walk away and become one of the inoffensive, nameless thousands who live a peaceful life in a far-off place. Surely Jacob Weatherby, as a name, is less threatening than Kid Barry or Jack Winter or Jason Frost, or any other fighting name I might've once been known by.*

But no, that's not to happen. I knew the consequences of saying, 'I'm in'. I knew the mantle of leadership would pass to me. And I know, as a result, that my days on the Stinkingwater are numbered. If it's kill or be killed, I lose if I win. When it's all over—if I'm still alive—I'll be running again. If not from a Wyoming grand jury, then from a murky vengeance wreaked in a long-ago Dakota army post. When I said 'I'm in' I lost the future I'd hoped for here in this country. And Lillian—the most exciting, most beautiful, most intelligent woman I've ever known—you'll never know that when you forced me into this Stinkingwater War, you drove a wedge that will keep us apart forever.

The best I can hope for is to shield you and your father and mother from what is to come. Possibly the best course would be to just go ahead and kill Burroughs and Bunting. Probably an even better course would be to get my Winchester and walk down to Morgan's and kill Burroughs and Wills now, then get Bunting later and clear out. That was the New Mexico way; the way both sides figured it in Lincoln County. That might not be the Stinkingwater way, but probably I don't have a choice. Whichever way this Stinkingwater War develops, it'll be chosen by someone else and it'll be up to me to respond.

Jethro sighed. "All right, we know we can count on the Mathers family and on you and your three sons, Mr. Marquardt."

"And on Sam Buttercut," Sam said as he slammed the table with a fist.

"And we can count on Sam Buttercut and me. That makes at least a half-dozen fighting men if we need 'em. What about Corbin?"

"Ain't no love lost between Corbin and Burroughs," Marquardt said. "And I think you can count on him in a pinch."

"Ashland?"

"Hates Burroughs. Dunno, though, whether he'll count when the chips are down."

"You said Kluster defied the quarantine?"

August Mathers cleared his throat. "Yes, but only because he thinks well of Lillian and Mattie and me. He does very little business with the Burroughs outfit, but he hasn't all that much to gain with us, either. I'm not sure he would become involved if this thing turned violent."

"The store owners?"

"Too dependent on the Burroughs outfit," Marquardt said.

"How about some of the other small ranchers?"

August Mathers shook his head. "We've not approached everyone up to this point; only those who have actually suffered from the Lazy T Bar."

"Well," Jethro mused, "we're talking about some sort of 'association'. You know the kind; where everybody pays a dollar and belongs to a group. We'll make it as easy as possible for them to belong." He focused on Marquardt. "Dad, you're the most respected man in the entire Stinkingwater country. Could you sound them out and get their responses to an organized resistance to the Lazy T Bar?"

"I reckon so," Marquardt replied. "But it'll take a little time. And if I ask 'em to get in, they'll want to know

into what, and how deep we plan to go a-fightin'
Burroughs."

Here it was! The all important question. *Resist force
with force? How do you fight someone who's fighting you
unless you're willing to deliver a telling blow? I know that,
but these people may not. Yet I know it doesn't always work
and they may never find that out. I know fighting and retaliation can become a scourge that consumes all parties. That's
what happened in New Mexico. Yet it's a necessary tool in the
arsenal. How to use it carefully without becoming consumed
by it? How can I explain that to these people? They'll want
vengeance, and that's the attitude that will spell my doom.*

"Whatever steps we take," August Mathers murmured,
"should always be strictly within the law. I think you
should tell them that, Dad. We might have to, at some
point, respond to force with force. But I think that
response should always be irreproachable, as far as its legality is concerned."

Jethro closed his eyes for a moment, nodding to himself. *Thank God for August Mathers. At least our methods
are beginning well enough. Down in New Mexico, legality
was never considered. Don't kid yourself, though. No matter
how legal it starts, it won't end that way. And you'll be the
one who pays.*

"You demonstrated that, Mr. Weatherby, in your two
years in Blood Canyon," August continued. "Even if the
Burroughs Empire was to employ unscrupulous legal strat-
egy against you—and that is a favorite tactic of theirs, it
could not succeed because your own methods have been so
exemplary. We would do well to emulate them, no matter
what the provocation."

"Okay," Jethro said, "what about the big ranchers—
Chapman, Frank, and Lovell?"

"I question whether they'll cooperate with an association against one of their own," Mathers replied, "no matter how much they might detest him personally.

Supporting small ranchers, they might think, could lead to an organized move against their own holdings."

"I can see that possibility," Jethro said. "But perhaps it would be in our interests to try to insure they remain neutral."

"How?"

"Someone should discuss our plans with them and explain that they need not feel threatened; that we plan only to resist Burroughs. And August, I believe you are the one for that job. Since you are neither a rancher, nor disposed to become one, you might offer proof of the broad base of our group."

"Then I shall do it."

"Now, what we need is a visible organization with a real charter and bylaws. We need a definite purpose and operational rules to follow. We need to enlist as many people as we can into the organization. It requires a clearly defined name with broad appeal—like, umm, Stinkingwater Protective Association, or something like that. We need ..."

"Shhh!" hissed Lillian. Then they all heard running footsteps. Dad, Sam, and Jethro started for Lillian's bedroom as the pounding began on the front door. "Pa! Pa!"

Marquardt jerked open the door. His son Billy stood there gasping for breath. "What is it, boy! What's wrong?"

"The ... barn's on ... fire! We cain't ... find Tom!"

CHAPTER NINETEEN

The elder Marquardt shoved through the door with Sam and Jethro at his heels. A red glow lit the sky to the south. Marquardt took off at a shambling run. Jethro looked at Sam and nodded as the little man thumped his chest and gestured with an outflung right hand, then disappeared into the night. Jethro dashed for his Winchester, then followed.

There was no chance of fighting the fire by the time help arrived. Even as Jethro ran toward the glow, a shower of sparks rose into the air and he knew the roof had collapsed. When he arrived and took in the scene with a glance, he turned away, scouting into the night—to the left.

A night scout is tough, but not impossible. Jethro knew it was better to look for tracks made that same night, for tracks are difficult to hide when they can't be seen by the individual making them, but crushed grass has a way of righting itself over time. He reached Sam an hour before daylight and had found nothing. They came together in a small coulee that lay a short distance from the barn and Sam said, "They's tracks here. Looks like they'uns held their hosses here and went on foot t'the barn."

"How many?"

"I reckon three, maybe four hosses. One man might o' held the hosses whilst the others stalked the barn. I make out two others."

"Is that coal oil I smell?"

"That's the way I make it. One can musta sprung a leak whilst on the packsaddle. But they had more'n one can. I see marks whar they set two o' 'em down t'once."

Jethro sighed. "How big were the cans?"

"I guess leastways fives."

They approached the Marquardt house a few minutes later, coming to it on the side opposite to the burned-out barn. They could see the figures of two men standing near the barn's glowing coals and one walking between the coals and the house.

"Hold it right there, or you'll have a bunch of holes in you!"

Jethro and Sam halted. "Friend," Jethro said.

"Who?"

"Sam Buttercut," Sam said.

"I don't know no Sam Buttercut."

"Friend o' your pa."

"Still don't know no Sam Buttercut."

"Damn it, boy, are you Joe or Billy?"

"We're talkin' about who you is, not me."

"My name's Weatherby," Jethro cut in. "We're both from Blood Canyon."

"Come on in."

Lillian and her father were in Marquardt's home. Mrs. Mathers sat along a far wall comforting Mrs. Marquardt. "They think they've discovered Tom's body in the embers," Lillian said. "But it's still too hot for them to be certain."

Dad Marquardt's eyes were steely blue. "Did you find anything?"

Jethro nodded. "Sam did. They left their tracks in a little coulee behind your barn."

Dad turned to Sam. "Tell me more."

"They'uns used coal oil. There was leastways three of 'em and they had leastways four hosses. One I reckon was to haul the coal oil."

"They'll pay," Marquardt muttered. "They'll pay."

"Oh Gray Eyes," Lillian said, leaning in to him, "it can't be true. Tell me it's not true."

He said nothing.

Sam tried unraveling the tracks after daylight. But it was as expected—they disappeared into a maze of other tracks as soon as they hit the main road.

After Tom's body was recovered from the ashes, it was with some difficulty that August and Jethro kept Marquardt and his two sons from riding to the T Bar. "It's a terrible thing, Dad," August Mathers said. "But you must give the law a chance to respond. We've sent a message to the Sheriff in Lander. He or a Deputy will come to investigate. We don't know with certainty who killed Tom. His death might even have been accidental. Besides, while we suspect Burroughs and Bunting of the arson, being able to prove it is something else."

Jethro took a different tack. "If you and Joe and Billy ride to the Lazy T Bar now, it'll be suicide. Dammit, man, that's what they'll expect you to do. Then, instead of losing Tom, your wife will be a lonely widow with three dead sons."

"If the High Sheriff comes, what'll he find that we don't already know?" Marquardt said.

"Probably nothing," Jethro conceded. "But at least he'll find you still alive instead of laying under a white sheet at the Lazy T Bar with a gun in your hand and murder under the pennies on your eyes."

August Mathers was more far-seeing than others the morning after the fire. As the sun rose and he and Jethro each had an arm on the white-bearded man's shoulders, he said, "Dad, this last act of Burroughs' will outrage the countryside. I'm sure those men—Bunting and Burroughs—have no idea what it's like to be held in such high regard as you. How could they? They're nothing but vermin!" The scholarly white-thatched gentleman, eyes flashing, spat the last word.

"They mustn't get away with this, and they won't!" Mathers continued. "But they won't not because you and your sons ride up to their ranch and try to kill them all. Mr. Weatherby is right about that, of course, and you know you'd never succeed. If Burroughs and the Lazy T Bar fail, it will be because of the force of public opinion and public reaction. This terrible act of theirs will so outrage the good people of this country that they will rally to your side. Please wait. Give the people of the area a chance to respond. I'm certain you'll be surprised, perhaps overwhelmed, to find the degree of esteem in which you and your family are held by everyone in northwestern Wyoming. For God's sake, man, wait long enough, at the least, to give your friends and neighbors a chance to join you."

Old Marquardt was silent, standing with his head bowed. When he finally broke into a wrenching sob, Jethro turned to one of the man's sons and said, "Turn your saddlehorses loose, Joe, and find a couple of shovels. Sam and I will dig the grave if you folks will tell us where you think Tom should be laid to rest."

Even as Sam and Jethro worked on the grave, August Mathers' prediction was proving true—the first of a host of Marquardt friends and neighbors began arriving....

The Burroughs Empire made a mistake by attacking the two points they did. No man in northwestern Wyoming was as well liked as Dad Marquardt. The rotund, friendly man was easily the best fiddler within a hundred miles in any direction, always in demand for any social occasion that arose within the district. And never, as far as memory served, had he turned down a request to play. Though Dad's three sons were not considered cut from the same cloth as their father, they, too, were happy-go-lucky and well liked. And Molly Marquardt was a quiet, smiling, portly woman whose life was centered around her family; a good, decent soul who never, ever, had a bad word to say about either friend or foe.

To top it all off, at least half the sturdy log buildings in the Stinkingwater and upper Greybull country had been built by Dad Marquardt and his three sons, each building standing as a monument to a craftsman's art. Both Otto Frank's and John Chapman's spreads contained Marquardt-constructed log buildings and Dad was a personal friend of each. If an election for Territorial Governor were to be held on the morrow, Dad Marquardt would easily receive ninety percent of the Stinkingwater vote.

The Mathers family was, of course, the second point of attack for Burroughs' displeasure. Though the family had only been in the Stinkingwater for less than two years, they were already entrenched in the hearts of its people, both for their inoffensive modesty and Lillian's feisty spirit. And in two seasons as the country's schoolteacher, Lillian had won the heart of each of her students; and through them, their parents' also. August Mathers was known for the thoughtful, curious man he was, his counsel often sought and always welcome. And Lillian's mother was fast earning a reputation far and wide for the sumptuous meals served at the Mathers' Place.

By revoking August Mathers' rightfully earned pension—news that soon spread via Sam and Jethro and Dad

Marquardt—Burroughs created a wave of sympathy for the entire family. As a result, people often traveled from afar merely to take lodging in one of Mathers' Place cabins.

Within a week after the fire, a majority of people in the northern half of Fremont County had been by to offer the Marquardts their condolences. As they came, August Mathers considered their prospective influence. Those he judged trustworthy, Sam and Jethro took to the coulee and pointed out the tell-tale tracks, as well as the imprints where coal oil cans had been set. Those among the first on the scene could even smell the oil. Jethro thought that strange until he caught Sam 'freshening up' the odor with a small jar of coal oil from his pocket.

Kluster from the stable, store owner Judson, and saloon keeper Morton all witnessed the tracks and smelled the oil, as did a couple of dozen others. They all shook their heads and some of their eyes and faces turned hard before they expressed their sorrow to Dad and Mrs. Marquardt.

George Corbin arrived around noon. August had sent a message to Corbin's Crossing before daylight. Corbin told the folks assembled at Marquardt that he'd managed to get a rider traveling to Red Lodge to pass word on to Chapman and to the north, while the news was headed for Meeteetse by stagecoach. Corbin thought the Fremont County Sheriff would have the message within two days, at the latest.

The people came—the following day from Oregon Basin and Cottonwood Creek and Ralston Station; the next from Lovell and Polecat Bench. Then they came from Meeteetse and Two Dot and Pitchfork and the Greybull.

The first night after the fire, somebody tried to steal in to blot the tracks and Sam almost got him. But he had friends, so they all got away in a blaze of gunfire—and one big blast from an old Hawken. Now there were more tracks to show Chapman and Frank and Lovell.

"Ve'll rebuilt the barn," said Otto Frank. "Just you vait and see. It vill be big like the first, und ve'll have dances like before."

"Be nice if that'd bring Tom back," Dad Marquardt said.

"Ve have notified der Sheriff und he vill be here soon. Then ve'll find who set the fire und who killed Tom."

Both Frank and Chapman had walked out to see the tracks Sam found. The whole coulee area and the arsonists' route to the barn had been cordoned off, with considerable care taken to see the tracks were preserved as long as possible. But it snowed before the Sheriff arrived from Lander—a week after the fire. By then it didn't matter whether tracks existed or not because there were enough witnesses who would swear affidavits to prove those tracks and what they meant; enough to convince any judge, no matter how partial to Burroughs' money he might be.

The Sheriff was a big, older man with long hair and handlebar mustache. He brought with him authority from Lander District Court Judge Kittleson to impanel a grand jury to investigate the fire and Tom Marquardt's death.

Sam and Jethro were among the first to testify; then they headed back to Blood Canyon. By then, of course, there was no longer any question about whether Jethro was alive, and Sam's presence was no longer secret.

There was still considerable snow in Blood Canyon when they hiked in around mid-March. But two sets of horse tracks preceded them. Nothing seemed amiss. In fact, the unknown riders had not entered the cabin, but they'd ridden their horses around where Jethro set his corner posts for the new fence, and around the gate posts. And it looked like one of the horses had accidentally stepped into a line fence posthole Jethro had dug last fall.

The weather turned blustery through the end of March, but spring breakup settled in up at the Rock House right after Sam and Jethro returned. Thus the younger man returned to work on his fence.

———◆·◆·◆———

A man came through Blood Canyon in early May. He was tall, riding, of all things, sidesaddle. Jethro understood why when he dropped from his horse to open the gate. After leading his animal through, the man turned toward the cabin, moving at a halting, shambling walk.

"Howdy," Jethro said as the man approached.

"How do. Y'all must be Gray Eyes Weatherby."

"Some would call me that. Tie your horse and come on in. Coffee'll be hot in a minute."

"Thankee. Ah'll do just that."

"Texas?" Jethro asked.

"Originally. Just now up from the Ralston Station." The man limped around the hitchrail. "I always did think it purty up heah." He carried a revolver low on his crippled leg and the holster's leather was oiled and worn. A rifle butt stuck over his horse's neck, too. He must have sensed Jethro's curiosity because he thrust out a hand as he entered the cabin. "The name's Curlew, Mr. Weatherby. Ah don't know y'all, but any enemy of Levi Bunting is a friend of mine."

Jethro took the man's hand and pumped it. The grip was firm. "Ah used to work fo' the Swede down to Ishawooa." Curlew explained. "'Til Bunting killed him."

"Now I got it, Jethro said. "You were one of Swenson's men. Curlew you say? You were cut down by Bunting in Marquardt. And the limp tells the story."

"Y'all got it about right. Ah been workin' at Ralston Station, down the lower Stinkingwater, a-waitin' for somebody to come along and put the run on Burroughs outfit."

Jethro poured two mugs of coffee and handed the man one. The newcomer gingerly lowered himself to a bench by the table and said, "Thankee."

"You didn't ride all the way up here to Blood Canyon for a cup of coffee. Especially not in your painful condition."

His grin was lopsided. "Miss Lillian said to tell y'all that the meetin' will be at Marquardt's on the fifteenth."

"Okay, Mr. Curlew. You can tell her I'll be there."

"'Fraid y'all will have to tell her that. I ain't a-goin' back."

"You'll never get over any of the high passes this time of year," Jethro told him.

Curlew's eyes met Jethro's over the top of his coffee mug. "Ain't a-thinkin' to try, Mr. Weatherby. Thinkin' I'll stay on heah and he'p y'all."

Jethro spluttered.

"There's a lot of things ah cain't do, Mr. Weatherby. Y'all can see ah cain't ride a horse much no more. But there's lots of things ah can do, too. Like when ah come in, ah see you are a-stringin' wire, and ah can do that as well or better than y'all. Ah can set posts and build corrals and ah can cook better than most cowhands. Ah can feed stock and water them, too. And ah wash a mean bunch of dishes and swamp out a cabin so it shines. It's just that ah cain't do nothin' quick no more."

"My God, fellow," Jethro said, "I wish there was a place for you here, but there's no way I could pay you."

"Ain't a-lookin' for pay. Just a place to sleep and a little grub for my gut."

"Why? Why would you do all that for so little?"

Curlew set his mug down on the table with a thud, and his angular face pinched. "Why?" he asked in a tone that would run chills down a rattlesnake's spine. "Ah'll tell you why. 'Cause this is where Bunting has got to come. Some day he will have to come here. And ah don't want to miss it when he does."

Jethro stared out a window while Curlew waited for an answer. After a while, the crippled man whispered, "Ah can shoot a rifle with anyone, Mr. Weatherby. And ah ought to be right deadly from this here cabin."

"You want another cup of coffee, Mr. Curlew?"

"Josh."

"You want another cup of coffee, Josh?"

"Ah'd be right proud."

⇒ CHAPTER TWENTY ⇐

With Josh Curlew's help, the fence was finished before Sam and Jethro left for Marquardt and the organizational meeting of the anti-Burroughs movement. They'd learned from Josh that the big group roundup, held each spring, was to be headquartered out of Marquardt, and that the organizational meeting was timed to coincide with that roundup.

Jethro could see the idea had considerable merit and could sense behind the scenes maneuvers by someone trying to ensure a big turnout for the meeting. He wondered if Chapman or Frank had a hand in the planning. If so, that would go a long way toward answering how they'd feel about the resistance to Burroughs—another big cattleman.

Jethro jogged away from Blood Canyon in the afternoon of the thirteenth day of May, heading for Marquardt. Sam was to come the following day, riding Curlew's horse. Their plan was to bring in their own horses from Corbin's place on the return journey. He crossed the Stinkingwater at the north canyon mouth—no small feat for a swimming man who pushed a log raft that carried his guns and clothes, even though the water was still below flood. But the day was pleasant and, after the crossing, he reveled in the smell of new flowers and new growth, the pungent aroma of sage floating in the breeze, and the pleasant feel of a warm sun lifting moisture from his river-soaked clothing. As he trotted, a bead of sweat coursed behind an ear, down the neck, paused for a moment at the shoulder blade, then picked up speed under the loose fitting shirt until colliding with constrictions around his waist.

He carried the Winchester, switching from one hand to the other as the notion struck, and he carried the Colt in its familiar place—its rightful place—where it was down in New Mexico and on the Uncompahgre in Colorado. His thought turned there.

"For a good man ay look, ya?"

I was sitting at the counter in a little mud and wattle cafe near Fall Creek. It was five years and two months to the day after Colorado became a state. I was sucking a cup of coffee and wondering where to head next. When I swung around on my stool, he was no taller than eye-level—and me sitting on my butt. He had blonde stubble on his cheeks, and dirt beneath his fingernails and imbedded deep into the cracks and wrinkles of his clenched fists. He wore a wool cap that was too big for him, a wool coat that was too big for him and wool pants that were tied around the waist with what looked to be a chunk of five-eighths hemp. His boots were run over on both heels and one sole flapped as he walked.

"You talking to me?" I asked.

It was only after I got to his mine that I discovered Gunnar Einarssen was one more innocent, bucking Amalgamated Minerals and Mining's stacked deck.

We held out for a while, Gunnar and me, along wih a couple of other small mine owners. But the real truth was we lasted so long only because I came on the scene when I did.

Amalgamated toughs made a couple of runs at me and came out second best. Then they brought in the gunman they called Benjamin Pack, from New Mexico. Only thing was, Benjamin Pack was really Jesse Evans, with whom I had a score to settle. So I kicked open the saloon door and said, "I understand Benjamin Pack wants to see me!" Jesse Evans wheeled, eyes widening, crying my New Mexico name: "Winter!" It was the last thing he ever said.

But Amalgamated got Gunnar—killed him when I wasn't around to protect him.

Night was falling as Jethro trotted past the mouth of the Ishawooa. He still felt strong and decided to keep going.

God only knows how much dynamite they used to blow that mountain down like that, entombing my little friend. I was saddling up when the lawyer wandered up to tell me Gunnar had left me the Nordic Summer and all of his estate.

So here I am in northwestern Wyoming, the recipient of a little Swede's bequest. There wasn't as much money as the lawyer thought, but only because I refused to sell to Amalgamated. Even so, there was enough money to carry a careful man for a few years.

I knew what I wanted to do as I rode out of Fall Creek ahead of the bitter winter of '82-'83. I planned to do just enough assessment work on Gunnar's mine to keep it from Amalgamated hands, and I wanted to find a quiet, peaceful country where I could mind my own business. So, come spring, I'd wound up along the Stinkingwater, settling on Blood Canyon for my homestead chiefly because there could not possibly be any conflict between a homestead there and any serious cattleman. Even so, I figured it best to tell the owner of the country's biggest ranch what I planned to do so it'd not come as a surprise to him that a homestead had been taken up on the fringes of his territory. By plainly stating my case, I thought I could avoid trouble. Jethro's shrill laugh surprised him, echoing from the surrounding hills.

So now where am I headed? To put my life on the line for someone else again. You're a fool, you know. You'll never reap the benefits of that fence or the Rock House, or the waterfall and pool and stream. So why go to Marquardt at all?

Because that's what life's laid out for you, that's why. It's the way God made you—God and a thoughtful, gray-eyed, mountain man father and a loving, raven haired Blackfeet mother. And your life has been honed by knowing and loving, of all people, an Irishman, a Chinaman, a New Mexico Englishman, and a Colorado Swede. Again, his peeling laughter echoed about him.

———•·•———

The sun rose while Jethro Spring slumbered in a patch of willows, not far from Marquardt. As chance had it, he lay less than a mile from where an important, impromptu meeting of a few of the district's leading cattlemen was taking place. Had he known, he'd have given much to be lying nearby....

———•·•———

Four riders sat their horses near the banks of the Southfork of the Stinkingwater. The river was still a month from the flooding that occurred annually during the high country snow melt of June. The riders were Ellis Burroughs, John Chapman, Otto Frank, and Levi Bunting. One rider seemed agitated.

"You can't be serious!" Ellis Burroughs exclaimed. "Why, our information is that the association is aimed at nothing less than a rendering of every big cattle operation in the Territory!"

"That ain't our information, Burroughs," growled Chapman. "Our information is that it's bein' formed as a fire fighting outfit—to help see that local barns don't burn down in the middle of the night."

"What's that supposed to mean?" Levi Bunting demanded.

"Exactly what you heared, Bunting. I have a habit of saying what I mean, and meaning what I say," Chapman growled.

Bunting shot back, "If you're accusing ..."

"Ve are accusing no vun of nothing," Frank cut in. "Und I'm surprised you vould think so. Dere vill be a meeting to promote northvest Vyoming, and it vill be held tomorrow at my friend Dad Marquardt's place. Dat is all I know, but I think I vill go, for I am interested in vot happens in northvest Vyoming."

"Surely you know the Grand Jury's indictment!" Burroughs said.

"We read it," Chapman replied. "It reads arson—and murder!"

"By 'parties unknown', for God's sake!"

"Yeah, Burroughs. That's the scary part—`by parties unknown'. That's what this meeting tomorrow is all about—a way to respond to these 'parties unknown'."

"Surely you don't believe for one minute that the T Bar had anything to do with Marquardt's barn catching fire?"

Chapman's eyes were veiled; Levi Bunting squared his horse around to better face the rancher. "No vun accuses anyvun of nothing," Otto Frank said. "But ve vould not like to see another such terrible thing happen."

"Maybe you'd ought to go to the meeting, Burroughs," Chapman said. "Most ever'body else in the county's north half plans to be there. Leastways, ever'body who don't like what happened to Marquardt's barn will be."

"Mr. Chapman and Mr. Frank." Burroughs tried a smile and a lighter tone. "You must know this association is aimed right now at the T Bar, but it is certain to spread to the Pitchfork and to the Two Dot. Again, I tell you the Lazy T Bar had nothing whatever to do with that fire, or with young Tom Marquardt's unfortunate demise. But surely you know that many people think so. And merely because Tom Marquardt had the misfortune to escort my once-intended to a dance. I know they think that, and it's the most absurd thing I've ever heard. Surely you must believe that."

Both Chapman and Frank stared stonily at the two men from the Lazy T Bar.

Burroughs tried again. "Surely you realize the T Bar has bigger problems than personality conflicts with a girl who once loved me—like that nester in Blood Canyon. Surely you'll not support one of those unwashed multitudes who, like vultures on a fence, wait to strip bare every viable cattle operation in the West. Surely you won't take a nester's part in a cattleman's war!"

"Surely ve von't, Mr. Burroughs," Otto Frank murmured. "I can assure you ve both vant nothing to do with dat man. Und maybe you vould be vise if you had nothing to do mit such a man also. But ve are to have something to do with those who burn barns by stealth, and who kills people mitout a just reason."

"Well, good. That leaves us clear," said Burroughs.

"Does it?" Chapman said.

"What is that supposed to mean?" again demanded Bunting.

"That's the second time you butted in, Bunting!" snapped Chapman. "I asked Burroughs a question. I don't want a question back from you."

There was a moment's silence, then Bunting muttered, "You'll be lucky if you live to ride away from the Stinkingwater, Chapman."

"Just a moment, Mr. Bunting," Otto Frank said. "There might be something you overlook here. If vun or both of us are to die, neither you nor Mr. Burroughs vill live to see the sunset. Und by tomorrow the Lazy T Bar vill be no more."

"Please! Please! Gentlemen!" Ellis Burroughs cried. "Let's think this through. Surely we can yet come to an understanding."

"I've got a question I want to hear answered, Burroughs," Chapman glanced pointedly at Bunting, "without interruption. You claim your outfit is too busy to retaliate against someone merely 'cause he dances with your old girl friend?"

"Yes, of course—that's right."

"Does that mean you don't retaliate against the girl, too?"

"Certainly not! Miss Mathers is free to do as she wishes."

"Then," Chapman said, "why did you stop her father's pension?"

Burroughs' face drained. "I don't know where you ever heard such an outrageous thing, Mr. Chapman. I certainly never … Did the Mathers family tell you such a preposterous story? If so, they lied. I would never …"

"Marquardt told me, Burroughs," Chapman lashed out. "He was in the Mathers' house that night when you stopped by to gloat over your telegram. The same night his barn burned and his oldest boy was killed."

"And so vas Mr. Weatherby and Mr. Buttercut, from up in Blood Canyon," Frank added. "You are a lucky man you vas not killed that night, Mr. Burroughs."

Chapman's voice was low, but ominous. "That wasn't a very nice thing to do to a lady, Mr. Burroughs. Most real men I know thinks poorly of a low-down bastard who'd pull such a rotten trick."

Burroughs jerked his horse around and lashed him away from the Stinkingwater. Bunting followed slowly, backing his horse from the two ranchers for the first ten feet, then reining him around and, with his own back square and straight, walked the animal away.

CHAPTER TWENTY ONE

The crowd was swelled by crews from every ranch participating in the annual spring gather. With August Mathers temporarily presiding and men like John Chapman and Otto Frank attending, it was much easier for weaker men to follow. Still, with the ashes of Dad Marquardt's barn offering graphic evidence during the reading of the Grand Jury indictment, the crowd's mood was ugly.

A voice near the rear shouted, "They might not know who done it, but by God we do!"

"Hear! Hear!" came another.

"Twenty feet of hemp'd save the Stinkingwater a peck of trouble," a man standing near Sam, Lillian, and Jethro muttered.

Without really listening, Jethro heard August Mathers' voice rise: "… can no longer ignore the fact that lawlessness is loose in the Stinkingwater … a committee formed to address the problem…" Jethro gazed around at the faces. He knew Kluster, Corbin, Morton, Judson, Ashland, Chapman, Frank, Duerr, and of course, the Marquardt family. "... recommend formation of an organization designed to protect and promote the legitimate affairs of the residents of this district. Therefore, be it resolved ..." Jethro began counting the people present. Finally he leaped atop an anvil for a better view.

"I get a hundred and thirty-three," he whispered to Lillian as he dropped to the ground. "But I'll bet I missed a dozen, give or take."

"... our desire to follow such dictates of the people of this district as they express it. The chair recognizes Mr. Chapman!"

"Mr. Chairman, I make a motion that this bunch should be limited only to action against issues that are clearly illegal."

"I'll second that!" came from a half-dozen sources.

"It has been moved and seconded ..."

Amazing! Jethro thought. *To muster such unity. Is there hope for me?*

The sun was sinking when temporary chairman August Mathers concluded the meeting. During its course, directional rules were developed for the StinkingWater Association for Promotion and Protection, and a constitution and bylaws committee formed by acclamation. In addition, a nominating committee was charged with compiling a list of names from which regular officers and directors would be chosen. It was determined the next meeting for S.W.A.P.P. would be held again at the Marquardt ranch during a barn-raising scheduled for late July. Formal elections would be held then.

Jethro squeezed Lillian's arm and said, "Looks good!" Inside, a tiny spark of hope was glowing. *Is it possible this thing on the Stinkingwater will turn out different from the others? From New Mexico and Colorado?*

213

Another meeting took place in the Stinkingwater, its timing coinciding with that of the StinkingWater Association for Promotion and Protection. The second meeting also concerned itself with area affairs and was limited to just two participants. The second meeting was held in the study of Ellis Burroughs' Lazy T Bar ranch house.

Levi Bunting sat in Burroughs' favorite overstuffed chair. The fact that his foreman had a habit of appropriating the best chair in any room was a source of considerable irritation to Ellis —not so much the act itself, but Levi's sheer impertinence.

"It seems apparent we are facing a crisis of substantial proportions," Burroughs began. "What are we to do now that the entire district is alienated and aligned against us?"

The darker man scowled. Infuriatingly, he pulled paper and tobacco from his shirt pocket and rolled a cigarette. Loose tobacco fell onto the chair. Bunting licked the edge of the wrinkled tube he'd fashioned, then finished the roll, twisting each end. He stuck the cigarette in a mouth corner and while fumbling for a match said, "I know what we're *not* going to do, Burroughs—we're not going to run scared merely 'cause a pack of rabbits banded together for protection from the wolves." To punctuate the pronouncement, he scratched a match across a polished end-table near his chair.

Burroughs frowned at the mark the match left, and at subsequent marks as Bunting scratched again and again until the match flared. The rancher said, "Rabbits?"

Bunting cupped the flare against his cigarette and inhaled deeply before exhaling. "Rabbits are rabbits, whether they're in a herd or by 'emselves."

"I shouldn't think one would consider Chapman and

Frank as 'rabbits'," the blonde man retorted. "Only a fool could fail to see you did a stupid thing by burning Marquardt's barn."

Bunting's scowl deepened and the dark man's unblinking eyes stared at his employer until Burroughs twisted uncomfortably on the window sofa. "Like I said, Boss"— his choice of words were dripping with sarcasm— "we're not gonna run scared. Whether you like it or not, you're in this as deep as me, and you'd be makin' a mistake if you think there's any way you can step out now and leave me hangin' in the stocks."

There was no humor in the younger man's thin smile. "That statement could be interpreted as a threat, and I shall not tolerate such an attitude for one moment."

Bunting's eyes glinted. He took the cigarette from his mouth and carelessly flipped ashes, ignoring the ashtray by his side. "The thing we oughta be doin'," he said, "is figuring what we're gonna do to bring this new bunch to its knees. I don't see we're doing anything by second guessing, or by runnin' scared on account of the rabbits squeaked."

Burroughs turned to stare out his window. Two horses were tied outside the blacksmith's shop, switching tails at the first of the spring's flies, awaiting their turn for Schulte to heat and bend and hammer and nail on new shoes. Two cowboys worked new horses in the corrals while several hands lounged around the cookhouse and bunkhouse. Ordinarily a workday, most of his hands enjoyed an unusual free day as the huge, collective spring roundup ground to a halt when other ranchers and their hands chose to attend the Marquardt meeting.

Even a dunce could see that a new order lay across the land. When Chapman and Frank and Lovell chose to cast their lots with the dozen-odd small ranchers in the district and they, in turn, were joined by the small businessmen and farmers and freighters and tradesmen, it created an unbeatable array of opposition poised against the Lazy T Bar. Even the wealth and political connections of his father paled against the righteous anger of men such as Otto Frank and John Chapman. And yes, of the anger of August Mathers and Dad Marquardt.

The T Bar owner contemplated the current situation: *What manner of people are these in Wyoming? How could they pretend to ignore the political and financial influence of the Burroughs family connections and revere a bumbling old fiddle player? What kind of people would welcome a penniless nester into their midst? Have I, Ellis Burroughs, erred? The books don't reveal it. My ledgers disclosed a healthy return on investment—the second such year in a row. If that's fair measure of success—and it is—then I've definitely not erred. In fact, I'd like to match books with Frank and Chapman and Lovell.*

Judson and Morton will come around. Without the T Bar, both their businesses would soon be in receivership. Or perhaps the Burroughs Cattle Company could start competing stores and the end would be the same. Money buys influence, doesn't it? We still have Judge Kittleson's past as a lever, don't we? Perhaps not. What was it the man said as he signed over his Stinkingwater assets to the T Bar?

"All right, Burroughs. You win this one. But tell your minions we're even now. If you ever again try to blackmail me, I'll spill my guts, even to the point where I disclose how you've blackmailed a Territorial Judge. Just in case you don't know what that means, until Wyoming is a state, it's a **Federal** *offense, under* **Federal** *jurisdiction."*

One of the loungers at the cookhouse stood up, stretched lazily and ambled to the corral where the two cowboys had eared down an unruly young bronc and were cinching a saddle on him.

Ellis Burroughs saw them, but it didn't register. His father was unmistakably proud of what his younger son had accomplished. If he were here he'd be scheming a counter-attack. Whatever course Douglas Burroughs chose, Ellis knew it would be subtle. As for the offending merchants, his father would never be so crass as to overtly retaliate; instead, valves would be turned while, at the same time, carrots were extended. The effect was the same, but appearances were not.

What would Father do? Most assuredly, political influence would be brought to bear—economically, of course. That means at the county level. It appears there will be a Deputy Sheriff and a Justice of the Peace appointed for the northern portion of Fremont County by the county commission.

There was a puff of dust from the corral as the saddled bronc danced in the dust; a cowboy made to mount.

How does one go about purchasing a county commissioner? Certainly it should be through an intermediary.

Levi Bunting slipped from Ellis's overstuffed chair and strode to a side cabinet where he poured a glass of whiskey. Turning, he said, "It's going to take time for cracks to begin showin' up in any new coalition against us. Likely there's a dozen ways to break up that bunch from inside, but that ain't my field. However, we've got to do something. Even rabbits take courage while in a bunch, especially if the wolves tuck their tails and run."

Ellis turned his idle gaze from his ranch yard. "There would be no, as you call it, herd of rabbits if you'd not had the brilliant inspiration to cower them by burning their nest." He returned to staring at the twisting, leaping, bouncing dervish of a horse in his corral, and at the cowboy atop, waving his hat and spurring the bronc on to greater action. As he watched, he observed, "Fire, as a tool in your arsenal, has not proven very effective, Levi. Burning the nester's cabin hasn't exactly discouraged him. And torching Marquardt's barn was such a grand idea, it's alienated the entire district."

Ellis spun on his window seat as Bunting's whiskey glass dashed against the stone fireplace, smashing into a hundred shards. "Don't mess with me, Burroughs," the foreman snarled. "Marquardt's barn was as much your decision as mine. You said the natives were getting restless and needed a lesson. It was you ..."

"I certainly did not authorize young Marquardt's murder!"

"Hell no, you never! You only said the Marquardt that had his tongue hangin' out around that schoolmarm bitch would be the perfect one to give an object lesson to!"

"But I never ..."

"You only said we'd fooled around long enough givin' 'em a chance to line up behind the T bar and now we'd oughta turn a few screws! You only said the natives had quit gettin' restless and started gettin' reckless, and that the dance was the last straw! You only said it had to be the Marquardts and the Mathers behind it, and if I'd give a lesson to Marquardt, you'd give one to Mathers!"

"Just a minute ..."

"Well, Burroughs, I'd say your lesson to the Mathers family fell flat, too, didn't it?"

"You have no right ... I won't stand for it! You cannot talk to me that way, Bunting. Do you think I'm a common cowboy? I own this ranch!"

The foreman ambled over to stand spraddle-legged in front of Ellis Burroughs, staring down at the fairer man with barely concealed contempt. "What are you gonna do, Burroughs? Fire me? Ha, ha! That's a good one. You wouldn't last five minutes and you know it." Then Bunting's voice turned ominous. "Don't ever get the idea you're gonna fire me, because it won't happen. I ain't an old shoe to be throwed away when you think you don't need me no more. I made you, Burroughs. Without me, you'd never even got by Bledsoe, and sure as hell not past Swenson. Without me, the best you coulda done would be to have Morgan's old spread, a feisty bitch for a wife, and a half-dozen snot-nosed kids runnin' around underfoot."

Reining in his temper, Ellis again turned his gaze out the window. The bronc was standing, its sides heaving as the rider leaned forward and fanned its head with his hat. The exhausted animal never moved. *Morgan's two thousand acres? Lillian for a wife? And children, too? Perhaps the thought is not as unattractive as this idiot foreman is trying to make it sound. Is he actually telling me I cannot fire him?*

As if reading his thoughts, Bunting continued. "No, Burroughs, you and me are in this together, right out to the end. Fact is, you ain't gonna get rid of me for lots of reason. Most of all, though, is 'cause I might get mad if you tried. Real mad."

Ellis swiveled his head back to stare into Levi Bunting's unblinking eyes. He shivered in spite of himself. "Please go back and sit down, Levi," he said, "and tell me what we should do."

The dark man wheeled and strode to Burroughs' chair. As he settled down, he said, "You work on upsetting their bunch from inside. Me? I think I'll hit 'em."

"That's insane at this point."

"No it ain't, Burroughs. What did Otto Frank tell you?"

Ellis shook his head. "He threatened us."

"Naw, that ain't what I mean."

"Please. I'm in no mood for guessing games."

"He said he and Chapman would remain neutral in our fight with the nester. Without Chapman and Frank, it's doubtful if the other cattlemen would fight on the nester's side either. Without the cattlemen, how many others would want to ride better than forty miles up the Southfork to fight the T Bar. The nester might belong to whatever bunch they're forming up, but right now, the way I figure it, he's their weakest link."

Burroughs shook his head. "There may be a Deputy Sheriff and a Justice of Peace here soon, Levi. That's reason enough for us to remain impeccably legitimate in our affairs. I should not think it would be to our advantage to have open warfare start between us and even the nester if we could be held responsible. He could hardly be considered the aggressor if we shoot at him in his cabin."

"C'mon, Boss, give me more credit than that. What I got in mind is perfectly legal. That nester is tryin' to keep us out of our upper Southfork graze. I don't think he shoulda built that fence, do you?"

"The fence?" Burroughs asked.

"The fence," replied Levi Bunting.

CHAPTER TWENTY TWO

Days were lengthening in northern Wyoming and night was barely falling as the young couple stepped from Mathers' Place for an evening stroll. The air was brisk, even though summer was on its way. They walked hand in hand, laughing together with a freedom that only those in love have, going first to Kluster's stables to look at the horses Sam brought in from Corbin's. Buck came to the fence and nudged Jethro's elbow. Despite their separation during a long winter, Jethro was so absorbed by the girl that he only absent-mindedly scratched the big buckskin's ear.

The couple strolled on until they found themselves in front of Lillian's school. A moon two nights past full, peeped over the southeastern horizon. Its brilliance lit the landscape until Cedar Mountain, towering to the north, seemed to leap out.

"Sam says the Indians called it Spirit Mountain," the gray-eyed man said. "They called it that, I guess, because of the two hot springs on it. Sam says there's a cave up there."

Lillian stood very close, smiling up at him in the moonlight. She tilted her face further and leaned even nearer so that he stared deep into moonlight-reflecting eyes until he thought he would explode. Their kiss was tender and long, and soft and long, and moist and long. It was full of two years of pent-up yearnings, yet gentle and as reserved as the man could permit it. He broke it off and she laid her head on his shoulder and sighed. Then, on tiptoes, she reached up to kiss again.

"I love you, Gray Eyes," she whispered as he broke off for the second time.

"It won't work, Lillian."

The startled girl stepped back and said, "I beg your pardon!" Dismay was mirrored in the moonlight. "Tell me why!"

"Lillian, we come from different worlds."

"I don't understand! I'm from Wyoming. You're from Wyoming. Why are we different?"

"You know nothing of me."

"I know you're a man of character who follows the guidance of his conscience. I know you're handsome, rugged, and strong. I know you are one of the most respected men in the entire Stinkingwater district. I know you're determined, industrious, and have modest plans. I know I love you very deeply and would certainly consider playing a minor role in those plans."

She laughed lightly and tried to move close, but his fingertips bit into her shoulders. "Do you know that I'm also half Indian?"

She stood so still his hands fell to his sides. "No, I didn't," she murmured. "We suspected you had some Indian lineage, my parents and I. Do you know it makes no difference?"

"Oh God!" he moaned as they came together. In a few moments he again broke their embrace.

Lillian was no wanton. But after a sparse two year relationship with this strange, fierce, shy, gentle man she'd concluded that if their relationship was ever to burgeon into something more fruitful, she must overcome what she interpreted as his inherent shyness. "Is there something else wrong?" she whispered.

His laugh was harsh. "Lots of things."

"Like what, my love?"

"Like the kind of man I am," he said, releasing her and gently prying her hands from his neck.

She folded her arms across her breast. "Gray Eyes, I do not understand. Can you explain?"

He scuffed at the road with his soft-soled boot, thrusting his hands deep into his pockets while his broad shoulders pulled in to appear a shrug. "You are so refined, Lillian." He paused, then continued, "You're so cultured and sweet, and your parents are genteel and educated. Aww, what the hell! What do you know about me?"

Tears welled in the girl's hazel eyes. She grasped the man's upper right arm with both of her hands. When he looked down at her, she whispered, "I told you everything I thought I needed to know about you. Do I need to know more? If I do, for God's sake, tell me! And it still wouldn't make the slightest difference to the way I feel."

Then she released him and turned her back. But her words were firm and carried easily. "I've talked with father about you, Gray Eyes. Frankly we *do* wonder about you. Father considers you to be a brilliant young man with a better than average western education. He wonders how what he calls a 'rough-cut diamond' developed in the far-off West without schools of higher learning." She wheeled to face him.

"Mission school," he mumbled. "Just a miserable mission school near a miserable reservation. And a kindly, loving preacher who went out of his way to give a miserable half-breed kid a miserable chance...."

"And my father envies your superb health. He thinks a

combination of hard work and outdoor living is responsible. The reason he envies you is because he was never in your kind of physical condition. His life was spent indoors and entailed little physical exercise."

He saw a tear spill down her cheek. She shivered. "Lillian, you're cold. We'd better walk home."

"No!" Then she said, "The school! There's a stove. And wood, too. We can build a fire."

Once inside, Jethro hurried a fire to life in the big, pot-bellied stove. Then he pulled a bench to the stove and he and Lillian sat together in the darkness. A loose-fitting lid allowed a crack of firelight to dance eerily on the ceiling of the tiny schoolhouse. Moonlight filtered through the window. Lillian's hand stole into one of his rough, calloused ones. "Can you tell me more of yourself?" she asked.

He said nothing for a long time as they absorbed the welcome warmth, then he began.

"It's not a pretty life, Lillian. Mostly the schools I attended were rough ones. Survival of the fittest. I've kicked around most of my life. I've been over much of the West and some of the East. Most of the time, I just wandered. I've worked cattle, drove nails on a railroad track, been a hardrock miner, an Oregon logger, and a levee man on the Mississippi docks. My parents are dead and until I came here, most everyone else I knew and cared for was also dead. As far as I know, I don't have any living relatives. I guess I'd not been able to get my life straight before coming to the Stinkingwater, and I can't tell whether I'll be able to hold on to them here, either."

He paused to think, then turned his head to the girl. "Until Blood Canyon, Lillian, I guess I've never had a real purpose in life. It's not much, but at least now I know where I want to be. But ..." Again, he paused. "You must realize Blood Canyon is no place for a woman. Not yet, anyway. I would not consider taking a woman—any woman—to Blood Canyon until this thing with Burroughs is settled. Especially one I ... I love."

She came to him with a moan, but he was not finished. She laid her head on his shoulder.

"Lillian, you can do better than me."

"Hush," she whispered. "There is none better than you."

"My prospect is, at best, an isolated life in a remote canyon. It will probably always be a struggle to find enough money for the necessities of life. At worst, a woman could be alone and a widow up there."

"But I want to go to Blood Canyon." She turned her face up to his and this time their lips met. Then they met again and again as passion begat passion.

Once more, it was Jethro who broke off. This time, however, he stared deeply into Lillian's shadowed face. "I love you," he said simply.

"Oh, darling!"

She tried to burrow to him, but he held her back. "We've waited this long, Lillian. We must wait a little longer—at least through the summer." He sensed her disappointment, and added, "I promise you, if this thing with Burroughs is settled and I'm still alive come fall, I'll ask your father for your hand in marriage."

She whispered, "I'll wait." And as her mouth found his, her lips parted.

Forever passed, came again and passed again as they embraced. Then he shook his head as if to clear it and said, "We'd best be going back to Mathers' Place. We don't want to keep Burroughs waiting."

➤ CHAPTER TWENTY THREE ≪

Early in the morning of May 17, Jethro and Sam moved their horse band from Marquardt, eventually to reach Blood Canyon. Later the same morning, Ellis Burroughs passed through Marquardt in his carriage, driven by the T Bar gunman, Cletus Wills. The fast-moving carriage trailed a spare harness horse that was twice alternated with the high-stepping first horse as the carriage rolled over the Meeteetse Divide. From there it was all downhill to Meeteetse where two fresh horses were hired to replace the first pair.

From Meeteetse, Burroughs and Wills guided their fresh horses up and over the Greybull Divide where they came to the Lander stage road fork at Wagonhound Bench. Here the two men turned their buggy left and drove down the long gentle grade across Mud Creek and to the hot springs along the Bighorn River, where they took shelter for what was left of the night.

At noon on the third day, Burroughs' carriage rolled

into Casper. There, Burroughs exerted some of his considerable influence with Wyoming Central Railroad, and he and Wills were afforded accommodations in the caboose of the first train headed for Cheyenne.

At 10:30 a.m., May 20th, Ellis Burroughs was ushered into the expansive office of Daniel E. McAllister, senior member in the prestigious Cheyenne legal firm of McAllister, Keaton and Murphy. Daniel McAllister and Ellis Burroughs were closeted in close conference for some hours, sending out for a light noon meal. At 2:30 p.m. a junior staff member of McAllister's firm was called into the conference. The meeting between the two barristers and Ellis Burroughs continued until 4:15 p.m., at which time Ellis Burroughs left the offices of McAllister, Keaton and Murphy for his room at the exclusive Cattleman's Association Cheyenne Club, where he fell asleep and remained so for twelve hours.

An hour after Ellis Burroughs awoke on the 21st, Andrew Thornton boarded a Union Pacific passenger train bound for points west. He disembarked two hundred and seventy miles later at Green River where he had a few drinks, ate a leisurely evening meal, and took lodging at Green River's finest hotel, which left—in Thornton's opinion—something to be desired.

The following morning, Andrew Thornton boarded a stage destined for Lander, one hundred and thirty miles north.

Upon arrival at Lander, he ate another sumptuous meal and took accommodations in that community's best lodging house—again barely tolerable.

The next morning Andrew Thornton closeted with Jay Hammond, one of three well-respected Fremont County Commissioners and a close personal friend of Cheyenne barrister, Daniel McAllister.

While Andrew Thornton was engaged on his behalf, Ellis Burroughs gave vent to long-pent bacchanalian passions. As a result, he and Cletus Wills—who'd also vented his own suppressed fantasies—were tardy leaving Cheyenne. But at Casper, the two men felt sufficiently recovered from their Cheyenne forays to sample the fleshpots of the new locale.

Consequently, Ellis Burroughs' leisurely driven, dusty carriage rolled into Marquardt on the afternoon of May 29. Ellis directed Wills to pull up at the A. JUDSON - GENERAL MERCANTILE. Once inside, he asked to speak privately with the store owner.

"The reason I've stopped in, Judson," Burroughs began, "is that I've decided to do considerable fencing of much of our T Bar bottomlands for hay pastures."

Judson nodded, all the while smiling at the Lazy T Bar owner. His eyes had already begun calculating.

"I suppose," Burroughs continued, "we're eventually talking about many miles of wire and several hundred pounds of staples, gate hinges, fasteners, and so forth. Ordinarily we would order these kinds of supplies in bulk from a Billings supplier. However, I've carefully considered the relationship the T Bar has enjoyed with our major local supplier over the last few years and concluded that mutual loyalties deserve to be rewarded—mutually."

Judson's eyes narrowed and he stopped nodding, waiting for Burroughs to finish.

Ellis picked up a pair of fencing pliers from a shelf filled with tools and said, "It struck me that our local merchants deserve to reap the benefits of supplying locally and I think I should like to give them a try. What do you say?"

Judson nodded carefully.

"Why don't we order a keg of two-inch staples and about ten miles of Haish's S-barb wire for starters? That'll allow us to fence a couple of hundred acres. If it works like I think it will, we'll eventually require several hundred miles of fencing. Is this an order that would interest you?"

Judson hesitated no longer. "Yes indeed, Mr. Burroughs. And you may rest assured that I shall supply it to you at a reasonable price."

"I know you will, Judson. I'm not at all worried about that. Be sure, in fact, that you allow enough for a fair profit. Your loyalty has never been in question as far as I'm concerned. Fifty pounds of staples and ten miles of Haish's S-wire as a test, eh?"

Ellis Burroughs whistled softly as he left Judson's and turned toward Morton's saloon.

"Morton, I've just returned from a trip to Cheyenne," Ellis said as he and Schyler Morton seated themselves at a corner table in the empty saloon. "While there I had occasion to chat with an unusual gentleman. The fellow was actually a former sea captain in the English navy. This captain and I discussed an interesting tradition within that service. Apparently they furnish each of their seamen with what they call a 'tot' of rum each day. According to this English sea dog, the daily rum allowance to their men actually improves their crews' performance and keeps them happy. Have you heard of the custom?"

Morton shook his head, but Ellis had his full attention.

"No? Very well, that's not important. What may interest you is the fact that I've decided to experiment with the custom up at the T Bar. Of course we'll use whiskey instead of rum. In order to follow their lead and give my men what is called 'a tot per day', I've calculated that it would require about a half-gallon per month for each employee. That would total, if I've calculated properly, around fifteen gallons per month throughout the summer. That's a sizeable quantity of whiskey. I suppose I could order it direct from a Billings supplier at a favorable rate, but upon consideration of the loyal relationship we've had, one with the other over the years, I'm wondering if mutual loyalties shouldn't be rewarded."

Burroughs paused for effect, then smoothly continued. "Of course, over the years we could be talking about a considerable volume of spirits and a relatively large sum of money. Naturally I'd like to experiment for a shorter period of time to test the effectiveness of the program—say a couple of months. That would require approximately thirty gallons. Is a thirty gallon sale of moderately good whiskey, over and above your normal trade, of interest to you?"

Just as the Burroughs' carriage rolled out of Marquardt, a packstring plodded into the hamlet from the north. Twelve horses comprised the cavalcade; each horse was tied head to tail to the horse in front. The lead saddlehorse was a buckskin.

———

Jethro Spring spent considerable time during his and Sam's horse drive to Blood Canyon thinking of Lillian, SWAPP, Chapman and Frank, Dad Marquardt, August Mathers, and Levi Bunting and Ellis Burroughs. During the later stages of their drive, he confined his thoughts exclusively to Bunting and Burroughs and what he suspected they would do next....

Josh Curlew welcomed Jethro and Sam at the Rock House. He reported all quiet in the canyon and asked how their Marquardt organizational meeting had gone. Josh served a hearty meal of venison steaks, sourdough biscuits, beans, and canned peaches. Jethro turned in early, but was also up early the next morning, throwing sawbuck packsaddles on his packhorses, and rounding up ropes and canvas manty tarps, along with large packbags called panniers. At three in the afternoon, Jethro Spring started his empty packstring for Billings, Montana, one hundred and fifty miles away.

Jethro's cavalcade passed through the lower Southfork country under cover of darkness, through Marquardt just before daylight, and over the bridge at Corbin's Crossing two days after the carriage carrying Ellis Burroughs and Cletus Wills took the road to Cheyenne.

Jethro paused around noon at the head of Cottonwood Creek to graze his animals. Three hours later, he was again under way. They crossed the Skull Creek Divide into the Yellowstone Drainage, skirted around Chapman's Two Dot Ranch while the sun was still high, and continued on down Pat O'Hara Creek to its junction with the Clark's Fork of the Yellowstone. There the man unsaddled and hobbled his horses for the night.

The big buckskin horse and the string of packhorses plodded into Billings by mid-afternoon on May 21.

After making arrangements for his horses at Lowry's Stables, Jethro went to the largest mercantile supply store in Billings where he made inquiries. Disappointed with the response, he sent a telegraph message to St. Paul and was assured that certain requested supplies would be placed immediately on the next westbound Northern Pacific train.

The following day, Jethro dropped into the offices of Yellowstone Feed & Seed and ordered seventeen seventy-pound sacks of a specially prepared combination of grass seeds, including orchard, brome, and fescues. Then he strode back to Jonathon Bros. General Supply and purchased a hand-operated mechanical seed broadcaster and several hand tools. These included rakes, shovels, hoes, a pick, and a small horse-drawn cultivator that he dismantled for easier packing.

Jethro spent much of the following day making up packs for an early departure, but was disappointed to discover his St. Paul shipment was delayed at Bismarck due to some sort of design problem with Northern Pacific's new bridge across the Missouri River.

On the following day, Jethro went to the offices of Rocky Mountain Mining Supply and purchased one hundred and forty pounds of dynamite, with considerable fuse, and two-dozen blasting caps. The sturdy dynamite boxes were carefully wrapped in canvas and stored at Lowry's Stable. The dynamite caps—the most dangerous part—were already wrapped individually, but Jethro checked them over again, adding a wrap where he was dissatisfied.

By dark on the 24th, Jethro had assembled two packs of food supplies and was awaiting only his St. Paul shipment. This time it was a 'hot box' at Dickenson and it was actually daylight on May 26th before Jethro led his twelve packhorses out of Billings. The dynamite caps were in his breast pocket and one hundred and forty pounds of dynamite was on his first, most reliable packhorse. The second horse—also reliable—carried the St. Paul shipment.

Four days later, Jethro led his packstring into Marquardt as the Burroughs carriage rolled out of town.

—·—

Levi Bunting had also been busy. With completion of the joint gather by cattlemen of the Stinkingwater country, Levi devoted himself to sorting out the Lazy T Bar's livestock. Throughout the roundup and branding and castrating and dehorning, Levi left standing orders to separate the biggest, wildest steers into a holding pasture between the forks of the Stinkingwater.

Many of Bunting's cowboys considered the standing order unwise, for control of the growing 'wild bunch' required hard and constant riding. Some men even tried to avoid the order, but when Bunting caught four-year-hand Zeb Grattner failing to bring in a wild steer from over on Cottonwood Creek and fired him on the spot, any further resistance to Bunting's orders crumbled.

Eventually the wild bunch gather reached three hundred head. Holding the rangy steers within the forks became easier with the annual spring rise of the Stinkingwater, prompted by the high country snow melt and predictable June rains. Then Bunting gave the order to let the wild bunch drift south, up the valley of the Southfork.

———•◦•———

Jethro Spring left Marquardt shortly after daylight on May 30, leading his packstring toward Blood Canyon. Skies were overcast and he was praying for rain to obscure his passage from idle eyes. To further avoid a confrontation with Burroughs' men, he turned away from the Southfork wagon road just outside town and began working his way up into the foothills of Kittleson Mountain. Then he swung south, staying high so he could watch below. It was a nuisance dropping down into the deep Bledsoe Creek upper basin, then toiling out the other side, but Jethro thought it safer.

At the summit between Bledsoe and Rock Creeks, he paused for a half hour and studied the open land below through his telescope. Satisfied that the land was clear of T Bar riders all the way to the Southfork, Jethro pulled his Winchester from its scabbard and, with Buck and the packstring following, began hiking a gradual descent that took them across Rock Creek and finally to the river, near the mouth of the Ishawooa.

The first drops of rain fell as his last packhorse struggled from the Southfork to the west bank. Within seconds, rain hammered down, continuing all the way to the Rock House.

It was midnight when Jethro swung open the gate of his Rock House Ranch amid a driving downpour. Struggling into raincoats over their underwear, Josh and a grumbling Sam met him while holding coal oil lanterns high. Jethro directed them to the last ten horses while he carefully unpacked the first two.

Later, Sam sat on one of the two packs Jethro had set

inside the cabin to keep dry. The old trapper lifted a cup of whiskey-laced coffee and asked, "What air in these here packs that's so needful t'keep the rain off?"

"Dynamite," replied the gray-eyed man.

CHAPTER TWENTY FOUR

Except for Hoss and Buck, all Blood Canyon horses were kicked out beyond the upper fence, upriver. Sam took Buck and his pony back to their old pasture along the waterfall creek while Josh and Jethro made plans to broadcast the grass seed the gray-eyed man brought. The rain tapered off a couple of days after Jethro's arrival and broadcasting began both by hand and the mechanical broadcaster.

The two men sowed over a thousand pounds of seed in two days. Then Jethro built a lodgepole harrow and drove large spikes liberally around the bottom for harrow teeth. Using Buck as an unwilling harness horse, the Jethro-Buck team worked the seed into the soil as, luckily, the rains began again, continuing light and steady for two weeks.

To their surprise, the fire of the summer before seemed to help the old grass, such as it was, and so did the June rains. Adding to the green carpet of older grass was a dense, lighter green that was in place by late June.

By then, Jethro Spring paid scant attention. Instead, he was busy applying the practical dynamite knowledge he'd picked up from Gunnar Einarssen in a Colorado hardrock mine.

———•·•———

The first bawling horned blight stuck his nose into Blood Canyon on June 28. The men at the Rock House knew the cattle were on their way five days earlier, when Billy Marquardt brought word of the T Bar's wild bunch steers on the move. When Billy rode from Blood Canyon to once again brave crossing the flooding Southfork, Sam followed him to the Ishawooa to keep track on the oncoming herd.

Meanwhile, Jethro climbed the walls above the Canyon trail, where he planted his dynamite.

Blood Canyon is a not-unusual combination of sedimentary and igneous rock formations, with the igneous rock most often occurring as intrusions via the geological term 'dike'. A dike is usually considered as a rupture or crack in existing rock layers, allowing molten matter to escape the earth's core. The newer igneous rock is often more erosion-resistant than its surrounding layering and, as weathering takes place over millenniums, igneous dikes in either columns or walls can be found protruding from the surrounding rock. So it is in Blood Canyon. There, several dike-like columns, some rising as towers, protrude from the basic sedimentary cliffs.

Around one of those igneous columns, containing several hundred tons of rock, Jethro Spring meticulously 'single-jacked' holes with a rock drill and sledge hammer. In those holes, the gray-eyed man placed charge after charge of dynamite, methodically inserting and crimping the caps, then carefully measuring the fuse length for timed explosions—and to allow himself time to escape. At last he backfilled and tamped the waste material around the charges for maximum effect. On the day the first of the T Bar 'wild bunch' stuck his bellowing nose into Blood Canyon, Jethro had just finished checking his charges. Then he settled back to await Sam's signal.

Several considerations entered into Jethro's calculations as he prepared his charges. First and foremost, he did not wish to dynamite enough rock down from the Blood Canyon walls to block the now rampaging Southfork full with spring run-off. Nor did he wish to entirely block the wide trail bottom through the canyon, believing as he did that this incident might be the turning point in his battle with Bunting and Burroughs. But he did plan to drop enough rock to stop the stampede he was certain Bunting intended to set in motion.

Most important to Jethro's calculations was timing. Though he did not wish to drop the rock column directly on the cattle, he wanted it to be near enough the charging leaders so some animals would pile up against the avalanche of debris. In the man's warping mind, if cattle died against the avalanche instead of under it, the perpetrators of the stampede would be responsible for whatever losses were incurred.

But above all, according to Jethro's reckoning, cattle losses must occur in order to strike a telling blow against the Lazy T Bar.

Lillian Mathers was as happy as a girl could be. She was deeply in love with the strongest, bravest, kindest, gentlest, most handsome man she'd ever known; and he loved her. In addition, with the increased business her parents received because of the heavy hand of Ellis Burroughs, they seemed secure in their Mathers' Place lodging enterprise. Both appeared to enjoy good health. Tops on her list of wonderful things was the fact that the man she loved had promised to seek her hand in marriage, 'provided'.... And it was that proviso that threatened her perfect world.

The last words her Gray Eyes said in the schoolhouse that magic night, one month, four days, twenty-two hours, and six minutes ago were, "We'd best be going back. We don't want to keep Burroughs waiting." It was that specter, a confrontation between her Gray Eyes and the minions of T Bar that worried Lillian.

She knew the man she loved was capable and confident and, when teamed with Sam Buttercut, truly formidable. But Lillian suspected intuitively that her man was afflicted by some inner torment (as yet not diagnosed by her) that might lead to some kind of irrational behavior. Thus she prayed that no confrontation would occur. But what she heard when Dad Marquardt visited the evening of June 22 sounded ominous. "They're movin' that bunch of wild steers up the Southfork."

"That means they're going after his fence, doesn't it?" August Mathers asked. "Can we do anything to help?"

"I been thinkin' on it," Marquardt said, "and I don't see how we can stop it—even if we could get a big enough bunch of men to scare Bunting. If we try to stop 'em before they get to Blood Canyon, and if it comes to a shootin' match, we'd be outside the law 'cause they got a right to move them critters up there."

"Let me ask you this, then. Could we get any sort of group together to ride up there?"

"Yeah, me'n the boys, and probably Corbin. And you, of course, and maybe two, three others. A half dozen; eight maybe. Probably no more'n ten."

August Mathers pondered, then asked, "What if it comes to shooting between the Lazy T Bar and the men in Blood Canyon? After the stampede, I mean."

"Bound to, August. Weatherby can't set there and do nothing."

"Would ten men have the potential to alter the balance, say, if it came to the point the Blood Canyon people were defending themselves and the Burroughs outfit was clearly an illegal aggressor?"

"Y-e-a-h." Marquardt's answer was hesitant, but he warmed to the idea. "Ten men shootin' down on the shootin'-downers would panic 'em for sure."

Dad Marquardt left Mathers' Place shortly after ten p.m. He was to send Billy to Blood Canyon to warn the inhabitants, while he and August Mathers would try to raise a SWAPP posse to ride to Blood Canyon. The two men parted confident they were doing everything possible. But Lillian wasn't so sure.

———•+•———

The maid Charlot brought word of the approaching visitor and Ellis Burroughs rushed to the window to see for himself. By God! It is the girl—and she's walking to his ranch house.

Lillian strode past the bunkhouse, cookhouse, corrals, and blacksmith shop. She wore a white print dress, gathered at the waist, and a matching bonnet. Her shoes were practical—sturdy, high-laced ones with flat heels and thick soles. She'd taken a pail and told her parents she was walking into the foothills to pick strawberries. But as soon as she was away from Marquardt, she set out on the two-mile walk to the Lazy T Bar.

Schulte, the big blacksmith, stood in the shade of his smithy and watched her without change of expression. Lillian cheerfully called out, "Good morning, Mr. Washburn!" to the cook, who stood in the doorway of his domain.

The man seemed embarrassed, but he waved and returned the greeting, "Mornin', Miss Lillian."

Charlot opened the door at her knock. The maid

smiled shyly and curtsied. "Come in, Lillian, my dear," came a baritone voice from across the shadowed foyer. "This is indeed a surprise."

Charlot took Lillian's bonnet, then clasped her hands and turned questioningly to Burroughs.

"Some tea, Charlot, if you would be so kind. And I believe Lillian will want a spoon of sugar in hers."

As the maid left the room, Lillian said, "Thank you, Ellis. I'm flattered you remembered."

Ellis stood in front of his upholstered chair; an opened book lay covering the nearby table's scratch marks left by Levi Bunting's match. "You do me an injustice, Lillian," the man said. "I remember *everything* about you."

When the woman remained silent, Ellis threw out a hand and said, "Won't you have a seat? If you walked all the way from Marquardt, no doubt you are tired."

Lillian sat at the window sofa while Ellis settled into his chair. She motioned toward his open book and said, "May I ask what you are reading, Ellis?"

"Um, yes. It's an Horatio Alger. *Joe's Luck,* I believe. The usual Alger stuff—poor boy succeeds against all odds. You know the kind. This one is about California gold camps."

Ellis broke the ensuing silence. "I know you didn't walk all the way out here to discuss my reading habits, Lillian."

"No," she said as Charlot entered to serve tea. It was in a silver service that Lillian remembered. Again, Charlot curtsied as she departed. When Ellis raised his teacup—and his eyebrows—she began again. "You're right of course, Ellis. I didn't walk to the Lazy T Bar to discuss your reading habits. But perhaps your choice of books is coincidental; 'Success against all odds,' did you say?"

The corners of his mouth turned down and his eyes flashed.

"Ellis, I beg you to drop this vendetta against Mr.

Weatherby."

"I don't know what you are talking about."

"I'm appealing to you to honor the promises you made in our discussion at the schoolhouse a year ago. Do you remember them?"

"As I said earlier, Lillian, I forget nothing about you. I remember, for instance, that you failed to honor the commitment you made to me at the school. Do you deny that? Do you deny that you abandoned me at the dance like a brazen trollop to run off after a man you knew to be my sworn enemy?"

Here it is, Lillian thought. *Don't get angry. Reason with him.* "Ellis, let's reconstruct our schoolhouse discussion. You told me your ranch administration was committed to peaceful operations. You said you intended your ranch to function well within the law and that you were working to establish that fact in the opinion of others."

"So?"

"All I did was agree to go with you to the Pitchfork dance. Nothing else."

"You rode to the dance with me. You did not ..."

"I'll admit I had a moral obligation to return with you, Ellis, and I did not do so. In my defense, I'll plead that I had just provocation." She sighed. "From the exchange I heard between you and Levi Bunting, it sounded as though you had no intention of honoring your moral promises made at the schoolhouse."

The man glared at her.

"If my interpretation was correct, I felt justified in refusing to come home with you."

"You didn't refuse to come home with me," he sneered. "You simply chased off like a hussy after my enemy. Do you deny that?"

"Yes. I did not act like 'a hussy', as you call it. I will, however, admit my actions were impulsive and ill-advised. I'll even apologize if that will help."

The man stared moodily past her, out the window.

"Why do you call him your enemy?" she suddenly asked.

Ellis snorted. "The man threatens me. He steals my land. He burns my grass. And you have the audacity to sit there and ask why I call him an enemy!"

For a moment Lillian stared down at her folded hands. Finally she raised her eyes to his. "Ellis, we're grown now. We're adults. You know the things you've just said are not true. Really, who are you trying to convince? Surely not me."

Burroughs was mute under her firmness.

"You know the man you call your enemy did not threaten you, Ellis, but only told you he would protect his rights. I was there, remember?"

"I meant the time in Morgan's saloon," he mumbled.

"I do not believe that either," she said. "And as for taking land from you—that's simply not true. Any court in America would find that land is his without question. Surely you cannot even convince yourself of that."

"And what is your argument for his burning our grass?"

"Why did you first burn his cabin?" she retorted.

Silence fell between them, broken again when he said, "I find your defense of the man amusing."

"He is not your enemy."

Ellis rose and picked up the teapot. She lifted her cup and drank half, saying, "Thank you," as he refilled it.

"What is the purpose of this discussion, Lillian?" he asked as he settled back into his chair.

"I was hoping to persuade you to stop the cattle."

His eyes narrowed and a mouth corner lifted. "What cattle?" he asked.

She sighed again. "The cattle your men are driving to Blood Canyon."

"My dear, those steers are on their way to summer

pasture."

"Those steers are intended to be stampeded into Mr. Weatherby's new fence."

"That's absurd," he said slowly. "Who says so?"

"Oh Ellis, Ellis, we've known each other since we were children. Don't you think it's time for us to be entirely honest with each other?"

Burroughs reached for his teacup, drank from it.

"I loved you once, Ellis, before you became involved in the shady manipulations that now appear to be consuming you. I'm appealing to you to stop dealing in those manipulations and become again the man of innocence and virtue I once knew."

He sneered. "Are you offering your love?"

"No," she replied. "I no longer have that to give, since I'm pledged to another. I'm asking ..."

"What?" he broke in. "Did you say pledged? To whom?"

"To the man you're trying to harm."

"You must be joking! *The* Lillian Mathers marrying a ragtag ruffian from pauper's row. Now *that* is really absurd. You're joking, of course."

"No, Ellis, I'm not. Mr. Weatherby and I are to be married. Now you can see that I have a vested interest in whatever happens up there. Please order the cattle back. Quit this ugly thing between you and the people in Blood Canyon."

Ellis Burroughs did not move, apparently in momentary shock. At last, he said, "I really had hoped to win your hand, Lillian. I had thought our arguments were merely lovers' spats and as soon as my affairs here on the Stinkingwater were favorably established, I could once again win your affection."

Cheeks reddening, she said nothing.

"But that's not to be, is it Lillian?" He seemed to stare through her, as if speaking to someone else. "Now I can see if it's not that Blood Canyon lout it will be someone else. There's no place for an Ellis Burroughs love, is there?"

"No, Ellis, there isn't. But there can be a place for an Ellis Burroughs respect if you do respectable things. The Blood Canyon affair is not a respectable thing."

"I really am disappointed in you and your father, of all people, turning against me as you did."

"What you did to father," she gently said, "was a detestable thing."

"I thought I had just cause." Then Ellis gave a short bark and said, "To all indications, it looks as though that plan to bring Lillian Mathers into line backfired in every way. I shall authorize renewal of the pension."

"What about the other, Ellis?"

Ellis stared at her, then at his teacup.

"The cattle, Ellis."

"That's not so simple."

"Why? Because of Levi Bunting? You must get rid of him, Ellis. As long as Levi Bunting is part of your destiny, that destiny will embrace evil."

A clock chimed in another part of the house. Ellis listened until the chimes stopped, then said, "Again, it's not so simple."

"Ellis you already have one of the larger ranches in northwestern Wyoming. According to father, you have actual legal claim to most of the vital lands within your ranch. You no longer need Levi Bunting. At the schoolhouse that day you said you would get rid of the man the moment you no longer needed him. Ellis, the man is a millstone around your neck. Surely the Marquardt barn affair proved that."

Burroughs started to protest, but her voice lashed out. "No thinking person believes you to be responsible for that fire, Ellis. But I know no one who doesn't associate the Lazy T Bar in some way with it." Her voice softened.

"That leaves only Levi Bunting, doesn't it?" Ellis Burroughs confirmed Lillian's fears by his silence. "The man *must* go, Ellis, or he'll take you down, too."

Again silence fell. "It's not so simple, Lillian," he repeated.

Lillian picked up the teapot and poured them both more of the dark liquid. As she stood in front of Ellis, she said, "Ellis, this affair at Blood Canyon must stop. There must be no confrontation over that fence. The cattle drive into Blood Canyon must stop. Will you try to halt it?"

Ellis Burroughs said nothing.

———•~•———

The owner of the Lazy T Bar sat in his darkened ranch home, moodily drinking whiskey. Had it really been just yesterday when Lillian walked alone into the T Bar ranch house to present her convincing arguments for him to halt the developing range war? Her last argument was the most telling....

As Lillian had readied to leave, Burroughs called for Washburn, directing the cook to take the woman back to Marquardt in the carriage. It was while they waited for the carriage that Lillian said, "Ellis, if those cattle stampede through Blood Canyon, one of two things will surely happen. Perhaps both. There will be a confrontation between your people and those in Blood Canyon. I know Jacob Weatherby will fight and you know he is a clever and resourceful antagonist. I cannot guess who will win, but however it goes, you and I will both lose. I stand to lose either the man with whom I hope to spend the rest of my life, or the man I once loved and still want to respect and call a friend.

"And what will you win if Bunting is successful? Questionable access to the least productive grazing lands in all of Wyoming—and the undying enmity of every man, woman, and child for hundreds of miles around. This 'Stinkingwater Affair' will go down in such history as is written of Wyoming Territory as one of the most sordid periods ever to develop. It's a history that will leave the Burroughs name forever tarnished, while the name of the man Bunting insists on destroying will live forever as a rallying cry for the very forces your foreman plans to cow with the thunder of a thousand hooves.

"Think about it, Ellis. Think what you have to gain. Measure it carefully against what you have to lose."

Ellis Burroughs had thought about it. He'd thought all last night until he'd fallen asleep sitting in this very chair. He'd awakened this morning still thinking about it and had come to the conclusion Lillian was right. Bunting's way was certain to destroy them both.

Had not he, Ellis Burroughs, contributed the only really positive developments to the building of the Lazy T Bar? He was the one insisting on harvesting and storing hay. He was the one who'd really developed utilization of a variety of land laws to acquire legal title to much of the T Bar's bottomlands and waterholes. He was the one who'd recently decided to fence key hay pastures and he was the one just now thinking of experimenting with some modest grain farming in order to develop feeder cattle. Too, he was the one who'd insisted on importing blooded bulls, who was responsible for systematic improvement of blood lines and beefier, more profitable animals.

And what had Levi Bunting accomplished? He'd burned a cabin and a barn and created enmity against the entire population of the Stinkingwater country. Even Ellis didn't know how many men Bunting had killed in the development of the Lazy T Bar, but he shuddered to think of it. "Lillian is right," the rancher muttered. "Bunting is a killer. I have a cold-blooded killer loose on the T Bar."

But what to do? What would his father do? Ellis knew his grandfather had a reputation for ruthlessness and that his father's was considered similarly ruthless. *Think! What would those men do about the Bunting problem?* Ellis rubbed his fingers across the scratches made by Bunting's match. "Charlot!" he shouted. "Charlot!"

When the little Indian maid hurried into the darkened room, Ellis said, "Please bring Mr. Lyle to me at once."

When Henry Lyle appeared, Burroughs said, "I need to cross the Stinkingwater at daylight. I know it is near flood and that the crossing will be more difficult than I would normally prefer. That is why I wish you to escort me. I will require a saddlehorse and one packhorse for myself. The packhorse will have a somewhat unusual load—a little food, an overnight valise, and a chair."

"A chair, Mr. Burroughs?"

"Yes, a chair. It will be a straight-backed mahogany one, with armrests. Charlot will show you. It is in the south wing guest room, Charlot."

Lyle stared in bewilderment, but as the maid turned for the hallway, the cowboy shrugged and followed.

As they left, Ellis added a reminder. "Remember, Mr. Lyle, I want to leave at daylight."

"Yessir, Mr. Burroughs. I'll be ready."

As Lyle disappeared, Ellis again called for Charlot. When the round face of the maid reappeared from the hallway, the man said, "Would you be so kind as to fetch Mr. Schulte as soon as you show Mr. Lyle the chair?"

CHAPTER TWENTY FIVE

It was an hour past day-light on June 25 when two of the largest and strongest saddlehorses on the T Bar ranch entered the Southfork of the Stinkingwater just upstream from where the Southfork and Northfork come together. The saddlehorses were followed by a big packhorse carrying, of all things, a straight-backed mahogany chair lashed high on the upstream side of the horse's sawbuck packsaddle. Swinging from the other side in order to balance the heavier chair was a packbag loaded with several river-run rocks, food, and Ellis Burroughs' valise. The food and valise were wrapped in oilskins for added protection.

Henry Lyle led the packhorse. The old cowboy care-fully coached the younger man on flood-stage stream crossings. "You've gotta keep your eye on the far bank, Mr. Burroughs. For God's sake don't watch the water or you'll start goin' with the current. Pick a spot on the far bank and make your horse go to it. Make him buck the current. Okay?"

Burroughs' face was white, but he nodded.

Lyle loosened the cinches on their horses. "That's so they can get a bellyful of air an' float higher." Then the two men waited while a partially submerged pine tree drifted past. Lyle shouted, "Okay, Mr. Burroughs, feed him your spurs!"

Ellis's surprised horse bolted into the muddy water, then settled into a surging walk. Gritting his teeth against fear, Burroughs locked his eyes on the far shore as the raging torrent rushed against the horse. As the big animal began to drift, his rider reined him into the current, pointing him to the spot on the far bank. He heard Lyle shout encouragingly, "Attaboy, Mr. Burroughs. You're doin' fine!"

Then the water deepened and it surged against the animal's belly and chest. Suddenly the horse was swimming and the muddy flood washed across the top of Ellis's saddle. He panicked, dropping the reins, grabbing the saddlehorn with both hands, and clinching his eyes.

"It's okay, Mr. Burroughs," came a shout from the rear. "You're okay. Just hold on."

Ellis did, but all thought of his exit spot was gone as his horse drifted with the rushing current. Then the horse hit bottom and found his feet. He began to wade.

"Rein him to the bank, for God's sake! Don't let him drift now or you'll be into the Northfork, too! Pick out a spot and make him go to it, Mr. Burroughs!"

Grimly, Ellis retrieved the bridle reins and headed his saddlehorse more directly to shore. Soon the animal was in water only to his knees, then clambering out on the west bank.

"You did real good, Mr. Burroughs."

Ellis turned with an excited grin to see Lyle's horses alongside. The awkward chair was still in place.

"Lemme get this straight, Burroughs—you want me to pull back the herd from upriver. You don't want me to run 'em into Blood Canyon." Levi Bunting had entered only moments before, tilted the mahogany chair against a wall of the Swenson line cabin and rested his spurred boots on the cabin's kitchen table. "Are you out of your mind?"

Ellis Burroughs shook his head. "I've decided to stop this confrontation, Mr. Bunting. I wish to call it off."

Bunting shook his head. "You *are* crazy!"

"No, Levi. I'm not crazy. I'm just determined to put an end to it."

"Why? In your almighty Burroughs wisdom, why'd you decide that?"

"Levi, we have too much to lose. Think about it, man. We've got the biggest ranch on the Stinkingwater. That damned Blood Canyon nester doesn't interfere with the ranch or its productivity. He's not even taking up land we ever thought initially to include in this ranch. If we continue this confrontation, we're jeopardizing the present ranch for something we're not going to use anyway."

The mahogany chair struck the floor with a thump as Bunting leaped to his feet. "Burroughs, you go on back to your ranch house and leave this to men who can handle it. We're gonna take them steers through Blood Canyon and through that nester's fence. And when we get done, there won't be no nester up there, nor none to the Stinkingwater for a hundred years to come."

Ellis tried, but couldn't keep the fear from his eyes as Bunting snarled, "Now maybe you ain't got sand enough to run a big cattle spread, Burroughs, but you're damned lucky you hired a man who has. Look at me, damn it! I'm that man! I'm runnin' this ranch—and I have been since the day Morgan handed you the key. You can go ahead and live high on the hog in Billings or Cheyenne or Chicago. You can go ahead and experiment with Durham bulls and cuttin' hay like a farmer. You can even run fences if you've a mind to, and piddle with your ledger books and play the big high-tootin' rancher. But don't you ever try to tell me how to run this ranch, 'cause I won't stand for it!"

The smaller man seemed to shrink.

"We spent four goddamn days gettin' them wild steers drove up to the Ishawooa, Burroughs. It took plumb damn hard ridin' by most every cowhand on the T Bar. Now, all of a sudden, you come ridin' in and tell me, 'Please, why dontcha take 'em back, boys? We made a mistake.' Well, Burroughs, we ain't gonna take 'em back, 'cause I never made no mistake. They're gonna run through Blood Canyon just like we figgered and you can go up and watch it about day after tomorrow, or you can tuck your tail 'tween your legs and run back to your ranch house and pout. Makes no difference to me either way."

Burroughs broke off eye contact, but found enough courage to say, "I shall do neither, Mr. Bunting. Instead, I shall stay here in this cabin and wait for you to return. Then we shall discuss your future employment with the Lazy T Bar."

Bunting was still cackling as he mounted his horse.

Ellis Burroughs watched him ride away. Then he wheeled in the doorway and stared across the room at the mahogany chair.

The unruly herd moved from the Ishawooa at dawn. As soon as Burroughs was certain the men would not be returning, he slid the mahogany chair over by a window that was opposite the cabin's plank table. Then he reposi-tioned the table so that it stood a few inches from the opposite wall. The blonde man smiled at the rowel marks Bunting's spurs had cut. He took a hammer and several square-forged nails from his valise and used them to nail the back of the mahogany chair to the wall. When he finished nailing, Ellis sat in the chair for a moment, then tried moving it. Returning the hammer to his valise, he pulled out a wood brace and bit and began boring several holes in the plank tabletop. Then he disconnected the bit and placed both it and the brace back in the valise.

After lunch, Ellis went again to his valise and took out a small roll of heavy wire and a pair of pliers. Then he took out the broken-down, double-barreled, twelve-gauge shotgun from whose barrels Schulte had hacksawed a good eighteen inches the night before Ellis crossed the Stinkingwater. After reconnecting the stock, Ellis cut several lengths of wire and positioned the shotgun under the table, its barrels aimed squarely at the mahogany chair. Going to the woodpile outside the cabin, he cut several small wooden shims. Then he used the shims, along with some firm wire twists, to bring the shotgun to bear on the top of the chair.

After pondering over a cup of coffee, Ellis took a roll of twine from his valise, cutting two six-foot lengths. Doubling each length, he tied them to the shotgun triggers and ran them to the wall behind the table, where he tied the twine to a nail.

Ellis again went to the window and looked out. He glanced at his watch and was dismayed to find it was already late. He returned to the table and crawled beneath. He tried to cock the shotgun hammers, but discovered the triggers were tied too tightly to allow the hammers to cock. So he retied the twine, cocked the hammers, then climbed out and stood at the end of the table. He nudged the twine with his knee and heard the satisfying twin 'clicks' as the hammers fell. Crawling once more beneath the table, Ellis broke open the shotgun and inserted two twelve-gauge shotgun shells loaded with double-ought buck. Then he snapped the breech closed, and eared back the hammers. When the blonde man crawled from beneath the table for the last time, he did so gingerly.

At last, from the bottom of his valise, he took a linen tablecloth, which he draped over the plank table and its deadly additions. Then Ellis settled down to wait ... but not in the mahogany chair!

———•••———

The wild bunch began to crowd as they entered Blood Canyon. It was three o'clock in the afternoon when the last steer plodded into the canyon mouth. As it did, Levi Bunting took out his revolver and began firing methodically over the rear steers' heads, shouting, and waving his rain slicker. Other men did the same.

At first it appeared the herd wouldn't break. Then slowly the entire rear of the mass began to move in a lumbering trot, flowing in the direction of least resistance. With the shouting, shooting, waving men-dervishes behind and a raging river and sheer canyon walls left and right, the torrent of steers quickly overtook those unknowing dozens of cattle still ahead.

Within ten minutes the entire herd was one huge mass of bellowing reds and blacks and whites, horns clicking and cloven feet clattering over rocks, raising an enormous dust cloud.

Bunting reined his horse in and his men followed suit. Holstering his gun, the foreman twisted in the saddle to tie his slicker behind the cantle. As he straightened, he smiled. "Well boys, we'll have a little cleanup work ahead of us. Might as well get to it, huh?" With that, the man pulled his saddle gun, jacked a shell into the chamber and lowered the hammer with his thumb. Then with rifle butt against his thigh, the man spurred his horse after the stampeding steers. Twenty cowhands rode behind. They'd cantered several hundred yards when the roar hit them, reverberating from the canyon walls, bringing the group to a halt.

O'Brien was the first. "Dynamite!" he cried.

Bunting spurred his horse savagely, crying, "The sons-abitches have dynamited the canyon!" But before all the others had started after their boss, they heard the faintest of the herds' bawling, tinged with unnatural, unforgettable bellows of agony. Then the first of the wild herd hove into view. His tongue was out and his sides heaved, but he hooked his horns as he neared and nothing short of a bullet would've stopped him. Behind him came more … and more … and more, bearing down upon the milling group of riders. "God a-mighty!" Wills shouted. "Let's get outta here!"

Bunting found himself with O'Brien, high up where the talus slope butts against the sheer canyon walls, pushing their horses unmercifully uphill, away from the raging herd.

"Look out there!" O'Brien exclaimed, pointing toward the rampaging Southfork.

"Oh my God," moaned Bunting as the first drowned steer floated by. Then the first cripple limped into sight. Finally the two men led their horses down the talus. Near the bottom, Bunting mounted and turned his steed up-canyon toward the carnage. But O'Brien flatly refused to follow until more of the T Bar hands joined them. At last, Bunting wheeled and the two men rode downriver. Along the way, they passed crippled animals they methodically shot to put them beyond misery.

It was near dark before Bunting and O'Brien started collecting their scattered crew. It was morning before they had fifteen. As the T Bar men began their ride to the canyon, they were joined by twelve men of the StinkingWater Association for Promotion and Protection.

News of the Blood Canyon stampede debacle had filtered downriver via errant T Bar cowboys. It grew with each telling, reaching the encamped SWAPP twelve near Ishawooa Creek late in the evening of the day of the stampede. That news, coupled with visible evidence of dead steers drifting with the flooding Southfork, turned the cautious SWAPP group into an information-gathering body.

Paradoxically, the T Bar crew—Bunting included—welcomed the newcomers as unbiased witnesses to the canyon's terrible disclosures. Thus the twenty-nine men of the combined parties rode together, silent, somber. Along the river, scattered, drowned animals lay along the shore in unseemly heaps, their carcasses already beginning to bloat. Dead steers lay along the trail; crippled, they'd been dropped by Bunting's and O'Brien's bullets the previous evening.

As the party neared the focal point of the avalanche, cattle carnage increased. Many had obviously been trampled when the stampede turned against itself. A few crippled steers still lived and those were mercifully dispatched by the rider nearest. Finally the joint party rounded the last bend. Here, death and destruction was at its zenith—wave after wave of stampeded cattle piled up against an avalanche of boulders, dying both beneath and against the block.

Few words had been spoken throughout the morning's ride, and those only broken sentences at random: "Jesus Christ!" or "My God!" or "Lord, who woulda believed?" or "I can't look no more!"

As the party rode the last few feet, the man they all knew as Jacob Weatherby suddenly stood from behind a boulder and gazed down upon them. He cradled a rifle, and only he knew a shotgun and another rifle leaned behind his refuge. "Thought you might be along, Bunting," he said. "I reckon it's time you and I had a little talk, like maybe we should've had the first time we bumped into each other. Didn't expect half the

Stinkingwater to turn out for it, though."

"Guess it's time a-right, nester," Bunting replied. "I seen at least a hundred reasons today for you to answer to."

A white-haired man from the group urged his horse ahead, past a bloating, trampled steer. "Please gentlemen," August Mathers' voice rang out, "I simply do not believe the shedding of human blood will atone for what has happened here. Mr. Weatherby, Mr. Bunting, I ask that you ..."

"You're too late, Mr. Mathers," Jethro Spring snapped, his voice bouncing from boulder to boulder. "I'm not interested in atoning for cow blood with human blood, either. What I'm talking about is Bunting's blood for a real human's blood. Josh Curlew died in that bastard's stampede!"

Bunting stared at the rifleman on the rock above him. He sat his horse stolidly, but his thoughts were racing. *If Curlew's dead, that still leaves Buttercut up there somewhere.* From the corners of his eyes, he could see Corbin and Marquardt and Ashland and a half-dozen others edging away. As far as he knew, the SWAPP riders would join in an attack on the T Bar men. And Weatherby himself had good cover in the rocks. *It's a stacked deck,* he thought. Bunting glanced at his own men and could see the cattle carnage they'd witnessed earlier in the day had taken the fight from them. So he looked back at the man on the boulder above —and blinked. Declining combat, he reined his horse around and rode back through the silent group of riders. One by one, the T Bar men followed.

As Bunting and his crew disappeared, Jethro Spring said, "I'd invite you folks over, but we're not receiving at the Rock House today. Maybe it'd be for the best if you folks went on back home. Leave the Blood Canyon dead to those of us dead ones left up here." He leaped from his boulder and started away, then turned back. "Thank you for coming, though. I didn't think anyone would." He paused. "It might've made a difference if I'd known."

Jethro Spring had made several mistakes in his calculations for blasting the canyon walls. First was the amount of carnage resulting. Though Jethro wanted this strike to be costly to the Lazy T Bar, he never wished for so much devastation. In retrospect, the extent of the carnage was traceable in part to Sam.

Sam's signal—billowing smoke from a gunpowder ignited coal oil and brush fire—had been slow in coming. The old man had not been keen on the dynamite idea and even when Bunting's men began stampeding the herd, he hesitated as the first rush of cattle seemed to falter. Finally, when Sam saw the stampede actually in motion and started his fire, smoke came slowly.

Then, too, the speed of the stampede was surprising. The first Jethro knew it was under way was when the lead steer rounded the bend and he scampered with his slow match, lighting fuses. Then he'd thrown the match away and, before turning, clambered up a trail cleared earlier to the cliff heights above.

When the explosion came, the first of the stampeding herd was nearly under the huge rock column. As further explosions rocked the column, Jethro's final mistake became apparent—many precious seconds were lost between explosion and avalanche. The huge column hung in the air for ever so long, then began to settle and tilt. At last came its deadly rush to the canyon floor, breaking into thousands of stones from house-size to stove-size.

Nearly thirty steers were already past when the avalanche struck the canyon floor. Hundreds of tons of rock settled into place, spreading from cliff to river. A huge dust cloud rose above the debris, amid a cacophony of bellowing and screaming as the animals were crushed beneath or smashed against the stones, then washed back the other way.

It was later, when Jethro descended from the canyon walls to see what damage the through-steers had caused that he found the body of the crippled Texan. "Damn you, Curlew," he raged. "I told you to stay in the Rock House!"

Curlew died trying to help. The crippled man was standing behind one of the big gateposts when the first of the escaping twenty-nine steers broke from the upper mouth of Blood Canyon. Josh tried to stop them—five dead steers lying sprawled before the fence bore mute testimony to that fact. But with an empty rifle and no chance to reload, the crippled man had no alternative but to huddle behind his post as twenty-four rampaging steers struck the fence. Even then, Josh would've been safe behind his corner post had not some of the strands of screeching, breaking, whipping barbed wire jerked him from his shelter, directly into the path of several of the big steers.

Josh Curlew died wrapped in a shroud of broken Haish's 'S' barbed wire.

CHAPTER TWENTY-SIX

That Levi Bunting was a conscienceless killer could not be doubted. But he was a cattleman first. And he knew that his ranch had sustained a terrible blow in the aftermath of the stampede he'd engineered. As to how extensive were the losses to the Lazy T Bar, he wasn't sure. But the man was certain they were severe—perhaps as many as a hundred head of cattle. And as soon as the full T Bar crew was gathered, Levi ordered a general roundup and tally of the survivors of the wild bunch stampede.

For four long, hard days cowboys rode throughout the daylight hours, pushing exhausted and injured steers into a general gather a few miles up the Southfork from the old Swenson line cabin. Among the hard-riding, exhausted men, none rode harder or longer than Levi Bunting. He was everywhere, a wild man, unkempt, eating little, shouting orders, then changing horses and riding away again to charge up another isolated canyon, or through a clump of willows and cottonwoods to search for yet more steers. At the end of the fourth day, the foreman called a halt and a tally was begun.

When the count was completed at noon on July 4— Independence Day—Levi Bunting thrust the tally slip into his pocket. It read two hundred and ten able-bodied animals and thirty-four injured ones. Of the thirty-four injured, three were so seriously maimed they had to be destroyed. That left an overall total of two hundred and forty-one survivors of the stampede and avalanche in Blood Canyon.

Bunting knew his employer still awaited him at the Swenson line cabin from reports of several cowboys who'd stopped at the cabin while searching for lost steers. Those cowboys told Levi strange things about the rancher—like an unshaven, unkempt owner of the Lazy T Bar who stared wildly at them while cursing and refusing them entry into the cabin. The foreman knew he'd have to confront Burroughs sooner or later. That he had little time for a confrontation with the man was a foregone conclusion in the foreman's mind. Instead, he was obsessed with a decision he'd made on his return from Blood Canyon and during the subsequent four-day roundup—Weatherby and Buttercut would die!

However, avoid it though he tried, the specter of Ellis Burroughs would not go away. Not that any pending argument with Burroughs worried the foreman; he would simply wheedle or bully Burroughs into submission.

First though, he would order the healthy steers to Ishawooa Mesa. Two hundred steers stripping the horse pasture Weatherby had used in the past wasn't much of a blow, but it gave Bunting some satisfaction to give the order. After doing so, the foreman rode to Marquardt for a drink. Let Burroughs stew in his juices—Levi Bunting was running the Lazy T Bar.

Sam Buttercut had been unusually pensive after the explosions in Blood Canyon. The deaths of scores of cattle in the avalanche were, in Sam's mind, uncalled for; though his concern for the innocent steers seemed paradoxical, given that the little trapper had hunted buffalo merely for the hide market, priding himself in knowing that down on the Powder he'd killed thirty-two of the shaggy beasts from a single stand. In the case of Blood Canyon, however, Sam was confused. He'd watched Bunting and his minions start the stampede, and the old man had little choice but to concede that Jethro's method of stopping it was probably the only way.

Still, Sam couldn't put the terrible waste of dead animals out of his mind. Out of his nose either, for the stench from the decaying animals soon permeated the air for miles around.

Another problem for Sam was Jethro. The Blood Canyon affair had taken a toll on the younger man. Sam was troubled that his friend's gray eyes seemed to turn mean and fathomless. But most disquieting of all was that the younger man seemed to have lost interest in his ranch.

Actually, the only things Jethro and Sam had done in the six days following the stampede were to bury Josh Curlew and open up a single-file horse trail at the fast-dropping river's edge.

It was Sam who suggested they scout below and get away from the terrible stench. His friend merely nodded. So it was Sam who brought in Buck and Hoss and saddled them. It was Sam who led the way below. And it was Sam who discovered the cattle drive underway to Ishawooa Mesa....

The gray-eyed man sat his buckskin horse, staring stonily below as the now docile steers worked their way up the canyon from Ishawooa Creek. T Bar cowboys seemed to be letting them drift and Jethro estimated it would take two or three more days before the steers spread across the mesa. He cursed beneath his breath and jerked Buck savagely around to ride back across the mesa to the trail down into the Stinkingwater.

Sam followed, but it wasn't the same. He knew his friend was in a dangerous mood and the old trapper wasn't sure what he should do. When he asked where they were going, the only thing the younger man said was, "To the Rock House." So when they reached the Southfork trail, Sam decided, "I reckon I'll stay out an' look-see Snake Eyes."

Jethro rode away without a word. As he did, two men rode up to the Swenson line cabin. One of those men was Levi Bunting....

"What do you mean you sent an order to pull the herd back from Ishawooa Mesa?" the foreman demanded, hot with anger.

"Precisely what I said, Mr. Bunting," Ellis Burroughs replied. "I do not wish my cattle on Ishawooa Mesa. That was heavily grazed last year, and I do not believe it contains enough grass to make it worthwhile to push my cattle up there. In my opinion, my losses have been all too substantial with you giving directions. Now, I'm taking control."

Bunting and Cletus Wills had ridden up to the line cabin minutes before and both had stepped inside the cabin, despite Burroughs' insistence that he wished to talk to Bunting alone.

"Wills can listen in on anything we got to say to each other," Bunting growled. Then the man pushed past the ranch owner and strode directly to the mahogany chair.

Burroughs slid behind the plank table, leaning with both hands atop its surface and struggling to display outward calm to Bunting. Wills stood indolently in the doorway.

"My, my! Ain't we gettin' hoity-toity?" Bunting said as he spied the linen tablecloth. Then he tried to pull the mahogany chair from the wall so he could tilt back. "What the hell's the matter with this chair?"

"I nailed it to the wall." Then Burroughs told Bunting he'd ordered the cattle back from Ishawooa Mesa and that he was taking operational control....

"Are you now?" Bunting said, settling into the chair.

If Ellis Burroughs had any doubts before, the previous two weeks of impatient waiting convinced him Bunting must go—with or without Wills.

The foreman stared at his boss and a warning clicked. *Something ain't right here,* he thought. *Why is this chair nailed down?* His eyes narrowed.

"Bunting, you are fired!"

"Wha-a-a-t?" the foreman cried, lunging to his feet.

"You're fired. I don't want you on the Lazy T Bar any longer than it takes you to ride from my ranch." Burroughs' heart was in his throat. He licked his lips, glancing at Wills who'd shifted from the doorjamb and wore a puzzled look.

Bunting's reply came in a snarl. "Remember what I said about how mad I might get if somebody tried to get rid of me like an old shoe? Well," he said, voice dropping, "I'm that mad. Mad enough to carve you up for dog meat." He took a step in Burroughs' direction.

"Hold it!" Burroughs shouted. "Wills, are you in this?"

"Dammit, Burroughs, Wills is my man."

"You're fired," Burroughs said and went for his derringer. Just as Bunting's gun cleared leather—incredibly fast—Burroughs kicked the concealed trigger twine and the twin roar of the sawed-off twelve-gauge filled the room. The two barrels of double-ought buckshot caught Bunting full in the stomach and nearly cut him in half, hurling him back against the mahogany chair, splintering it with the impact. One outflung arm went through the window as the bloody mass of what had been Levi Bunting slid to the floor.

Ellis Burroughs saw none of it. His eyes were only for Cletus Wills and the gunman's deadly hand. The shotgun's blast had startled Wills and he'd spun to see Bunting hurled against the chair and wall and window. Comprehension sank in and he whirled back to Burroughs as Ellis brought the tiny derringer to bear.

"Hey! No, wait, I ..." A tiny hole appeared above Cletus Wills's left eye as his right eye widened in surprise. He tried belatedly for the revolver on his thigh, but died while tugging it up, helped along by the second barrel of Burroughs' derringer.

CHAPTER TWENTY-SEVEN

On the afternoon of July 8, a solitary horseman leading a packhorse crested Ishawooa Mesa. An hour later Jethro Spring let his horses fill from a clear pool of water, then slid from Buck and drank himself. Afterward, he lifted two wooden boxes from the packhorse and prized up their lids. Inside each was an eight-gallon jug with a cork stopper sealed with wax. A paper containing a skull and crossbones was affixed to each jug. Under the skull and crossbones was printed: MERCURIC BI-CHLORIDE.

Jethro cut the wax seals with his knife, then pulled the corks and poured the jars' contents into the pool.

Two hours later, at dusk, Jethro and his horses began the laborious descent from Ishawooa Mesa.

At precisely that same moment, a clean-shaven, scrubbed Ellis Burroughs knocked at the door of Mathers'

Place. Mrs. Mathers opened the door. "You!" she exclaimed, slamming the door.

Burroughs knocked again. No answer. Again he knocked and the door was opened, this time by August Mathers. "I'll not stay if you invite him in!" cried Mattie Mathers from across the room.

"Please, Mattie. Ellis, what is it you want?"

"I must speak with you and Lillian, sir. It's about something that needs to be said, sir. I promise you, this will not be as unpleasant as my last visit."

When August Mathers hesitated, Ellis said, "Please. I have many apologies to make—to Mrs. Mathers, too."

"Come in, Ellis. I'll call Lillian."

Once inside, the visitor was not asked to sit. He cleared his throat and said, "Mr. and Mrs. Mathers, I have many sins for which to atone, not the least of them being sins against you people." He paused, looked at Lillian, then continued. "I have behaved quite boorishly and rudely toward three of the kindest, most gentle people I've ever known." He focused on Mr. Mathers. "I'm not foolish enough, sir, ever to think I can repay you; or atone for my churlish treatment of you. But I can perhaps put your mind at ease by telling you that—thanks to Lillian—I've come to recognize the error of my ways. And to promise you—if I am to have anything to do with it—a new order of things to come on the Stinkingwater."

"May I take your hat, Ellis?" asked August Mathers. "And won't you have a chair? Perhaps there are things we can discuss."

Early on the morning of July 10, August and Lillian Mathers rode from Marquardt, bound for distant Blood Canyon. Despite being the bearers of good news, the two easterners-gone-western reveled in the delights of early summer on the Southfork. It was a warm, fleecy-cloud day. When August stopped to poke again around the rubble of Castle Rock, she joined him, picking flowers and smelling the blooms of shrubs. Later, August pointed to darting fish in a backwater pool of the now-clear Southfork, and she pointed to the manner in which distant mountain ranges stood out amid the clear air. What did it matter that they dawdled? Tomorrow they would easily ride to the Rock House and her Gray Eyes would know all things were well and good. Tomorrow he and Lillian could actually begin planning for their love to come to fruition. August Mathers threw another cottonwood limb on the fire. Lillian stared dreamily into the darting flames.

"Reckon you need some more wood," Sam Buttercut said as he stepped into the firelight and dumped an armload by the fire.

"Sam!" Lillian squealed. "You frightened me!"

The buckskin-clad old trapper grinned. "Don't rightfully know why. We'uns ought t'be gettin' used t'each other 'round a campfire by now. Any coffee in that pot?"

"For you? Certainly," Lillian said as her father rummaged in their gear for an extra cup.

"Well Sam, what brings you to the edge of civilization?" August asked as he handed a cup of the steaming liquid to his friend.

"Scoutin'," Sam replied, squatting by the fire. "Makin' shore Pansy Bottom an' Snake Eyes ain't up t'somethin'."

"Oh Sam, we have wonderful news for you!" Lillian gushed. "The war is over. Ellis said he will keep the peace. There is to be no more fighting. Isn't it wonderful?"

The little man sipped his coffee, clearly skeptical.

"He says he is sorry for all that has happened and has even ordered his men and cattle back from Ishawooa Mesa and the Upper Southfork. You and Gray Eyes can live as you'd like, and not have to look over your shoulders all the time. Isn't it wonderful?"

"And what do Snake Eyes say t'that?" Sam asked.

"The man is dead," replied Mr. Mathers.

"Ellis told of Bunting's death in an argument at the Swenson cabin," Lillian added. "He says he's firmly in control and he's stopping any further confrontation."

"An' you two are on your way t'Blood Canyon t'tell Gray Eyes."

"That's correct, Sam," August said. "But we must confess, we were caught up in the warmth and beauty of the Southfork summer and have dallied along the way."

Sam nodded. "Wal, the good word you bring upriver might be what Gray Eyes needs. He ain't been the same since the big cow run, an' Josh a-dyin', an' his fence an' ranch bein' wrecked again. Maybe this'll bring him out o' it."

"What's wrong?" Lillian said, suddenly somber.

"Cain't rightly tell you ma'am. But he ain't smiled for most a month now, an' them cows an' Josh an' losin' his fence has done shut his mouth. Why, he ain't speaked ten words since the stampede. An' his face an' eyes took on a plumb mean look when he seed them cows a-headin' for Ishawooa. Tell you the truth, ma'am, that boy's about t'bust loose. An' iff'n he ever turned mean at the same time he turned loose, hain't no tellin' what'd happen. Maybe it's a good thing Snake Eyes is dead, 'cause I got a feelin' he warn't goin' t'live much longer nohow."

August Mathers nodded. "I had a feeling something was wrong, but I never had your insight. Perhaps our message is more urgent than we realized."

Sam rose and disappeared into the night to hobble Hoss and turn him out with the Mathers' rented horses. When he returned, he said, "Whitetop, I been a-thinkin'."

Lillian and August looked expectantly at the wise little man.

"That boy ain't right. He's had a tough life, that un. I dunno the half, an' likely nobody never will. But he's got sand, an' gived a chance, he'll be a dandy and a half. But iff'n he cuts loose, this country'll never see a ring-tailed bear to match him. Now I don't know why he ain't a-busted loose afore, but I do know he's been fightin' the urge plumb powerful. That's why it's been a-buildin' an' why iff'n it pops loose, it'll pop loose big."

He paused. Lillian and her father both breathed, "Go on."

"Far as he can see, he's about t'lose what he tried double-hard t'keep. An' Pink Laigs here are a right smart kicker in the bargain, what any red-blooded man'd hate t'lose."

Lillian smiled.

"Even a cornered rat'll fight like pizen iff'n he's gonna lose nohow—and that's whar Gray Eyes figgers he be."

August Mathers said, "I can appreciate your assessment, Sam. But I'm not sure I see where you're leading. Won't the news we have rectify the problem in Mr. Weatherby's mind?"

"I think it oughter be Pink Laigs what delivers the goods."

"Eh?"

"Hit oughter be jest Pink Laigs what tells Gray Eyes his worries are over. An' they-uns oughter have some time t'talk t'themselves. You an' me, we oughter straggle in later on when Gray Eyes has a chance t'settle down an' we can kick out some more good news."

"More good news?" August said.

"Ishawooa," Sam replied. "We'uns will tell him thar ain't no cows on Ishawooa Mesa."

"Maximum effect!" August breathed. Then he asked, "But what about Lillian? She'd be required to ride through Blood Canyon alone. Past the aftermath of the stampede and avalanche. She'd be required to smell—it does smell up there, doesn't it?"

"Smells fierce," Sam said. "But she was goin' t'smell it nohow. What diff'rence would it make iff'n she smells it by herself or with a cavalry escort?"

"I can do it, father," Lillian blurted. "Let me do it Sam's way."

"What of the avalanche?" August Mathers asked. "Is there a way through it?"

"Just stay t'the water's edge, Pink Laigs. Me'n Gray Eyes cleared a way through. You'll have no trouble follerin' tracks."

"And us?" asked August Mathers. "Should we actually go up on the Mesa to make certain no cows are there?"

"Don't rightly see why not. It air purty up thar an' we kin still be t'the Rock House early 'nough t'see no hanky-panky goes on after dark."

August and Lillian smiled. "I've wanted to go back to that rock with all the bracheopods in it for some time," the father said. "Do you suppose we could ride that far and still return to the Rock House by dark?"

"Easy as could be, Whitetop," Sam said.

—•—

The two old men sat their horses along the mesa's east rim, with the Southfork valley stretched below, north and south. They'd parted early that morning of July 11, 1885, with Lillian taking the lightly loaded packhorse on up to the Rock House. Now, at mid-morning, the two elderly friends sat saddlehorses and stared about them. "Breathtakin'," Sam said.

August looked at the old trapper in disbelief.

Sam blushed and said, "I heered somebody say that once't," and he reined Hoss around so he could stare out over the Mesa. "Iff'n it's all right with you, Whitetop, I'd like t'swing over t'the west an' make double sure 'bout them cow critters not bein' here."

"Certainly, Sam. Do what you think best. But would it be all right if I went on to the fossil rock? I'm sure I could find it, and I've so wanted to try to track the rock for some time now. No doubt we could meet near the waterhole somewhere."

"Hit's plumb fine with me. We'uns'll meet somewhar, that's shore. Don'tcha fret none about it."

CHAPTER TWENTY-EIGHT

The stench was terrible, but so excited was the girl to reach the Rock House, she covered the lower half of her face and resolutely pushed on. She'd found her way through the avalanche boulders by following Sam's directions and had ridden through the desecrated remains of her beloved's fence. Eagerness caused her to take scant notice of the torn-up, violated, newly seeded pasture. As she neared the building, her heart was singing and skin tingling. Soon all would be right forever with her and her Gray Eyes!

"Hello the house!" she called as she rode to the hitchrail. No answer came. "Hello-o-o!" she shouted again, tethering her horses and pushing open the cabin door. It was empty, though the stove was still warm and a pot of lukewarm water on it.

Lillian went back outside and, with some effort, stripped the saddles from her two horses. Then she removed the bridle from her riding horse, went back inside, built a fire and boiled a pot of coffee, settling back to wait.

She waited all afternoon. As the sun went down, the woman walked to the waterfall and waded in the pool. Afterward, she sat against a cottonwood and dreamed. Here, beneath the cottonwoods, the rampaging steers hadn't reached, and the glade was still as beautiful as Lillian remembered.

"You're just as beautiful as I remember," Jethro said, startling her.

"Darling!" she cried, scrambling to her feet.

They held each other for a long moment, then kissed longingly and passionately. At last, the man held her away while his eyes devoured her from head to toe.

She searched his face—as he did hers—and thought his eyes sunken and haunted.

"You shouldn't have come," he said. "Blood Canyon is not pretty now."

"But the Rock House is, Gray Eyes. And the waterfall and the pool and the cottonwoods. And you are here."

He pulled her to him so that her voice was muffled in his shoulder. "Something wonderful has happened, my dear. The war is over."

He held her away. "Say that again."

"Levi Bunting is dead. Ellis Burroughs stopped by Mathers' Place to tell us. He is very contrite, dear, and father believes him. He's started father's pension again and he specifically said there'd be nothing further between you and him. In fact, he wishes us happiness, Gray Eyes—you and me. Isn't that wonderful?"

Jethro released Lillian and turned to the pool. He thrust his hands deep into the pockets of his trousers and walked away, all the while looking up at the waterfall, heart pounding. *If it were only true!* Lillian came to him and placed a hand on his shoulder. "Do you believe it, Lillian?" he asked.

"Oh yes dear! I know it's true."

He turned to her with tears in his eyes. "I'll be the happiest man in the world and I'll make you the happiest woman."

They embraced again and when they broke, both faces were radiant and both hearts in song. They began walking to the Rock House, hand in hand.

"I can't believe you came all the way up here alone," he said. "And through Blood Canyon by yourself."

"Silly," she said. "We women are stronger than you think. I tolerated the smell because all I could think of was that you were just ahead."

He stopped and smiled down at her and she said, "I didn't come alone to the Ishawooa. Father came that far with me. Then he and Sam rode to Ishawooa Mesa fossil hunting."

His mind suddenly went blank. "What did you say?" he demanded, grabbing her shoulders so hard his fingers dug.

"Father and Sam went fossil hunting on Ishawooa Mesa. Why? Gray Eyes, what is wrong?"

"Oh my God!" the man moaned. "Oh my God!" And he wheeled to run toward the Rock House.

"What is the matter?" she screamed, then ran after.

As she reached the Rock House, his face was tight and he was throwing his saddle on her livery horse. "Gray Eyes, what in the world is wrong?" And she screamed, "Tell me-e-e-e!"

Just then the two horses at the Rock House hitchrail threw up their heads and turned toward Blood Canyon, where a solitary buckskin-clad figure led a single laden saddlehorse.

"No!" whispered Jethro. "No! No! No!" He began to run, whirling to say, "Stay here!" But she caught up.

They reached the broken fence and gate as Sam neared. Then Lillian grasped Jethro Spring's arm and cried, "NO! NO-o-o-o-o!"

Crisis on the Stinkingwater

Jethro sagged against the gatepost as Sam trudged up, leading Hoss and the lifeless body of August Mathers. "I hain't never knowed nobody low enough t'pizen a water-hole afore," was all the old trapper said as he shuffled past.

Other Books by Roland Cheek

Fiction

Echoes of Vengeance 256 pgs. 5½ x 8½ $14.95 (postpaid)

A military outpost situated in an isolated region of the Department of the Upper Missouri. An embittered commandant who believes unkind fate kept him from fame and glory during the recent War of Secession. A band of starving Blackfeet too riddled with smallpox to withdraw to their reservation. A young mixed-breed army interpreter whose aging parents are with the Blackfeet tries to prevent a massacre-in-the-making; he's beaten and dragged to the guardhouse for the attempt.

Thus the stage is set and principal characters in place for the opening pages of *Echoes of Vengeance*. It's a tangled tale of daring and adventure as the youth flees echoes from his revenge. From Mississippi dock to Modesto prize ring, from Cherokee Strip to Colorado end-of-track, Jethro Spring treads the line between death and survival, merit and rascality, growth and degeneration.

Bloody Merchants' War 288 pgs. 5½ x 8½ $14.95 (postpaid)

Poor farmers and ranchers gripped in bondage by an iron triangle of crooked merchants, an oppressive military, and a corrupt Territorial government. Thus, the town of Lincoln, New Mexico Territory, was not a good place to be ambushed by events that spiral an unwilling fugitive into a conflict without clear distinctions between good and evil, right and wrong, friend and foe. Eventually Jethro Spring chooses, but did he make the right choice? With Billy the Kid? For John Chisum?

Book two in the *Valediction For Revenge* series features the adventures of Jethro Spring, wanted for killing a U.S. Army Major responsible for brutally murdering the young man's parents.

Lincoln County Crucible 288 pgs. 5½ x 8½ $14.95 (postpaid)

Third novel in the *Valediction For Revenge* series continues the life of Jethro Spring, a man torn between cultures.

The story opens after the terrible gunbattle where Alexander McSween and many of his partisans perish and with the "Santa Fe Ring," a crooked triumvirate of the United States Army, Territorial government, and merchant-stranglers in near-total economic control of southeastern New Mexico. Young Jethro is undecided about remaining, or riding into the sunset. His head tells him a man with a price on his own head should drift on. But what of the widowed Susan McSween? Or of his friend, Billy the Kid? Or the starving Mescalero Apaches? Or the poor Anglo farmers and Mexican peons strangling from "the ring's" bloody yoke?

And what of this new, incoming Territorial Governor, Lew Wallace? Might there be hope?

Gunnar's Mine 288 pgs. 5½ x 8½ $14.95 (postpaid)

Fourth novel in the *Valediction For Revenge* series continues the life of Jethro Spring, a man torn between cultures.

Wanted fugitive Jethro Spring is once again drawn into a hopeless cause, this time for helpless emigrants who dare to dream of riches amid Colorado's mountains of minerals. Jethro's head tells him to move on, but his heart rules through his love and admiration for a little Swede whose only sin is that he won't sell to the greedy corporation determined to obtain every independent claim in the entire Uncompahgre mining district. It's a tale that *Roundup Magazine* said had, "a plot with more twists than a sidewinder..."

Crisis on the Stinkingwater 288 pgs. 5½ x 8½ $14.95 (postpaid)

Fifth novel in the *Valediction For Revenge* series. Set in northwestern Wyoming's Stinkingwater Valley.

Non-fiction on next page

Non-Fiction

Learning To Talk Bear 320 pgs. 5½ x 8½ $19.95 (postpaid)

God's music is wind soughing through treetops, dove wings whispering at waterholes, the mournful cry of a lost-in-the-fog honker. It's a harmony that became addictive, and carries even into my dotage. Elk music took me to the dance. Bears—particularly grizzly bears—keep me dancing. Grizzlies, you see, are the Marine Band of the animal world. They swagger with the calm indifference of an animal who knows he has nothing left to prove. So why does this John Philip Sousa of wildlife resonance—an animal who not only fears not, but cares not—receive such a bum rap from the planet's most fearsome other creatures—us?

Good question. Not all grizzly bears are Jeffrey Dahmers in fur coats. That's the why for this book. An important book for anyone wishing to understand what makes bears tick. Humorous high adventure and spine-tingling suspense, seasoned with understanding through a lifetime of walking where bears walk.

The Phantom Ghost of Harriet Lou 352 pgs. 5½ x 8½ $19.95 (postpaid)

In the beginning there was heaven and earth; and the earth was without form and void and little tow-headed boys wandered around barefoot with hands in pockets because there was nothing upon the land to catch their imagination. And God looked upon His work and saw it was not yet good that no thing existed to challenge those boys. And so an autumn came to pass when eerie whistlings drifted into the valleys from distant mountainsides and the by-then lanky teenage boys threw away their toys and accepted the wapiti challenge that would make them men! And God and girls saw that it was good.

If you've heard a different version of this story, that's your problem. I heard it but once—this way. And so I became an elk hunter. Then I became infatuated with all creatures, and eventually a believer that God's handiwork is composed of such intracacies that a quest to understand has taken the rest of my life. The Phantom Ghost of Harriet Lou is about that quest.

Dance on the Wild Side 352 pgs. 5½ x 8½ $19.95 (postpaid) by Roland *and* Jane Cheek

It was her idea to compete in a man's world. "Competing in a man's world" is the way Jane referred to her growing enchantment with outdoors adventure. That upsets me. I understand that people must struggle with relationships. I realize love must be learned and earned, and that it can be lost through choices made. Some might applaud the thought of a lady determined to become her "own woman" in a man's world. Not me. What bothers me is not that my petite wife of more than four decades wants to compete in outdoors proficiency, but where in the hell does she—or anyone else—get the idea that all in nature belongs to men?

This book, then, is about two people in love sharing a life of exciting adventure and growing in the process. In reality it's about everyone over forty who has lived and loved and struggled together toward a common dream. What makes this particular book's storyline remarkable is how many times these people fell on their butts while doing it.

My Best Work is Done at the Office 320 pgs. 5½ x 8½ $19.95 (postpaid)

Roland Cheek's popular stories of low chuckles and high adventure got their start far from bierstube and beltway, around wilderness campfires. The best of those riveting tales of wild people, wild places, and wild things eventually made their way into the guy's newspaper columns and radio scripts. As a result, Roland's audience exploded from a handful of campfire gatherers to a coast-to-coast mushroom cloud numbering in the hundreds of thousands.

Now there's a book composed of the choicest of those stories. You can see for yourself why Roland is widely known as America's Rocky Mountain Sage; why his tongue-in-cheek wit is so irreverent, but so relevant; why fans re-read old newspapers for his columns and pause in their work or sleep to listen to him on the radio.

Chocolate Legs 320 pgs. 5½ x 8½ $19.95 (postpaid)

Her story begins as an ursid Shirley Temple, a cute blond phenom amid the real-life Shangri-la of Glacier National Park's most scenic mountain valleys. In time, however, the curtsying knockout zoomed to Princess Diana-sized celebrity, demanding more than admiring glances and the flashing bulbs of paparazzi cameras. It was those outsized demands and an ever-growing haughtiness that attracted official attention.

Chocolate Legs is an investigative journey into the controversial life and death of one of the best-known grizzly bears in the world; by a long-time journalist who has lived (and sometimes brushed near death) with the great beasts.

Montana's Bob Marshall Wilderness 80 pgs. 9 x 12 (coffee table size) $15.95 hardcover, $10.95 softcover (postpaid)

97 full-color photos, over 10,000 words of where-to, how-to text about America's favorite wilderness.

See order form on reverse side

Order form for Roland Cheek's Books

See list of books on page 278

Telephone orders: 1-800-821-6784. *Visa, MasterCard or Discover only.*

Website orders: www.rolandcheek.com

Postal orders: Skyline Publishing
P.O. Box 1118 • Columbia Falls, MT 59912
Telephone: (406) 892-5560   Fax (406) 892-1922

Please send the following books:
(I understand I may return any Skyline Publishing book for a full refund—no questions asked.)

Title	Qty.	Cost Ea.	Total
_____	____$	_____$	
_____	____$	_____$	
_____	____$	_____$	
_____	____$	_____$	
_____	____$	_____$	
_____	____$	_____$	
_____	____$	_____$	

Total Order: _____$

We pay cost of shipping and handling inside U.S.

Ship to: Name _____

Address _____

City _____ State _____ Zip _____

Daytime phone number (____) _____-_____

Payment: ☐ Check or Money Order

   Credit card: ☐ Visa ☐ MasterCard ☐ Discover

Card number _____

Name on card _____ Exp. date ___/___

Signature: _____